THE
THIRTEENTH STEP:
ZOMBIE RECOVERY

MICHELE W. MILLER

The Thirteenth Step: Zombie Recovery

Copyright © 2013, Michele Weinstat

This is a work of fiction. All people, places, events, and organizations are the product of the author's imagination or are used fictitiously. Any resemblance to actual persons, living or dead, or to any places, events or organizations is purely coincidental.

Cover Art, © Kerry Brooks
Interior Design: JW Manus
ISBN: 978-0-9910668-1-0
A HOW Club Press Production

In memory of my mother.

"If I focus on a problem, the problem increases; if I focus on the answer, the answer increases."
   —The Big Book of Alcoholics Anonymous, p.419

"There's a Zombie on Your Lawn."
        —Plants vs. Zombies

CHAPTER 1

On the day humanity hit the fan, Bill was at the office: Midtown, Eastside. He paused before the glass doors to the Lotto Commission's reception area and quickly sized up the group that waited there. As Press Officer, he had the list of winners on a Plexiglass clipboard. None of them knew it and Bill certainly didn't, but they were lucky too late.

He looked down at the names and pushed through the door: Courtney Hayes, age 27. Although she was the youngest, she guided her six coworkers to him.

"Congratulations. I'm William Curtis." He smiled and shook each of their hands. He shook Courtney's last.

She stood slightly taller than his six feet. Pencil skirt, bright white pearls, hair swept up into a French chignon. She conveyed elegance, which Bill figured she'd learned through long-distance imitation, not privilege. She was unusual though. Most winners were a heart attack waiting to happen. Virtually no one took the twenty-year payoff even though it meant more money for the winner in the end. After a lifetime of Kentucky Fried Chicken and booze to wash it down, the winners usually chose the lump sum and spent it fast, racing against their narrowing arteries.

Bill took in Courtney's tight smile. She would keep her share of the 360 million dollar jackpot and live on the interest, he would bet on it. That was a nice thing to see in his line of work.

The group followed Bill down a quiet corridor past photo portraits of prior winners, many of whom Bill had escorted down this same hallway. It was Bill's job to know as much as possible about the winners. Today, they were all government workers from New York State's Department of Taxation. Four were middle-aged men with thinning hair and cheap suits. Courtney's supervisor was a working mom. The third woman—dumpy and 57—fidgeted with her pocketbook as she walked beside Bill. He looked down at his clipboard: Grace Leocata.

He committed her name to memory: Grace, gray hair, *not* graceful. Bill had learned working on the governor's campaign to get people's names and use them to make them feel comfortable and important. Sometimes his memory devices weren't exactly kind but they worked, and what people didn't know usually didn't hurt them. It was clear that Grace was the one who would need most of his attention today. She was switching back and forth between elation and anxiety, like one of those spook-house portraits that change when you walk by them.

He looked down at her and smiled, "It can be stressful winning fifty million dollars."

She nodded and sort of grimaced, her mouth a rigor mortis slash across her face. The reporters would be lucky to get one word from her.

Bill had Googled everyone. Only Courtney had an internet presence: a LinkedIn page, Twitter account, and a six-year-old news photo from a charitable event she'd organized at a small college upstate. Some of the others had vanilla Facebook pages, nothing more. It was because these winners were so ordinary that the press was interested in them. A bunch of civil servants winning a huge jackpot had riveted every working stiff in the country who struggled to support a family, get the kids through college, and put something away for retirement. At 35 and a government worker himself, Bill identified. Only he never played Lotto and still hadn't started on the marriage with children thing.

Unfortunately, days like today were rare. Bill was accustomed to hosting a couple of dismal winners and half a dozen hyperactive wire reporters. Most times, the Lotto videos got as many hits as a school concert on YouTube.

Bill had once been the "kid with a future" in the governor's Press Office, dealing with front-page issues every day. But that was before the governor got caught with his pants down, bumping a 25-year-old hooker. (Bill was sure it was the fact that he kept his socks on which had done him in. Who could forget that image?) Overnight, there had been a new governor, who had brought his own staff. Bill's governor had ended up with a show on CNN and Bill ended up in Lotto Office purgatory, lucky to have any job in a down economy. It sucked. But he was grateful that nowadays his greatest satisfaction in life came from things other than his career, like sponsoring guys, making meetings and solid friendships.

"Here we are." Bill showed the group into the green room, a windowless lounge with a TV and conference table along one wall. The winners and their spouses helped themselves to donuts, bagels and coffee, which an intern had arranged on a side table.

Bill started his spiel as the winners sat: "The interviewer's Maria Colon. You've probably seen her reading out the Lotto balls on TV. You'll line up on the podium behind her and she'll call each one of you up for a question. Everyone wants to know how you found out you were winners, what you've been doing the last few days, and how you want to spend the money."

"Jim and I had to go to the office and get the ticket," Christopher Stevens, the oldest white-haired man piped up. "We had to keep it safe from Saturday till Monday when your office opened."

Bill committed his name to memory: white-haired Christopher; Bill pictured him as Kris Kringle.

Jim, a guy with a concave chest and graying red mustache, nodded. "We wrapped the ticket in two plastic bags and put it in Courtney's basement inside a metal wastebasket."

"Good thinking, Jim." Bill ticked off Slim Jim's name in his mind, an easy one.

Courtney raised her hand and waved as if to say, *that's me.* "We poured in ten pounds of kitty litter in case of fire."

"Excellent. Maria will like that kind of detail. That's great."

The conference room was packed when Bill led the group there. Reporters filled seventy chairs on each side of a center aisle. The shades were drawn. Balloons in blue and yellow—the official state colors—surrounded the New York State Lotto backsplash, a burst of glitter and stars that covered the wall behind the podium. Cameramen filled the space in front of the first row of seats. The rent-a-cop security guard stood next to the entrance. Everything was in order.

The room quieted down in the glare of the klieg lights. The cameramen focused on Bill ushering the group in. He directed the family members to the reserved seats in the front and waited to the side of the raised platform with the winners.

Maria Colon bounded to the podium and took the microphone, a smile plastered across her face. She had put on a few pounds over the two decades since she'd started reading Lotto balls. But she was still attractive in a pale blue silk skirt and jacket. She held the microphone in her jeweled hand and began to speak.

"Hel—lo, I am Maria Colon, for the New York State Lotto," she announced into the mic as if she'd drunk a half dozen triple-shot venti lattes. "And today we have seven, that's right, seven lucky winners of the three hundred and sixty million dollar Powerball lotto. We have waited anxiously to learn their identities and he—re they are!"

Bill guided the winners to the podium.

"Are you all right, Grace?" He touched Grace's arm as she passed him. Her face had blanched a queasy gray, almost the color of her hair. He'd never seen anyone quite this nervous for the press conference. He'd lay odds she'd be spending her winnings on Xanax and a therapist's couch.

"I'll be okay," she said, looking up at him meekly.

"It'll be a breeze," he reassured her, modulating his voice to keep his annoyance out of it. Then he stood to the side and watched, not at all sure she'd find her voice and knowing that whatever went wrong at the press conference would be his fault. The buck stopped with him. Boy, he could use a drink. Totally out of the question.

A movement caught his eye ten rows deep into the audience. A reporter, BlackBerry in hand, was making a quick exit toward the back of the room. The way he walked, Bill thought it more likely the guy had to make an emergency bathroom visit than a private phone call. The reporter weaved as he ran out, his face gray and stressed like Grace's. Someone coughed on the other side of the aisle. A woman leaned forward, forehead on her knees. Was she sick? The thought of Legionnaire's Disease flitted across Bill's mind, gone as fast as he thought it.

"First up," Maria said into the mic, "we have Christopher Stevens."

White-haired Chris stepped forward and waved his hands above his head like a gold medalist.

"So," Maria said, "tell us how you found out you had the winning numbers."

Chris told the long version of the short story. Bill had heard the same story hundreds of times already. Groundhog Day. The old guy had checked and rechecked and rechecked the numbers then, zowwie, he was a millionaire.

"Jim, come up here," Maria said, good-naturedly gesturing Chris back to his place in line and bringing up Slim Jim.

Maria turned to the audience. "These guys are all tax auditors." She laughed and faked a shudder. "If we're lucky, there will be seven fewer auditors reviewing our taxes now!"

"You might be right, Maria," Jim said, "I'm leaving as soon as I can!"

The audience chuckled and Bill did, too, always glad for a light moment. He'd done this gig with Maria for six years, and enjoyed working with her. She was a pro. And the guys loved talking to her. He watched Maria's eyes taking in Grace's rattled state. Maria had to ask the woman a question—there was no getting around it—but she wasn't looking forward to it. She skipped Grace and went to Courtney, who stood tall, beaming as if born to be in front of the cameras. Courtney's coworkers looked like extras in her movie. It was hard to fathom why she'd ended up working as a bean counter at a state tax office. Lights flashed, the photographers loving her.

Courtney answered Maria's stock question: "No, I don't have any plans yet."

A reporter shouted out, "Are you married?"

The others laughed. She tilted her head, coyly. "Not yet."

Maria touched Courtney's arm as if they were girlfriends. "Well, honey, ya betta get a prenup!"

The flashbulbs went wild for a couple more seconds. Bill wanted to pump his hands, Courtney was their savior. She would be a front-page story all around the state. Maria reluctantly turned to Grace,

"Next, we have—"

Before Grace took a step, Bill heard a percussive blast, loud but distant. Gunshots? Then he heard the unmistakable squeal-bang-crunch of a car crash outside. He glanced toward the sound. Other heads in the audience turned, too.

Ever the professional, Maria kept her smiley focus on Grace, who tottered closer to the mic. Her face was drained of color and she walked with great effort. Bill inched toward the front in case she actually fainted. But, instead, Grace suddenly pivoted on her heels, hauled off and punched Slim Jim hard in the face. Maria reared back. A gasp escaped Bill's lips before he could stop it: *Whoa.* He hesitated, stunned. Then he took two steps toward the front of the room. He couldn't believe Grace could move so fast. This incident would be the way people remembered today, he knew. It would go viral. He had to end this.

Bill signaled to the security guard, who started toward the stage.

Grace gouged her fingernails along Slim Jim's cheeks. He howled and his wife shouted, running forward from the audience, fighting past the surging cameramen.

Still trying to wrap his mind around what was happening, Bill saw Courtney screaming at something in back of him. Her mouth formed a wet chasm of shock, her eyes wide. As Bill started to turn, he was knocked off balance by a cameraman. From one knee, he saw Grace leap on Jim, who now had a bloody river for a face. Her pleated skirt flying up over her thick rump, she took a huge bite out of him.

Bile and breakfast flew out of Bill's throat.

Screams warped the air. Bill straightened and saw a spout of blood arching over the winners and hitting Maria Colon. Her blue suit became a dripping Jackson Pollock. Maria went silent, mid-scream. A bloody mud hole appeared at her middle. She doubled over, an attacker from behind jumping on her ferociously as she fell.

Reporters ran toward Maria to help her, the cameramen still filming. But one of the reporters dove at Maria instead, yowling, mouth impossibly wide, and took a new chunk out of her bloody belly. It was a feeding frenzy. Simon, the office mail guy, rose to his feet behind Maria, his scalp reflecting the camera lights. Six foot five. 270 pounds of muscle. Bloody spittle covered his face. Blood-soaked inter-office mail lay at his feet. He yoked one of the cameramen, a thick forearm around the man's neck. Despite all the screaming, Bill thought he heard the cameraman's bones break then wet chomping as Simon's teeth clamped over the side of his face.

Mayhem had engulfed the entire room. Bill could just make out the security guard's blue uniform in the fray. He couldn't tell whether the guy was killing or being killed. The Lotto winners had scattered. He saw Courtney scrambling out of the way of the chaos, clambering up on a metal desk near the entrance. A five-foot-long reproduction check for three hundred sixty million dollars flew through the air toward her. She deflected it with a Wendy Murdoch smack, sending it spiraling madly into the bedlam.

Courtney's eyes darted around. Her single-mom supervisor ran to hide in the coatroom a few yards away. Bill wanted to help them but a screaming, crying, bloody marsh of winners, reporters and government workers lay between Bill and the women. The exits were filled, too, with the fighting and dying, people bitten and mangled.

Courtney slipped behind the desk, out of sight, before Bill could struggle across the room. Maybe she had managed to get outside. He looked beyond the mess of writhing bodies to find a path toward the exit for himself. But he was barely able to dodge the three reporters and the security guard running by. He watched as one of them pounced and wrestled the old guy, Chris, to the floor. Grunting with flesh-lust, it was Chris who turned on them one by one, his fingers clawing their clothes, his teeth sinking into their limbs.

The security guard tried to get up. He seemed to gain energy, despite the white of his ribs sticking out of his uniform shirt and his ear hanging off as if he'd fought Mike Tyson. He turned. His predator glare zeroed in on Bill as if Bill were the weak animal separated from a herd. The guard's stare couldn't have been human. Even his bone structure seemed transformed in some fundamental way. His eyes had sunk deep into their sockets, his blood-covered jaw bulged, as strong as a shark's. Bill felt a million-year terror of this teeth-gnashing creature, oozing a hate-filled brutality. Moments ago, the man had been the friendly security guard Bill had known for a year; but he was a monster now.

Time stretched slowly like a rubber band but that was an illusion, Bill knew that. He needed a weapon fast, any kind of weapon to keep himself out of the predator's reach. But he didn't see anything. He was going to have to fight for his life, bare-handed.

Then the guard's fierce eyes set on a slow-motion running, screaming woman. His head snapped toward her. He leapt instantly, roaring after her instead of Bill.

Bill barely saw the tackle and blood spray at the farthest reach of his peripheral vision. He sprinted to a supply closet just off an entryway at the back of the room. He reached it in time and shut himself in, standing in pitch black, his face against the cold wall, his back lodged against a metal shelf. Screams, howls, moans, and the stench of blood and feces filtered into the closet. His trembling fingers reached inside his pocket for his cell phone. Not there. It was at his desk. He was alone in the noisy dark, praying.

CHAPTER 2

The death racket quieted outside the supply closet. Bill pressed the button on his sports watch. It glowed green: 1:02 PM. It had been a half hour since the press conference began. He took a deep breath and opened the closet a crack. Light flooded in. Silence. No moans of the injured, no screams. For a moment, Bill doubted his sanity. Would he walk out and find his coworkers back at their desks pounding away at their computers? Would they be talking quietly on their phones as if nothing had happened? No . . . he could still smell it: the blood and guts, thick enough to taste and sticky beneath his feet as he approached the conference room.

Blood covered the walls. He was alone, no sign of any of his coworkers, the attackers, or Courtney and her supervisor. Of the winners, the two of them had still been alive, still normal the last time he'd seen them. He reared back, almost bumping into a leg draped across a chair. It had been gnawed to the bone, the shoe still attached. There were no whole corpses, just body parts strewn haphazardly: a hand on the floor, what looked like a neck bone, clumps of hair still attached to scalps.

Bill threw up again. Jeez, so much for his belief that he was steely under fire. He wiped his mouth with the back of his sleeve and inched along the wall, heading toward the security desk and phone near the entrance to the room. He cut a path around deep patches of blood on the carpet. Courtney was cowering underneath the desk.

She looked up at him and sobbed, "Please don't kill me."

He held up his hands, palms out, whispering just in case, "I think it's over."

She crawled out with his help, trembling and weak. He picked up the phone and dialed 911.

A recording announced: "I'm sorry, all lines are busy. An operator will be with you in a moment."

"It's a recording." He waited for an operator to pick up.

Courtney shivered.

"They're not picking up," Bill told her, waiting anyway.

Courtney spoke, words barely coming out, "My boss . . . she got up."

"What?"

"But she couldn't have gotten up." Courtney whispered and wept the words. "They found her in the closet. They ripped her lungs out. I saw her lungs." Courtney forced the words, "She got up . . . afterwards. I saw. They stopped eating her. She got up and went with them. She looked like them, vicious, crazy . . . grabbing. I saw her attack a woman."

"Zombies. They're zombies," Bill said almost to himself, the words scraping out of his throat as if saying them was what made the carnage real. Bill set the phone receiver on the desk, the canned police operator still repeating her please-hold mantra.

From the street, a human shriek and a car alarm's warble penetrated the double-glazed windows.

For the first time since the car crash during the press conference, Bill realized that something was going on outside. He rushed to the window, Courtney following. Ominous cries, hundreds of voices. His nerves on fire, Bill lifted the blinds. Below, twelve flights down on wide Third Avenue, the street overflowed with fighting, howling people. The chaos they had just witnessed at the press conference was still unfolding—to the 1000th power.

It reminded Bill of Church Street near the World Trade Center, where he'd been on 9/11. Only, on that day, before the towers collapsed, the crowds had been looking up at the fire or streaming away in a sort of stunned and frightened but sensible way. Not today.

A group of four men and a woman in office attire ran out of a black-glass office building across the street. The instant they stepped outside, hundreds of frenzied zombies climbed over each other to rip them apart. A cry caught in Courtney's throat. Bill didn't hear his own voice doing the same. He reached over to Courtney, who had started to whimper. The keening of the four stopped. The zombies seemed to go even crazier then: shrieking, howling. A wide swath of the mob broke off and swarmed into the black-glass building like army ants overwhelming a tropical plantation.

Courtney stuttered out words, "Are they looking for survivors . . . to eat?"

Bill felt as if his head were a shaken snow globe. He couldn't put his thoughts together. Then it dawned on him: On 9/11, the air had been filled with sirens coming from every direction; he'd seen police and firemen all over the place. But now there were no sirens, no firemen, no police at all.

Bill grabbed Courtney's arm. "There's a TV in the Commissioner's office. The door locks, too. Maybe people are hiding in there."

"My pocketbook. My cell. I have to call my father."

"Okay."

At the green room, Bill pressed his ear against the door before opening it. There was nobody there. On the chairs and tables, the winners' belongings were already incongruous artifacts of another time. Courtney grabbed her shoulder bag while Bill kept watch in the hallway outside.

On the way to the Lotto Commissioner's office, they passed empty, blood-splattered cubicles. Bill recognized the torso of the college intern who had cheerfully arranged the balloons that morning, lying near her cubicle. Courtney almost stumbled over the partial corpse. Bill put out his hand to steady her while scanning the glass-front offices along the wall. No sign of life anywhere. He went into his office and picked up his North Face backpack from under his desk. Bill heard Courtney mumbling, "But we won the Lotto."

The door to the Commissioner's corner office was open. The room was empty and clean. Air conditioning battled with afternoon sun that heated the large windows, but there was no sign of human struggle. Legal pads and pens, and a couple of stray water bottles sat on a small glass conference table. It looked as if a meeting had been interrupted.

Bill locked the door behind them. He went to the back of the room, listened at the door to the Commissioner's private bathroom then pulled it open. No sign of life or death. Bill closed the door again and took a deep breath.

A TV was mounted near the ceiling in a corner, where the Commissioner could watch from behind his desk. Courtney picked up the remote control from the conference table. Out of the corner of her eye, she caught a glimpse of a bloody madman banging from inside the window of an office building across 53rd street. She leapt backward and let out a yelp. It seemed as if he wanted to jump through the glass to get her. "He's seen us! They're going to come back!"

Bill ran to the window and slammed the blinds shut. "He wouldn't know where we are from outside."

Courtney helped Bill shut the other Venetian blinds. "He'd know the floor."

Bill moved from window to window, lowering blinds. "I don't think they're able to reason like that . . . you saw them."

Courtney and Bill moved to the office's second wall of windows, which overlooked the black-glass office building. Next door to it was the block-long, Lipstick Building, an oblong, rouge-colored tube of offices where Bernie Madoff used to work. The high-rent business district had been transformed by the masses of bodies crowding the street, all zombies now.

Courtney dropped to the floor, feeling safest out of the line of sight even with the blinds closed. She sobbed for a moment, the fear overwhelming. Then she wiped her nose with the back of her hand and talked to herself: *Pull yourself together, NOW.*

She crawled and aimed the remote control, finding the 24-hour cable news station, NY1. Snow. Then Channel 4. Snow. On the next channel, the emergency broadcast system buzzed. Then on Channel 9, snow again.

Bill shook his head. "Jes—"

Courtney cut him off, sharply, unwilling to think about what it meant. "The cable's out. They'll fix it."

Bill gave Courtney a long look. She wasn't getting it. He took in her terror, her face blotchy and streaked with tears. He returned to the window and peeked out the side of the blinds. The man Courtney had seen was still banging at the window across the street. "He's there. He's not coming for us."

Courtney took a deep breath.

Bill sat at the Commissioner's desk and logged on to the computer. Courtney pulled out her iPhone and scrolled through her contacts. Then she stood behind Bill to look at what he was doing. The CNN homepage came up on the PC first. Courtney read over his shoulder. It had a breaking news item, only a sentence, not even large type: *Worldwide Reports of Terrorist Attacks*. The report was logged in at the same moment the news conference began, 12:30 PM. Bill clicked but there was no link to a story.

Bill double-clicked into the Drudge Report. As a PR person, he checked it sometimes to see if a scandal was going to break. Drudge didn't waste time confirming facts and sources, which had its benefits.

At the top in bold caps, the headline said: *ZOMBIES??*

Bill clicked: *Starting at 12:30 PM EST worldwide reports of massacres. Unconfirmed reports that the dead are reanimating as zombies, bringing the number of attackers to world-threatening levels.*

Bill laughed, something about reading the headline overloaded his brain like a crashing website. He exhaled a ragged breath and peered at the screen, trying to focus. His voice came out a harsh whisper, "This hasn't been updated since 12:30. The attack must have happened everywhere at the same time."

"It happened all over the world . . ." Courtney's voice drifted off, no longer able to deny it. She dialed her father's number but his phone went straight to voicemail. "My father always forgets his phone," she said almost to herself, feeling as if her thoughts were passing through cheesecloth. "Half the time it's out of juice even if he has it with him."

"My dad, too."

Bill went to Twitter on the PC. There were pages of calls for help. People under attack, hiding out, then they'd tapered off. Only one in the last few minutes.

Courtney tweeted from her own phone: "East Side Manhattan— two survivors. Help!" She didn't dare put in an address. They didn't know who their enemies were.

While she concentrated on calling her contact list, Bill pulled his phone from his backpack and tried his parents. No one picked up.

They each left half a dozen messages before Courtney put her phone down. For a second, the image of her father, alone and fighting off attackers in his Inwood apartment, came to her. Her throat closed. She had to force herself to breathe.

"I can't believe this," Bill whispered to himself. "I can't believe this."

Nothing more to do. Courtney sat on the floor with her back to the wall and cried into her hands. Bill used his thumb and index fingers to stanch his tears, his own throat tight. He was hanging on by a frayed thread—how could he look out for Courtney, too?

A squeal of tires and a loud crash downstairs launched them to their feet. They opened the slats to the blinds and peered out. A fire truck had crashed head-on into the Lipstick Building. Someone was still alive to drive that truck . . . or had been.

The shrieks from the street became more urgent. The mob of zombies surged on the fire truck. They all tried to get a piece of the driver; but the truck exploded into a fireball, shattering windows on the first few floors of the building and sending zombies flying backward like flaming spears. Fire shot up the side of the Lipstick Building. The crowd receded and expanded haphazardly, some charred, some not. The moans and screams didn't change. The zombies showed no sign of pain, although some of their bodies incinerated down to ash and bone. The smoke from across the street began seeping into the Commissioner's office. No one was coming to fight the fire.

Bill sat on the carpeted floor, a couple of feet from Courtney. He closed his eyes and rested his head against the wall, worrying about his parents. Were they safe in their house in New Jersey? He thought about the woman he'd had a date with on Saturday. It had actually been a promising evening, although he still didn't know her that well. He didn't even know her exact address. He wondered if he would ever see her again.

"Whenever I had Lotto fantasies," Courtney said, quietly, "I'd always think about the vacations I'd take, the homes I'd own. I would meet Mr. Right, raise kids, travel, not have to work, all of that. But in the end I would always end up getting a thought like: terminal cancer. I couldn't get through a Lotto fantasy without envisioning some kind of disaster. But when I won the Lotto for real—nineteen million dollars lump sum after taxes was my share," she told him even though he knew. "I really thought all my dreams would come true."

Bill looked at Courtney. The last thing he cared about was her Lotto millions. He might be at the office, but he was definitely off duty, probably forever. "If it's any consolation, Courtney, I'm sure the world isn't ending because you won the Lotto."

"Are you adding insult to apocalypse, really?" she said, angrily.

"I'm sorry," Bill said, immediately wishing he hadn't said anything. "It's been a long day." The greatest understatement ever told.

She waved it off and rested her back against the wall, staring at nothing.

They sat on the floor for hours that way, the sky darkening outside. Courtney dozed off—as much from emotional overload as fatigue. She startled awake to the sound of another nearby explosion. Screams rose from downstairs as if the explosions and shrieks from the zombies were an evangelical call and response. Reality crashed back on her and she had a sense of déjà vu. For weeks after her mother's death, she had opened her eyes to the sunlight each morning thinking it was a normal day, but then the devastating reality would crash down on her like a wrecking ball. She had been only eleven when her mother died. Now, she listened to the hellish cries of the undead moving toward the explosion and harsh reality sank back in. Shivers scurried up her spine.

Bill's red-rimmed eyes hadn't closed for more than a moment while she slept. The office lights went out, and Bill waved his arm in the air as he'd done twenty times already. The motion-sensor lights popped back on.

Courtney breathed in the smoky air. "We can't possibly be all alone. If we're alive, other people are alive, too, hiding just like we are. We should try to get to a police station."

"A police station? We wouldn't get ten feet out there. The first responders aren't responding . . . they've eaten each other, Courtney."

She shuddered. "Maybe there are some left. It would take time for them to get to us, to help us."

"You're right . . . it would take time," Bill pondered aloud. "There must be two ways of becoming a zombie. The ones who were sick could have picked up the infection earlier, hours or even weeks earlier. But when they attack, they give it to others instantly. That's why everything went crazy right away." He thought back to the distorted face of the security guard with the Mike Tyson ear. "But I can't really believe anything as mundane as an infection could cause all this . . . That Grace lady, the one who started the attacks by biting Jim . . . did you have any idea that something was wrong with her? Did anything happen to her before?"

"Nothing that I saw. She was such a bland person, not someone I paid much attention to. I didn't really take in how odd she looked with the gray skin and all until she hit him. I didn't hear her make any funny noises until right before. I remember thinking it was strange, how nervous she was, that she would gasp like that." Courtney took a deep breath. "My boss . . . I think they didn't want to eat her after a certain point. They lost interest all at once. Then she became one of them."

Bill palmed the sides of his face, rubbing his skin downward, listening to the cacophony of howls and moans downstairs. "Zombies don't eat each other once their flesh is infected . . . or maybe they're dead. That's why a zombie virus would be such a good weapon for terrorists. Their numbers would only increase."

"No terrorist would do that. It would destroy *their* people, too." Courtney hugged her arms. "But I've been thinking it must be passed by body fluids, saliva to blood . . . like on TV."

"The Walking Dead."

"Right, and like vampires, too."

She watched Bill as he stared straight ahead, only moving from time to time to wave the lights back on. His slick corporate look had been replaced by a five o'clock shadow and tousled hair. He was a center-of-the-herd kind of guy, she figured, someone who would set up a press conference but didn't want to be in the spotlight. Brown hair, brown eyes, pleasant-looking but maybe headed prematurely to middle age. Now that his suit jacket was off, she noticed he had an extra ten pounds around his middle. She found herself wondering whether he was one of those people who paid for a monthly gym membership as if it were a charitable donation. She hoped he could run.

Courtney unconsciously reverted to an old habit: she bit off her index-finger nail to the quick then shook her finger, the pain setting in instantly. She looked at the drop of blood that appeared. "I read once that it takes up to a minute for blood to circulate through the body. The zombie infection or whatever it is must shoot straight from the bite through the bloodstream to the brain."

Bill took a sip of the bottle of water he'd kept in his knapsack. "After a few seconds, you can see there's nothing human in their eyes. And they're not just limping along like in *Night of the Living Dead*. Some of them are fast and strong." Bill took a hard look at his water bottle. "We better stick to bottled water."

"What?"

"We don't know how the first zombie got sick. It could have been from a contaminated water supply. I always drink bottled water. I'm going to stick to that. You should, too."

Courtney's mouth clamped into an anxious line. She didn't want to think they could still become zombies by drinking the wrong drink or eating the wrong food. It was bad enough they were under siege and outnumbered by thousands, maybe millions of murderous monsters. She shook her head. "It couldn't be food or water. People would have eaten and drunk at different times, so the first people wouldn't have all gotten sick at the same time."

"You're right. It could have been something in the air . . . that only affected a small number of people. Beyond explanation. I don't know why I have a hard time believing there's something supernatural going on. It's not like that's a stretch of imagination after everything we've seen."

Courtney leaned her head back again. Thoughts smashed around inside her skull until she couldn't keep her eyes closed anymore. She looked around at the office that had become their bunker. It had been such a great day, an amazing day, at first. She had won the Lotto. She had done great at the press conference, especially when Maria asked her about being married. Everything had been perfect. Courtney looked at Bill. She should count her blessings. She could have been alone. She couldn't imagine getting through this alone. "You know, you run one hell of a press conference."

Bill let out a clipped laugh. "Was that before or after I shipped in the zombies for the video?"

Courtney giggled with Bill, both of them wiping tears away, half out of their minds as they waited for the long night to be over.

CHAPTER 3

When the sky lightened, Bill stood by the window, getting a sliver-glimpse of Third Avenue's overnight destruction. Dozens of cars were mangled or just sitting in the middle of the street, their windows shattered. It was the same for the half dozen blocks he could see up and down Third Avenue. Twisted metal, flaming refuse and dead bodies littered the ravine between tall office buildings.

The smoke seeping steadily into the office had become uncomfortably thick. From behind him, Courtney spoke, hoarsely, "It's like breathing glass."

Bill turned back to her. "The street's almost empty. Now may be our best chance."

Courtney was glad to hear Bill talking about leaving, even though her breath quickened with panic at the thought of it. "We'll find other people. Find out what's happening in the outside world."

"If there is an outside world."

Courtney wheeled away, his comment terrifying her. In the Commissioner's bathroom, she grabbed a pair of men's trousers from a hook on the door. She pulled them on and rolled them up at the waist to make up for their being too big. Then she returned to the office and put on ballet-style flats she'd brought to the press conference in her shoulder bag. Luckily, she wouldn't be running in high heels like in the old horror movies.

They left the office fast, not wanting to give their fear time to paralyze them, and they made their way down cement stairs to the building's lobby. The sun glared sideways through the lobby's tall windows. Their heads swam with a toxic speedball of adrenaline and sleep deprivation; both flattened themselves against a rectangular marble column. The smell of human remains thickened the air. Tangled, mostly-eaten bodies—two, maybe three—were piled near the newsstand at the back of the atrium. Courtney averted her eyes to avoid sorting the bodies out in her mind.

Bill gripped a baseball bat he'd taken from the empty office of one of his work buddies who'd played in a Central Park league on Wednesdays after work. Bill already thought of him and most everybody else in past tense, although the lack of internet news and total silence of the phones kept playing tricks on him. His mind still created pictures of himself walking through a door and finding everyone alive.

The bat had been the only weapon Bill could think of. Unfortunately, he didn't have much hope for its effectiveness against multiple attackers. Courtney held a butcher knife she'd taken from the office pantry. They needed to get hold of guns, which he only wished he knew how to use.

From where they hid, the lobby windows looked out on the corner of Third Avenue and 53rd Street. The same cars they'd seen from above were stopped at a traffic light, which changed from red to green now. Some of the cars had crashed, others had burned, others had simply been abandoned with their doors left open.

"Could we take one of them?" Courtney whispered. "They could have keys in them."

Bill recalled the section of Third Avenue they'd seen from the window. "The streets are jammed with cars and there's debris and crashed cars blocking the sidewalks. The noise of the car moving could attract *them* . . . and we'd be—"

"Never mind. I get the picture."

A noise near the lobby security desk jolted them. They pressed their backs against the marble column. From the corner of her eye, Courtney glimpsed a bloodied man. He emitted something between a moan and a growl as he came closer, not yet seeing them.

Bill's muscles cinched tight, waiting to swing.

The man's yellowed eyes swiveled to fix on them. Snarling, he turned to grab Courtney. Bill swung with terror-powered force. The man's ribs crushed inward as he flew backward, but he didn't even wince. He regained his balance and came toward them again. Bill swung at the man's head, once, twice, three times. The skull imploded. Courtney leapt backward. Brain splattered and spilled in her direction, and the man fell. She and Bill exhaled simultaneously.

"So, it's true . . . we have to destroy the brain," Bill said.

They heard the collective shrieks of a mob approaching from the Third Avenue side of the building. There was a ferocity to the sound: Predator spotting prey.

Courtney and Bill froze, unsure what to do. A group of the zombies appeared in the street, but they weren't headed toward where the two of them were barely hidden. They had converged on a white Incredible Edibles truck. The crowd pounded with their fists against the truck's metal. The truck rocked back and forth. Metal screeched under the assault of dozens of attackers, who seemed to feel no pain as their fists slammed into the side of the truck. The fruit bouquets etched onto the side of the truck became three dimensional: punched-in chocolate-covered strawberries, buckled pineapple, and a widening hole in the cantaloupes.

As the mob tried to reach through the hole, a man's boot slammed the hole from inside. They could hear him yell and wished they could help. He kicked at the hands of his attackers, hands that were steadily widening the hole. One finally grabbed the man's leg and, joined by dozens of grappling hands, pulled it out through the hole. The metal cut the leg open. The crowd's roar rose. They crashed through to consume him.

Bill and Courtney crept back behind the column.

"How did they know he was in there?" Bill whispered.

Courtney's eyes burned from smoke and horror. "They sensed him somehow. If it was smell, why didn't they smell him before?"

"Maybe it was refrigerated until now . . . and he ran out of gas?"

"Why haven't they smelled us?" Courtney peered out at the Incredible Edibles feast still going on. "Are we upwind?"

"Jeez . . . we better go while they're still eating."

Courtney and Bill ran toward the lobby doors farthest from the crowd. They slipped out into the acrid spring air and ran west toward Lexington Avenue. Panting with fear, they sprinted a few yards to the first recessed space in the building's granite facade, a closed metal service entrance. It gave them a few inches of cover. They peered out then ran to the next one.

At each entryway, they mentally took measure of the distance to the next doorway. They sprinted a zigzag around blood puddles and fly-infested body scraps that looked like trash left carelessly after a garbage truck run. They ducked for cover a half dozen times before they crouched across the street from an entrance to the silver Citicorp building with its iconic slanted roof above.

Bill peeked around the wall. Zombie crowds were moving down Lexington Avenue. He pointed across the street to the Derek Jeter health club on the first floor of the Citicorp building. Jeter's useless face looked down at them, fifteen feet tall.

Bill grabbed Courtney's hand. "Go!"

They dashed across the street, unnoticed, and silently slammed into the high-powered air conditioning of the health club, scanning the reception area. No sign of zombies. The smell of decay wrinkled the cold air.

Courtney's eyes lit on the gym's clothing shop. "I need clothes." She touched the trousers she wore. "I can't run fast in these."

They stayed low and ran across the reception area to the glass-walled room with one side open to aisles of hanging shorts and t-shirts. Mannequins in workout clothes lined one wall. A zombie in skin tight spandex, her nose just two holes in her face, lurched out from among the plastic people. Courtney had time to see the bare six-pack of her midriff as the woman bore down on her. Without thinking, she round-housed the butcher knife through the woman's temple, then jumped out of the way. Bill's baseball bat finished the job.

Courtney backed up in shock, making contact with a rack full of clothes. She fell, landing in a pile of jog bras, shorts and noisy hangers. She looked at her brain-drenched hand in disgust, forced herself to pull the knife from the woman's temple. The stink of the infected woman was almost too much to bear in close quarters. Courtney wiped the knife and her hand on t-shirts scattered next to her.

Bill looked at her, in awe.

Courtney's eyes opened wide, her breath turning ragged. She held up her finger where she'd bitten off her nail the night before, leaving a tiny wound. They could both see the wetness where the woman's brains had coated it.

Bill counted the seconds. How long would it take for the infection to travel her blood stream? Courtney crumpled into herself, mewling. Bill would have tried to comfort her but his lips were sealed shut and his heart beat too wildly. He gripped the baseball bat, his knuckles whitening. His thoughts became a tornado as he braced himself for what he'd have to do if she turned into one of them.

He silently counted—one Mississippi, two Mississippi—sixty times before he relaxed his grip. He spoke softly, "You don't have it. You're fine."

Courtney wiped her tears with her sleeve, her breath smoothing out. Her voice came out a shaky murmur, "I don't think 'fine' is a word I'd use right now." She took a deep breath. "Maybe 'better.' That might be the word: Better. Whew." She lay her palm on her chest. "Too close."

Crouched low, they cased out the rest of the tiny store. Courtney forced herself to focus on the task at hand. She snatched a pair of black running shorts, a jog bra and a t-shirt from hangers. She changed between clothing racks, not giving any thought to Bill's seeing her. Bill traded in his suit pants and wrinkled dress shirt for a pair of shorts and a t-shirt. He took a pair of sneakers from a male mannequin. She put her ballet-style shoes back on. She'd need to find a sneaker store—the only sneakers here were on the mannequins. The men's were too big and the women's too small for her size eleven feet.

Then they snuck around to the gym snack bar. Courtney washed her arm and the knife at a steel sink, built into a pocket of space that was shielded from view of the lobby and street. She found a sharp knife at the juice bar, which she put into her pocketbook as a backup. They both stashed some bottled waters and energy bars in their bags and sat behind the snack bar counter, downing bottled smoothies.

"Your first shopping spree since the Lotto," Bill said.

"So, you're an asshole."

"Sometimes." Bill put down his empty smoothie container. "Really, you did a great job in there. Amazing."

"Thanks." Courtney took a sweet sip. "You pack a pretty good punch yourself."

Bill finished one smoothie and opened another. "We're gonna need real supplies and larger backpacks to carry them."

"I still want to go to the police station."

"If there were police, we would have heard gunshots . . . sirens."

"People could be hiding there."

"Maybe you're right. We'll at least try to get weapons there. But I have to go downstairs first."

"Downstairs?"

"The basement. There are meeting rooms three flights down."

Courtney looked quizzically at him. "I don't understand."

"I know it's a chance in hell," Bill said, "but I have some friends who met there at noon yesterday. I'd have been there, too, if it hadn't been for the press conference. I want to check if anyone's there."

"What were they doing down there?" Courtney asked, but the puzzle pieces were already clicking into place for her.

"It was an AA meeting."

"You're an alcoholic."

"Yes. Eleven years sober."

Courtney grimaced and rested her head back against the wall, looking up as if talking to God. "Great, really great."

"Wow," he said, blindsided by her dismay. "You'd have thought I said I was an undercover zombie."

Courtney took a deep breath, surprised she could actually feel less safe. "I'm sorry. My parents were alcoholics . . . and addicts."

"Well, you've definitely got the righteous indignation part down." Bill laughed bitterly. "Now we know there's a fate worse than being the child of an addict."

"Screw you. Just don't get fucking drunk on me. I want to live."

"No kidding," Bill said, angrily. "Me, too."

Trying to work up courage to move out from their hiding place, Courtney looked sideways at Bill. "I still can't believe you'd rather look for a bunch of drunks than find the police station. Don't you think that's a little weird, even for an AA guy?"

"You're a piece of work, you know that?" Bill wouldn't say what he thought—this was no time for a therapy session—but he knew now that Courtney wasn't halfway as together as she'd seemed at the Lotto podium. She'd been the screwed-up child of addicts, working under deep cover in an accounting office. He was impressed though. She was doing incredibly well, all things considered. "So, are you coming or not?"

"As long as we go to the police station next. The police are our friends, even if you were probably a criminal once."

"Thanks for the vote of confidence."

They walked through the Citicorp Building's basement atrium, passing café tables and a grand piano, which had set the mood each day for the lunchtime crowds. Smoke seeped from a restaurant's open entryway. Opaque air above confirmed that they needed to get in and out of the building fast. Bill realized that no building in Midtown would be safe. The restaurant workers wouldn't have had time to turn off their ovens and stovetops, all of which would have been working double time at the height of lunch hour.

At the far end of the atrium, they passed an empty security desk, skipped the elevator and entered an unmarked, orange-walled staircase. The first flight down led to a community center, which usually served five-dollar lunches to senior citizens. One more flight down and they'd get to the meeting rooms. Bill checked for movement in the senior center, looking through a narrow glass window in the metal double doors.

A face met his, right at the glass. He reared back with a yelp. He started to grab Courtney's arm to run.

"Wait," he heard a female voice through the door. "Help."

"Oh shit," Bill said.

Courtney held her stomach, recovering from the flood of anxiety.

A woman pushed the door open. She was petite, fit, wearing stretch jeans and a disheveled silk blouse. She appeared shocked or it might have been Botox. Courtney recognized the alien look: the woman had been artificially frozen at early middle age. Her $500 page-boy—short in back, long in front—was worse for her night in hell, but it still accentuated her strong jaw line and stretched-tight cheekbones.

Smelling of urine and sweat, the woman grasped and hugged both of them. Courtney resisted her impulse to pull away. The woman's gold watch glinted. She turned to Bill. "You're from the meeting."

"Yeah."

"I know you, Bill, right?"

"Patty?" Bill guessed her name. He remembered—her hair had reminded him of Patty Duke when he'd once heard her share.

She took his arm, kindly. "There's no one left. I'm the only one who made it."

Bill felt as if he'd been punched in the stomach even though he'd guessed that his friends, sponsor and sponsees would be dead. "What happened?"

"I was running late. When I walked out of the stairwell, people were stampeding from the meeting room, screaming, others chasing. I didn't have time for a long look. But some of the ones chasing were people I saw here all the time. I ran to the ladies room, locked myself into a stall and stood on the toilet. Another woman did the same in the next stall. The killers filled up the bathroom. They banged at her stall with the most horrible howling and screaming. They banged until the door crashed in. At the last minute, the girl . . . she jumped down from the toilet and tried to get under the wall to me. From where I was, I could see . . ." Patty tore up, her lips closed tight. She took a breath before continuing, "They dragged her out . . .

"I stood on the toilet for hours. The weirdest part, I can't understand . . . the killers never knew I was there but—I've thought about this a lot—they smelled that girl out like a cat stalking a hidden mouse."

CHAPTER 4

They didn't see anyone alive as they ran doorway-to-doorway to the Midtown East Precinct. The City was disintegrating by the minute. Flammable items exploded in the distance, sending jarring booms from across the East River in Queens. The smoke was getting thicker, and Bill wondered what toxic chemicals the factories there were spewing.

They caught their breath in a service entrance to one of Third Avenue's office towers. Savage war cries, hundreds of demented voices, echoed off the glistening building.

Patty whispered to the others, "I keep searching for human faces in windows. But there's no one. Yesterday I walked down the stairs to the meeting. It took two minutes for me to get to the bottom. The whole world turned upside down in two minutes."

"Let's go," Bill said, worrying that Patty might freak out. "We're almost to the precinct."

They moved from their hiding place, staying close to the buildings.

Despite the explosions and undead cacophony, the absence of car engines, sirens, horns, ringing cell phones and people talking, created momentary silences deeper than any Bill had ever experienced: dead silence. It reminded him of 9/11 again. When he'd gotten home that day, there had been no cars on the highway near his apartment. The summer day had become as hushed as the City after a blizzard. Things had never been quite the same after the attack, but daily life had returned to a new normal that wasn't so different from the old. Bill had gone back to work in the same office with the same coworkers. Later on, he'd gone to graduate school then moved to his power-job-in-training with the Governor's office. The subways had been screwed up for a year, worse than anyone would ever have imagined, but he hadn't even lost any close friends. His life had gone on. Yet, the inhuman noises in the distance and the fires that raged unattended made it clear that what was happening now was an entirely new kind of horror.

Bill chastised himself for letting his mind wander. He couldn't blame his mind for wanting to shut down. Things were bad, really bad, but he had to keep a grip on himself. AA had taught him that 90% of life was about showing up, and now it was a matter of life and death . . . or worse.

All their faces dropped with dismay when they saw the police station from across 52nd Street. Even Bill, who had warned they shouldn't expect help there, was devastated by its condition. He'd hoped to get weapons, and despite himself, he'd imagined finding at least one Rambo cop holding down the fort. It would have been nice to let someone else do the thinking for them. But after almost an hour spent traveling three blocks of human holocaust to get there, they could only stare at the precinct, burnt black.

"It looks like a news photo of a terrorist bombing," Patty whispered.

Courtney pointed to a couple of scorched police cars parked on the sidewalk. "They tried to barricade it."

"If it was anything like what we went through, it must have been cops fighting cops," Bill said. "And the bad guys had the element of surprise."

"Where are the survivors?" Patty murmured almost to herself. "We can't be all alone."

"There's nothing for us here." Courtney turned away.

They ran with their hearts in their throats across Third Avenue, dodging stranded cars and sprinting across the empty bus lane and sidewalk. They rested in the entryway to a Korean nail salon then dashed to the Sports Authority, taking in its empty cashier stations and clothing aisles. The place looked pretty much intact as if human beings had been zapped from Earth. They inched warily past each empty aisle.

On the second floor, Patty pointed to the backpack section and turned a corner. A store clerk in a bloody Izod shirt and urine-soaked khakis, lurched to his feet from where he'd crouched in a corner. His bloodshot eyes zoomed in on her. Doubt flashed across her mind: *Was he infected, alive, dead?*

"Ahh," she started to speak, stepping back as he advanced toward her.

Her eyes lowered to the place where he'd crouched. A pile of raw meat. It could have been human or animal but it sure wasn't a Big Mac. She jumped back. The man charged.

"Look out!" Courtney pushed her.

The clerk's head exploded, Bill's bat slamming through it.

"Oh my God!" Patty gasped.

Courtney grabbed Patty's arm. "Come on."

Courtney picked out a baseball bat, and Bill handed one to Patty. They looted flashlights and sturdy backpacks, filling them with bottles of water, trail mix and beef jerky. Courtney and Patty found sneakers and put them on.

"It's getting late," Patty said when they peered out at Third Avenue from the entrance. "I live just a few blocks from here. If we can get there, we can stay safe for a while."

The sun had lowered behind the buildings.

"We don't want to be out after dark," Courtney agreed.

"If we can get to your place, we can figure out our next move," Bill said.

"Let's go, then. This way."

They made their way down a long residential side street to Patty's building on First Avenue. The neighborhood changed from a commercial district to residential, mostly small mix-and-match apartment buildings on the side blocks anchored by luxury high rises on the corners. A mangled woman and a snarling doctor in a soiled Sloan Kettering medical coat leapt at them from a doorway. Bill batted down the woman. He heard Courtney in the background, chanting with each swing at the doctor, "Motherfucker, motherfucker!"

Courtney straightened up, her face red.

At her feet, the doctor moved his hand, almost imperceptibly. Patty swung down at him, the final blow pulverizing his face. He went still.

Tears ran down Patty's cheeks. She pointed a trembling finger toward her building. It was a brown brick high rise with a circular driveway and fountain out front. The fountain with its lit-up, pink-tinted water seemed incongruously elegant and inviting to Bill and Courtney—like an oasis in the desert.

On First Avenue, they wove through an obstacle course of cars, trucks and buses. Bill made his way around a gargantuan, black-glassed limo, almost as long as a bus.

Nearly at Patty's place, they heard a noise.

"What the—?" Bill's eyes opened wide, realizing the source of the sound as his words formed.

The roar sounded like a 50-foot tsunami washing through Manhattan's canyons. Disharmonious wails, moans and stomps, all getting louder. It had to be thousands of zombies, tens of thousands . . . heading their way. Bill froze amidst the stalled vehicles, his eyes darting around. No time to make it to Patty's building. No time to even get to the other side of the street.

Bill grabbed Patty's arm and ran two steps, Courtney following. He grasped the door handle to the limo. It opened. "Come on!"

The inside of the limo—dark and as long as a living room—was filled with gnawed corpses, at least a dozen of them. Chinese men in business suits were sprawled on the floor and couches that lined the car below its black windows. The death-stench blasted out just as the gangrenous stink of the oncoming zombie mob filled the outside air. The one-two punch of air was so thick Bill could taste it.

No choice. He and the women dove inside among the corpses just as the first zombies rounded the corner onto First Avenue. The last in, fighting not to gag, Courtney slammed the door shut behind them.

A Chinese businessman pounced at Bill from among the corpses. Bill bunted his bat defensively, the man on top of him. Patty yelled and swung her bat but tripped over a corpse leg.

The street and sidewalk filled with milling, shuffling, stomping dead on the other side of the limo's tinted glass, while Bill fought off the Chinese man. A zombie outside turned toward the glass, hearing the noise.

"A little help here!" Bill called, desperately.

"Not enough room!" Courtney couldn't get a full swing with her bat under the low ceiling. She dropped it and picked up a crystal decanter from the limo bar, which she slammed twice into the businessman's skull. He fell on Bill. She hit him again then dropped the bottle.

"Stay under him!" Patty said to Bill, forcing herself to get underneath the corpse she'd tripped over.

Courtney swallowed bile and buried herself, too.

From under the corpses they could see the curious zombie peering through the glass toward them. They couldn't tell what he could see through the dark windows from so close. They held their breath. Another zombie banged into him, and he allowed himself to be jostled away, moving in the direction of the crowd.

They watched the zombies crashing into each other on the far side of the glass. Courtney couldn't shut out the memory of the Incredible Edible guy being pulled into the crowd. Her heart jumped each time one of the zombies banged the glass with an arm or elbow. Burrowed as deeply as possible under the horrifying body, she stared at the glass as if she could will it to hold.

The mob thickened still more, as tight as sardines. The limo rocked with the force of the jostling dead.

"It's gonna flip!" Courtney sobbed.

The limo rose on two wheels then fall back again. Corpses rolled off the couches on top of them like items falling off shelves during an earthquake. A spider web of cracks formed on a back window.

They all gasped: This was it.

The vibrations of the marching dead on pavement pounded into their bones and muscles. The cracks in the spider-web glass grew longer. They barely breathed. The mob all churned in the same general direction, brushing past both sides of the car. One horrible being after the next passed the windows. Eventually, though, the crowd thinned out. The tidal wave of dead dissipated. They were on the far side of its crest.

Bill took in the sight of the upended liquor decanter next to the dead zombie's face. He tried to make a joke of it. "That's a damn shame."

Courtney looked at Bill. "Better him then you."

When the back end of the crowd disappeared, they left the limo.

THERE WERE NO light bulbs tinting the water in the fountain outside Patty's building. It was circulating blood through its drains and back out the top again. The pink water splashed down on a pile of corpses, their skulls crushed by what must have been a fall from above. In Patty's lobby, an old dead guy with a walker appended to his hands as if by habit tried to have a go at them. But he was slower than those who had been younger in life. When Bill hit him, his skull gave way like an eggshell.

Afraid to take the elevator in case of a blackout, they walked up 25 flights, climbing slowly, trying not to get so winded that they'd be unable to fight. Despite her 55 years, Patty handled the stairs more easily than Bill or Courtney. They stopped to rest between the eleventh and twelfth floors.

"I've been climbing the 'stairs to nowhere' for decades—the Stairmaster," Patty said, her voice quaking from shivers, which hadn't stopped since she'd killed the doctor. "Always while reading the *New York Times.*"

At the 25th floor, they cautiously opened the stairwell door and scoped out the empty hallway. Patty unlocked her apartment door, closing it fast behind them. She lived alone and didn't expect unwanted company. She double locked and chained the door, and they entered a wide foyer and Persian-carpeted living room. Picture windows overlooked a commanding city view. They walked to the windows as if mesmerized, tracking bloody, unnoticed footprints. The city was a checkerboard of fire as far as they could see. Pillars of smoke rose into the air, charbroiling the colors of the sunset, though no fires appeared close enough to threaten them.

"There's nothing in the air," Bill said.

"What do you mean?" Patty asked.

"There are no rescue helicopters, not even planes surveying the damage that we might not have seen from the ground. We're really on our own."

Courtney turned to Patty, trying to ignore Bill's pronouncement. *Did it need to be said again that they were all alone?* "Do you have a charger that fits an iPhone?"

They entered Patty's home office, a comfortable room with a computer desk and deep armchairs. Patty took Courtney's dead phone and plugged it in. Through the window, they could see the industrial fires on the far shore of the East River.

Courtney's phone buzzed.

"*Yes!*" She picked it up, pushing aside her disappointment when the message wasn't from her father. "A tweet." She read aloud: "Am at 114th/Broadway. Church upstairs. Have food & safe place 4 now. Broken leg. Could use help & team 4 best survival." Courtney stared at the message and silently reread it. "It's the only tweet since yesterday afternoon. It's twelve hours old."

"He's probably dead by now," Bill said.

"There you go again, Bill. A bundle of optimism." Courtney tweeted back. *Are you still there? We r three. East 53rd Street.* Courtney looked at her phone. "The message isn't going out. It says 'no data network.' But it sometimes says that even on a regular day. It could just be slow."

Bill didn't say what he thought about the unlikelihood that Twitter would still be functioning.

They showered in separate bathrooms and threw out their slimy clothes. Courtney and Bill returned, wearing new shorts and t-shirts they'd boosted from the sporting goods store. Courtney scanned Patty's kitchen with yearning: Granite counters, stainless appliances and a center island. The lights flickered.

Patty pulled salad greens and meat from the refrigerator. "We better eat it before it goes bad."

It was dark outside by the time they ate—barely ate—with baseball bats within arm's reach and the front door in sight. Everything was surreally quiet again. Bill found himself wishing for X-ray vision as his eyes repeatedly returned to the front door.

"I've been sober for twenty-five years. My husband was a businessman and did very well," Patty told them, trying to fill the traumatized silence. "We met in the Program. He was the love of my life, fifteen years older than me. He died much younger than either of us expected, five years after we were married. The only other relative I have is my sister in Florida, but we're not close. There was nothing on my email from her . . . I emailed a few minutes ago and I think the email went. But I don't think there's any hope she's alive."

"If I ever get to spend my winnings, I'll have a place like this," Courtney said, looking around. An angry wave surged through her. "Goddammit." She laughed humorlessly. "I win the Lotto and there's a fucking zombie outbreak."

"You're kidding."

"Nineteen million, after taxes," Bill said.

"Bill and I met at the press conference."

"Wow . . . well, look at it this way," Patty said. "You may be the only Lotto winner alive."

"That's a positive spin on it." Bill looked around at the room. "All this is over anyway."

Patty's stomach contracted. She knew he was right. Her days in her home were numbered. Her old life was dead. "I would have given all this up in a heartbeat—the apartment, the vacations—to have my husband with me."

Courtney tried not to cry. She wanted her father to be alive so badly. "I grew up in the AA rooms."

"Really?" Patty was surprised and pleased. Twelve Steppers shared common ground rules. At least they had a sense of the need for honesty and had learned to work as a group.

Courtney turned to Bill with a snarky tilt of the head. "So, did you Thirteenth Step women?"

"What?"

"You know, hit on the new girls? Big recovered dude with double-digit sobriety."

"Wow, Courtney, what's your deal?"

Patty looked at the two of them. She knew they'd just met, but they got at each other like siblings. "The proverbial Thirteenth Step: Sometimes the men took advantage of the newly sober women. How shall I put this? There will always be that one asshole who preys on the new women who don't know any better. Anyone can join the Program and no one gets kicked out. Of course, there are only twelve steps. Problem is, not everyone worked them."

"It was my father who was in AA," Courtney said. "He was okay. My mother tried the Rooms once after she and my father were divorced. A guy Thirteenth Stepped her. The next thing you know, I had a new stepfather. Lucky I didn't live with her. Asshole is right. The guy lasted about two minutes . . . like my mother's sobriety."

"I'm sorry about what you went through," Bill said, trying to tamp down his anger, "but there's only one Thirteenth Step as far as I'm concerned, and it's new." He leaned forward and lowered his voice. "It's called 'How to Survive a Fucking Zombie Apocalypse.' So, can we focus on that?"

Courtney sat back, on the verge of tears, her nerves raw.

"Soon, we're going to have to move on." Bill forced himself to keep the coldness out of his voice. "This place isn't sustainable. So high up, it's a fire trap. The electricity is already shaky and the water won't work on such a high floor in a blackout. And it's not like we can hole up until help comes. As I said before, it doesn't look like any help is coming."

Courtney looked at the others. "Are we gonna find the guy on 114th Street?"

Bill shrugged. "Not if we don't know he's still alive."

Courtney put aside her plate and got up to get her phone. She'd always been addicted to her cell phone. Even now, checking for messages comforted her. She just couldn't believe there weren't people hiding like them, tweeting like crazy.

Through the window of Patty's office, an orange pall of fire ate away at the horizon across the East River. She could see the 59th Street Bridge and the lights of the RFK Bridge at 125th Street to the north. Courtney took the phone charger from the wall, planning to bring it back to the foyer and plug it in there. She had a message, printed across the screen. She smiled and swiped the phone open. It was the person at 114th Street.

"Get bikes. Bikes r faster than zombies & beat traffic jams. Quieter than cars. Stay quiet. Jared."

Courtney looked up, out the window. A blanket of darkness cascaded over Queens and Manhattan toward her. Bridges, buildings and street lights winked out, block by block. In an instant, Courtney stood in the dark. Swatches of fire outside provided the only light for as far as she could see.

CHAPTER 5

"I know this subway station." Bill crouched between cars, scoping out Third Avenue.

It was a bright spring day, still early morning. Undead wandered around stalled cars and picked-apart corpses. An impassable mob remained on Lexington Avenue, a block away.

"We can't make it across Lexington to the bike kiosk on Fifty-fifth Street," he said, "but we can tunnel under the wide avenues and get to the Westside if the subway's not overrun below."

"A big *if*," Patty said.

Courtney sighed. "We have no choice."

Bill noticed how she'd been trying to smooth things over. No snarky comments today.

"The tunnels should take us straight across town," Bill added. "The Midtown North precinct is on Eighth Avenue and Fifty-fourth. We can look for guns then double around to the Park for bikes and try to get to that guy on 114th Street. I don't know what we'll be able to do for someone with a broken leg, but if it's a safe place and we could stay for a while, it would be worth it."

They passed watchfully through an office building's lobby, its huge windows providing sunlight. The building's basement atrium had its own subway entrance. They climbed down a stalled escalator into the darkness. Smoke and smells of sweet human rot filled the air, more intense indoors than out. They passed the Incredible Edible shop, its windows smashed out except for a few shards of glass that glinted in Patty's flashlight beam. The black air buzzed with silence.

They pushed through Plexiglass doors to the underground labyrinth of the subway station, the floor changing from slippery polish to cement under their feet. The flashlight lit up the token booth. Inside, the token clerk howled and dove at the booth's glass. They all froze, then realized he was stuck in the booth. His face banged against the bulletproof glass, painting it with coagulated blood, and ricocheted backward only to try again. They didn't stick around to get a good look at him. Who knew whether his noise would attract his brethren like a whale's siren, or whether a burst of strength would allow him to break out of his cage.

They walked into a wide passageway. Darkness crowded the edges of the flashlight beam, weighing heavily as if a solid mass. Their footsteps echoed disconcertingly. The stench of the dead intensified. A rat ran across their path. They leapt backward. The information crossed all their minds like tickertape: Not a zombie.

The three stayed close together, their ears attuned to the slightest sound of movement. Courtney thumbed on her own flashlight. She began walking half backwards, sweeping her light in a semi-circle, watching for sudden attack. The passageway—where Bill had entered the subway every day for years without giving much thought to it—was now a maze of dismembered corpses, the squeaking of rats their funeral dirge.

Patty's flashlight beam picked up the top of the escalator, which would lead to the train platform below. The red glow of rat eyes shone back at them like brake lights on the Cross-Bronx Expressway. Groups of rats were satiating themselves on human remains. They looked up when the humans approached then returned to their feast. They were the dominant species in the subway system now. They were either too fast for zombies or weren't on the "A list" of dining choices. Patty tightly grasped her flashlight. She never thought she'd welcome seeing a bunch of rats eating human corpses. But if rats could get the zombie infection, she would surely be under a pile of them now.

Terrified of what lay beyond their flashlight beam, they descended three flights of metal steps to the black abyss of the train platform. When they hit bottom, their flashlights lit up a train stalled in the station, its windows and doors busted out. Thousands of zombies must have been temporarily trapped inside three days before. They didn't see any now. There were noises, though, scraping and moaning, which echoed off the tile walls down the platform. Coming closer.

They ran toward the front of the train. At the front edge of the platform, Bill tried to unlatch the yellow metal gate he'd seen workmen go through many times. Courtney looked back, the noises getting closer.

At last, the gate clicked open. They sprinted down to the tracks, five steps below. Endless pockets of darkness surrounded them: ahead, behind, to the sides. Avoiding the third rail just in case, they jogged awkwardly over the slats that stretched between rails. After a few minutes, the darkness behind them blotted out the groans and wails of the undead. They slowed to a walk.

They shone their flashlights around each blind crevasse as they passed. Each recess in the wall, they knew, could hold an attacker. Most were just shallow places where workers could stand when trains passed. Others were corridors. Bill's flashlight lit upon flesh. They made out the bas relief features of a man's filthy, bearded face. Not a zombie: he squinted in the light then pulled back into the shadows of a man-sized tunnel. Gone. Not interested in humanity.

Zombie cries sounded behind them, attracted to their slight noise. No choice but forward, they ran until the sounds faded again.

Their flashlights illuminated writing on a tile wall: Seventh Avenue. The tunnel opened to the station. There was movement on the platform. They couldn't turn back. They cupped the light of their flashlights to dim them.

They moved out at a half crouch, staying low, under the platform, crawling over and around long-discarded garbage, which had found its way there during normal times. Midway through the station, they heard the sounds of zombies eating above them on the platform. Breath labored and faces hot with fear, they inched past underneath, the platform only a thin cement layer between them and death. They picked their way through on hands and knees. Bill signaled silently to the women to warn them of broken glass in their path. At last, they emerged at the end of the platform. They walked into the next tunnel, unaccompanied.

Their flashlights lit up the sign for the next stop on the E-line, 51st Street, and they listened warily. Bill felt his first moment of hope. The only sound they heard was the drip of water and a chorus of rats. He signaled with a thumbs-up to the women. They mounted the stairs to the platform. Silence. They passed through turnstiles and climbed up the stairs to the street.

CHAPTER 6

At midday, Patty and Courtney hunkered down in shadow under the Studio 54 marquis on West 54th Street, waiting while Bill cased out the police station across Eighth Avenue. Patty remembered dancing all night inside the throbbing club. But mostly she remembered the ladies bathroom, its elegant lounge filled with as many men as women, all sniffing coke. The irony wasn't lost on her that she was back at the place which, over thirty years ago, had launched her into an ugly time of addiction and alcoholism.

Bill saw that the police station wasn't burnt out. There were a couple of zombies outside. One was an armed cop, literally without arms. He ambled in front, seeming to guard the place out of habit. Scattered around him were several blue-uniformed corpses, the leftovers from yesterday's brunch.

There was a teenage girl, too. Her face was half eaten but she still had the skinny rigid back and duck feet of a ballerina. She must have been one of the girls who attended the elite ballet schools near Lincoln

Center. Even undead, she had perfect turnout.

"We have to get across the street fast and come out swinging," he said when he returned to the women. "There's only two of them."

A moment later, they ran across Eighth Avenue with Bill and Courtney ready to take on the two undead. Bill held his hand against Patty's back to keep up her speed. Patty was sure she could handle a bike ride to 114th Street; but she couldn't sprint worth a damn and knew she'd be useless, too, when it came to swinging a bat. Her shoulder was sore from killing the doctor yesterday—weak from injuries she'd sustained lifting weights in her thirties. She kicked herself now for being such a gym rat when she was young. Who knew her life might depend on her baseball swing?

Bill ran right at the cop, swinging at his head. Courtney went for the girl. She was fast, side-stepping and moving in on Courtney. But the zombies didn't seem to have the adrenalin that pumped up their human enemies. With a grunt, Courtney shattered the girl's head. Bill grabbed the cop's gun from its holster and put it in the waistband of his own shorts.

"More coming," Patty called.

A group of a dozen zombies had heard the commotion and now set their sights on human meat. Patty, Bill and Courtney darted to the police station door, no time to collect the guns of the other dead cops. They slammed and locked the doors behind them, praying that a bunch of zombie cops weren't inside and that the door would hold.

With their backs against the wall of the entryway, they peered warily toward the dim innards of the precinct. Bill vaguely remembered the place. As a teenager, he'd been busted once for smoking marijuana in Central Park. The cops had taken him in then released him with a desk appearance ticket. All he'd seen that day was a small cell. His memory of the long-distant, inebriated day was too murky to depend on.

They inched through a second doorway framed with plastered pre-war moldings. Behind them, fists banged against the outer door, rattling its frame. But they soon realized, even though they'd been spotted, that the undead were few. The pounding was tapering off. Then it stopped. The zombies seemed to forget about them once they were out of sight and earshot. They each gnawed on the mystery.

Bill examined the cop's gun to see where the safety was. He had never shot a gun in his life and had no idea what to expect in terms of kick. He wondered whether he would be better off with just a baseball bat. He looked at Patty. "Have you ever shot one of these?"

"I once went to a shooting range with my husband, after 9/11."

"You're elected." He handed her the gun.

She shakily put aside her bat and took it.

They entered the large room of desks behind a counter topped with safety glass. They didn't see any movement inside, alive or undead. The place had been abandoned.

"We have to look for the weapons room," Patty said, sure about that after years of watching *Law and Order.*

A sound above: zombie shrieks.

They nearly tripped over each other, backing up.

"Oh shit," Courtney whispered.

There were zombies inside.

"STUPID DEAD MOTHERFUCKERS!" A man's voice shouted above them, "Ya wanna piece of me? Ya wanna piece of this." The undead shrieks got louder. "Kiss my black motherfucking ass!"

The three looked at each other, trying to compute. Zombies. Shouting. Coming from the same place?

They crept further into the precinct. An open door at the end of the room led to a staircase. They followed the sound of the man's voice up the stairs.

"Bite on this, motherfucker!"

At the top of the staircase, a metal door with a barred window had been left ajar.

The sour, nauseating zombie stench buffeted them when they neared it. They'd come to know that smell already. It was human rot combined with the gangrenous, shit-pee stink of the most incorrigible unwashed person. Inside the door, they beheld a sea of sinewy men, stripped to the waist, mostly Latino and Black. All muscle, blood and rage. And all dead. They roared, climbing and pounding against the bars trying to get to the new human arrivals.

Dozens of cells each contained a metal bed, sink, toilet and one or two zombies. Light streamed in through barred windows across a corridor that ran the length of the cells. A bizarre pattern of shadows striped the mutilated inmates.

Bill turned off his flashlight. "It's an overnight lockup."

A man stood alone in one of the cells a few yards from the entryway door. His hand shot out in warning. "LOOK OUT!"

A dead cop launched at Bill from within the cellblock. The cop was inches taller than Bill, buff and strong.

The prisoner yelled again, "On your right, another one!"

The first cop reached for Bill. The second cop surged at him from the opposite direction. Bill could see yet another cop behind them.

The prisoner ran toward the front of his cell and waved his hands through the bars. "HEY! HEY! HEY!"

The cops paused for a split second.

Bill and the two women scrambled backward and slammed the door shut. The first cop body-slammed the door, his face at its barred windows.

"It's not locked!" Courtney cried out. "It's not gonna hold."

Patty put her gun through the bars, flush against the face of the zombie, and fired. The cop's head exploded. She flew backward. Her ears rang with the noise and her hip went hot with pain where she landed. She scrambled back to her feet. Courtney mouthed something Patty couldn't hear. The second cop appeared at the barred window, evidently too stupid to know better. Patty braced herself this time and shot again, metal on zombie skin, detonating. The next cop climbed over the others to be executed. Patty couldn't believe she was the executioner. She fired.

They heard the man shout from inside the cell block, "They're all dead."

Courtney opened the cellblock door.

The prisoner reached through the bars in excitement and relief. "Thank God!"

A zombie in the cell next to him lunged. He'd come too close to the bars that separated them. The man jumped back into a small corridor of space that was out of reach of the hands of the zombies in the cells on each side. He returned his attention to the three rescuers. "Can you get me out of here?"

Patty focused on his face rather than the pile of dead at her feet and the rest of the prisoners, anxious to murder all of them. In his mid to early twenties, he was brown-skinned with dreadlocks to his upper back. He would have been handsome if he weren't so filthy and exhausted. Under normal circumstances, Patty would have had a hard time looking at the bull ring through his septum but right now anyone alive was a glorious sight.

Bill stepped around the corpses, getting his first extended look at the locked-up zombies. They were in various states of disfigurement, mauled and hideous, starving and strong. The banging resumed at the precinct's front door. The noise of the gunshots had reminded the crowd outside that they were here.

Bill looked at the lock on the prisoner's cell door, wanting to get the hell out of there. "These open with keys."

"The big cop was guarding us when it started. He's been trying to eat me for days." The guy pointed. "See the keys there, on his belt."

Bill turned back to the tangle of zombies Patty had killed. He unclipped the keys from the big cop's belt. "I'll have you out in a second."

"Wait!" Courtney shouted over the din of the zombie prisoners. "What's he in for? Is he a rapist or a killer?"

Bill paused.

The man looked at them in stunned distress. "What?"

"What are you in for?" She turned back to the others. "Not that he'd tell us the truth."

The three stepped around the dead cops to talk with each other.

"She's right," Patty said. "We have enough problems . . . but we can't leave him here."

"Drug rap," the man said. "I'm in for a drug rap. Small time buy and bust. Retail." He stuttered out facts. "I had someone selling for me. I steered the undercover to him. Please, I never hurt anyone. You can't leave me here."

Courtney turned to him, skeptical.

"Listen, my name's Shane Taylor. Graduated Binghamton University. Couldn't get a job after I graduated. Look, I came from the hood. My boys were laughing at me for all the time I wasted cramming for tests while they were clocking dollars and getting the girls. I couldn't beat them, so I joined them."

Shane was crying, desperate, seeing Courtney's indecision. He'd been living with the dead in a narrow slice of cell for three days. He'd thought he'd starve to death, no food, drinking water from the toilet because he couldn't reach the sink.

"There wasn't a job anywhere when I graduated." Shane's eyes met Courtney's. "Come on, you know the deal. The Great Recession. Unemployment."

"The bull ring couldn't have helped in interviews," Patty said.

Shane's face twisted like a kid trying to keep from crying in front of his friends. "Miss, do I look like an idiot? I took the ring out for interviews." Then he stopped, catching himself. "God, is this a got-damn interview? A job interview from hell? Is this a joke? Miss, do you see where I am? Do I *look* like I interview well?" He turned back to Courtney. "I'm asking you, please don't let me die in here."

"Let him out," Courtney said, taking a deep breath. "At least he didn't say he was innocent."

"Oh, thank God. Thank you."

Courtney spoke to Bill but studied the hungry zombie in the cell next to Shane's. "How are we going to unlock it? That one is within arm's reach of the lock."

Bill and Courtney both turned to Patty.

Patty shook her head. "A moving target . . . through bars, and I'd have to stay out of his reach, too. I would hit the bars or I could kill Shane by mistake."

"Just call him," Shane said. "He'll come like a dog to breakfast. Call him away from my side of the cell. Then unlock it fast."

Courtney stood in front of the cell next to Shane's and the wiry zombie lunged toward her. She jumped back, instinctively, even though she was too far away for him. "He's right."

Bill sorted through the keys, finding the only one large enough for the cell lock. "On three."

Courtney and Patty stood just out of reach of Shane's zombie-neighbor, near the corner of its cell farthest from Shane's.

"Here kitty," Courtney taunted. "Here kitty, kitty, kitty."

The moment the zombie lurched toward the women, Bill moved swiftly to Shane's cell and shoved the key in the lock. The zombie lunged his way, not as stupid as they'd thought. Bill leapt back.

"Come on, you stupid ass!" Courtney called the zombie back to her and Patty.

When the zombie moved toward the women, Bill stepped forward, turned the lock and pulled the door open before jumping out of the way again.

Shane stumbled, left his cell and joined the women halfway down the staircase. Bill closed the metal door to the cellblock, dulling the zombie uproar. They paused and listened to the noise coming from the street outside the precinct. The banging had subsided at the front door, but it sounded as if a large crowd was gathering.

"What's going on out there?" Shane asked.

"The whole world is dead, we think," Patty said. "They've overrun everything."

"But we're alive for some reason," Bill told him. "We came looking for weapons."

Bill handed a gun to Courtney that he'd lifted from the cops Patty had killed. He paused, considering Shane. His gut told him Shane was not their problem, and they needed all the help they could get. But should he hand him a gun?

"Don't worry man, I come in peace." Shane held up the Vulcan peace sign.

Bill shook his head. "Shit. I hope so."

Courtney listened to the sound of the zombies outside. "What have we got to lose?"

Bill passed the gun to Shane.

Shane put the gun in his waistband. "Do you have any food?"

Courtney fished in her backpack and took out a power bar plus a small bottle of Poland Springs water.

"Thanks." His voice was hoarse with emotion.

After he'd gulped down the bar and downed the water, they surveyed the precinct the best they could. The gun room was protected by bulletproof glass and a locked, heavily fortified door. A zombie policeman was behind the glass, drooling and moaning at the sight of them. None of Bill's keys fit the lock. To get to the bigger weapons inside, they'd have to shoot the lock then kill the dead guy.

Bill turned to Shane. "Have you ever shot a gun?"

"Honestly. Never."

Bill turned to Patty. "It's on you. You'll have to shoot from a distance. I don't know whether we have to worry about flying pieces of metal but there could be ricochet."

Patty stood a few feet away, knowing she wouldn't have a chance of hitting the lock if she backed up any farther. Everyone stood behind her, rightfully wary of friendly fire.

She had to squeeze off five shots, plaster spraying wildly, before any hit. The lock was black and dented. The zombie cop in the weapons room nearly climbed the glass, trying to get at them. His fists were becoming bloody clubs. Every vein in the being's face stood out as if they would burst from his skin. The zombies upstairs shrieked and the din of dead fists against the precinct door resumed with new vengeance.

"We've gotta hurry!" Courtney said.

"You ready?" Shane asked Bill, reaching for the doorknob. "I'll jump away and let him run out."

Bill nodded, baseball bat poised. "Go 'head."

Shane gripped the knob and turned, but it didn't move. "It's still locked," he hissed. "Didn't work."

The noise was getting louder outside. Thousands of voices now, the mob still building. They heard the crash of splintering wood.

"Jesus!" Patty exclaimed. "There's no time!"

"Forget this shit." Shane opened desk drawers as fast as he could. He found a box of bullets, then another. "There's a back door where they move the prisoners in and out. We need to get out of here before it's too late."

Bill found a backpack sitting under a desk, emptied it. A cop's house keys and gym clothes fell out on the floor. He threw the backpack to Shane, who shoved the bullets inside. Courtney grabbed a police nightstick that was lying next to the desk and handed it to Shane as well. Patty collected shoulder holsters, trying to keep her panic at bay.

Shane led the others at a trot toward a back hallway. "I know a place uptown where we can probably get guns with silencers." He pointed to the gun in Courtney's hand. "Those are what we really need, not these zombie-attracting motherfuckers."

He had an indisputable point.

There were only a few zombies in the alleyway behind the precinct. Shane, Bill and Courtney did the swinging while Patty covered them with the police revolver. Hugging the buildings, they traveled east on 53rd Street, headed toward Central Park.

CHAPTER 7

Shane couldn't get over the changed city landscape, its emptiness of life, the shattered glass, gore and smoke. At least he knew he wasn't crazy, now that he had company. Pacing in the jail cell (his undead neighbors pacing with him), he'd wondered whether someone had spiked his drink before his bust. Looking at the grisly scene around him, he half wished he *were* crazy. At least then there might be a pill to cure him.

Outside the Seventh Avenue entrance to Central Park, abandoned bikes were strewn everywhere. Shane crouched behind cars with his new companions, scoping out likely ones. Courtney and Bill spotted bikes quickly, darted into the street and grabbed them.

Shane sized up a bike several yards from where he crouched. "That's a good one," he told Patty.

Patty began to rise to go after it.

Shane held up his hand. "I'll get it for you."

"I can do it."

"I'm faster."

"Thank you."

Shane sprinted out into the center of the street, lifted up the bike and ran back to Patty. Then he got his own, no problem.

"We should take the bike path by the River, not Central Park," Patty said to the others. "The Loop goes into a steep uphill for a long way once you get into the Seventies and Eighties. If we run into a group of them while we're climbing a hill, they'll overrun us."

Bill agreed. "Probably fewer zombies, too, if we get away from the office buildings and tourist traps."

"So, what's on 114th Street?" Shane asked.

"There's a guy there, he's hurt," Bill said. "But the internet doesn't work. We haven't heard from him since last night."

"He says he has a safe place," Courtney said.

Shane didn't have any better ideas. "Okay, let's do it then."

It took a lot for them to ride down the center of the street in plain view rather than hiding. Their blood raced and bodies coiled tight with the anxiety of it. They were going on faith that they'd hear any big mobs with enough time to hide. As long as they didn't run into smaller groups or strays head on, they hoped they could ride in full sight of the dead and still stay ahead. It was the only way anyway. They agreed with the tweet from Jared about riding bikes. They wouldn't make it all the way to 114th Street running doorway to doorway.

They cycled carefully, looking and listening for danger. Smoke from dozens of fires mingled with dark clouds gathering in the sky. A few of the dead noticed them and followed at a distance behind, the bikes seeming to work out so far. They pedaled around a horse's corpse, still attached to a carriage, the street wide enough to allow them to pass without slowing down. They cut a wide swath around Columbus Circle, where zombies crowded the street.

It was late afternoon when they reached the bike path that ran most of the length of Manhattan. Sandwiched between the West Side Highway and the Hudson River, the area bordering the path was sometimes wide enough for picnics and tennis courts. At others, it was a narrow slash of concrete between the car crashes of the highway and the choppy, gray water of the Hudson.

The group rode at a moderate speed for decent stretches, conserving energy for sprints when a dead jogger or picnicker spotted them. They were lucky the undead couldn't rollerblade. Courtney pointed one out as they passed: He couldn't stay on his feet and didn't know how to get the skates off. Courtney thought it a pity they had no time to watch.

On the river, the situation looked as bad as on land. At the 79th Street boat basin, the pier had burnt black. Fires flickered on some of the small boats. Others were burnt hulls. A barge floated in the middle of the river. Everything on the water looked dead, ghostly. There was no sign of life other than the seagulls, up to business as usual, bobbing for food.

A drizzle fell when they came out of Riverside Park on 104th Street. Shaded by a canopy of oak trees, they rode Riverside Drive with a trail of undead following in their wake. They hadn't gotten used to the terror of that but they were starting to believe they'd actually make it to their goal.

Bill saw a glimmer of shiny pavement ahead, no more than a couple of inches wide . . . too late. His tire skidded on a piece of shredded skin and gristle, muddied by slick rain. His bike sideswiped Courtney, who yelped in surprise. She jumped off her falling bike, catching herself upright, while Bill's calf and arm scraped along the pavement, his bike tangled up with him. Patty tried to avoid them but she ended up in the pile, her hand slicing open on the spokes of Bill's back wheel.

Shane braked in time and jumped off his bike, taking in the distance of the dead who followed them: Still almost a block away. He pulled Patty up.

Bill was trying to extricate himself from his bike. The zombies quickened their pace. A tall, skinny one—built like an Ethiopian marathon runner—emerged from behind a tree a few car lengths down. It would only take seconds for him to reach the street. And the rest would be right behind him.

"We've gotta move!" Courtney urged, frantically, pulling Bill's bike away from his legs.

Bill jumped to his feet, fear dulling any pain. "Let's go!"

Two dozen zombies shrieked behind them as if sensing weakened prey. They were closing in, fast.

The wheel askew, no time to adjust it, Bill got back on his bike. Patty started peddling. The zombies were only a couple of yards away, the tall skinny one out in front.

"Let's go!" Shane exhorted as they all took off.

They could hear the dead right behind them, no time to look back to see how close they were. Bill imagined fingers grasping him off his bike from behind as he picked up speed, the last in the pack.

They turned onto 114th Street, cycling past brownstones and wide, shady stoops, putting space between themselves and the zombies behind them. They spotted the entrance to the church rectory just short of Broadway, dropped their bikes and rushed up the stairs to the solid wooden doors. Locked. The dead rounded the corner onto 114th Street.

Bill rang the intercom but it didn't work. He banged on the door, all of them cringing at the necessary noise.

"Hurry up, hurry up," Courtney chanted, the group of dead closing in on them again.

They heard a voice above them, "Heads up."

A key on a thick brass ring clanged to the cement. Shane grabbed it and passed it forward. Bill unlocked the door and they rushed inside. Standing in a wood-paneled entryway, they latched the door behind them. Darkness. They smelled the church's pews before a distant flickering of a candle gave them fleeting glimpses of their surroundings. The candlelight came closer, above them.

The dark walnut staircase to the second floor had been destroyed, apparently butchered by an ax. A splintered pile of wood lay below it. From the landing Jared's head appeared over the edge. He smiled broadly. He was in his early twenties with large brown funky-nerd glasses, a no-foam-latte complexion and loose biracial curls. He called down, "Wait a minute. I have a ladder. Step back."

He tossed down a metal-link fire safety ladder. It fell and unfolded itself. Bill gave it a test pull.

"It's attached to a heating pipe," Jared said, "It'll hold."

Bill thought Jared seemed pretty nimble for someone who'd tweeted that he'd broken his leg. Bill had expected him to be dying if not dead by now.

Shane held the ladder taut for Patty. "Can you handle this?"

She patted Shane's arm. He obviously thought she was ancient. "I'm okay. Don't worry about me."

Shane held the ladder for Patty then Courtney before climbing up.

At the top, they made out the outlines of a center foyer with frayed carpet runners lapping dark wood floors. Open doors led to a residence on one side and offices on the other. Jared wore cutoffs and a t-shirt, a lanky five feet ten. A cast covered his leg from toes to above his knee. Holding the candle, he limped ahead into the rectory living room.

The rainy sky provided diffuse light through two windows at the far end. The living room was masculine but comfortable with beamed ceilings, chocolate-brown bookcases, a forest-green couch and armchairs. They could hear the banging of the zombies starting now at the front door, but the attack was lackluster.

"How the hell did you cast your own leg?" Bill asked after the banging ceased and they'd all introduced themselves.

"Oh you thought I'd just broken it. No. It's been broken for almost six weeks. Car accident." Jared motioned to Bill's leg. "It looks like you're in worse shape than me."

Bill examined his raw calf, scraped from ankle to knee. He rotated his sore shoulder. "I'm okay. Got lucky."

"I'll get you something for that."

Patty sat in a deep armchair. She examined herself, too. A scraped knee. The cut on her hand was a few inches long where the thumb met her palm. She normally wouldn't have given much thought to such minor injuries, but an infection might be a death sentence now.

Jared returned with peroxide and a bag of cotton balls. "I could use help cutting off the cast. Then I may need a few days before I'm strong enough to get out of here."

Courtney frowned. "Out of here?"

"Well, yeah. There's no future in the City. Too many zombies. Diseases from unburied corpses. Rats. Fires are bound to spread, releasing asbestos and who-knows-what." Jared rattled off the thoughts he'd obviously been alone with for three days, "If there's any government, it's more likely they'd nuke us than try to save a couple of people here or there. What's a few collateral casualties when you can kill millions of zombies?"

"I doubt there's any government anyway," Bill said, dabbing his leg with peroxide. "We haven't seen a single plane or helicopter."

"Me neither. Without electricity, there won't be any heat in winter and the water will run out. We'll want to head south. The highways will be clogged until we get a ways out of Dodge and then periodically after that. I have to get my leg ready for a long bike ride. Unless one of you guys knows how to sail. There should be boats at the Seventy-Ninth Street Boat Basin."

Everyone shook their heads.

"We're not a super qualified group to survive this," Courtney said. "I think we all majored in the wrong subjects."

"The boats were on fire anyway," Shane said.

"That was pretty impressive, breaking down the stairs," Bill said.

He passed the first aid supplies to Patty and walked to the window.

"Thanks. The dead can't climb a ladder. But if they were really onto our scent, they would probably keep coming until they piled on top of each other to get to us. So, whatever we do, we have to stay quiet. Noise is a big attractor. If we're quiet, they forget we're even here. It is a little weird, though. I've never heard of zombies giving up once they home in on prey."

"How do you know so much about them?" Shane asked.

"Didn't you ever read the *Zombie Survival Guide*, by Max Brooks?"

Bill turned away from the view of Broadway, already feeling like Ann Frank in her attic. "Dude, that's fiction."

Jared looked him in the eyes, deadly serious. "So you say."

Shane laughed. Patty found herself smiling, too, as she watched Bill struggle with that. Bill was also grappling with the marijuana clips he'd seen in an ashtray near the window. The kid had been smoking and watching the street. Bill couldn't blame him. He'd been alone for days. Even a civilian—someone who wasn't an alcoholic or addict—would get drunk or high under the circumstances. Unfortunately, though, Bill figured the kid was a regular user or else he wouldn't have had a supply of weed on him when the attack broke out. Their lives all depended on each other, and Bill was worried about the possibility that one of them might be chronically impaired.

"Do you have a shower?" Shane asked, knowing he reeked after three days in lockup. He was dying to feel some water and soap against his skin.

"It's cold but there's still water." Jared clomped in the direction of the hallway, showing Shane the way. He spoke over his shoulder to the others, who had arrayed themselves on the chairs and sofa. "We also have food, a whole pantry full of canned and bagged stuff. They used to have a soup kitchen here." Jared slapped Shane on the shoulder. "Man, it is good to see you guys."

A KITCHEN WINDOW overlooked 114th Street. The lowering sun cast an amber aura. Bill watched a mangled dead woman chase a cat down the puddled street. He could hear the snarls of more undead. When the zombies disappeared from sight, he began opening white wooden cabinets and drawers, searching for bowls and silverware.

The square rectory kitchen was big and old-fashioned with a heavy wood plank table, a slab bench against the wall and several 1950s aluminum-legged chairs arrayed around it.

Patty checked the water that boiled in a tall, pockmarked metal pot. She took charge of cooking Pasta Florentine from huge cans of vegetables and economy-size pasta. They had Parmalat milk for protein and plenty of gourmet parmesan cheese from the priest's private stash.

Shane came in and sat down at the table, barefoot, wearing a priest's black pants and shirt.

Patty laughed. "Wow, that's a change in image."

Shane laughed with her. He liked Patty. She struck him as kind, not brutally honest like some people.

She passed bowls of pasta. Bill stood near the window and ate standing up, too tense to sit. Shane took a famished bite then began shoveling the food into his mouth, his empty stomach a greedy creditor after three days without food.

"I'm a graduate student at Columbia, from California," Jared told them, his expression glum, "My kid brother left me a voicemail . . . he was hiding in a closet. He said my parents were dead. Then I heard the screaming. I've played the message over and over again. I know I shouldn't have . . . Phone's dead now."

"How did you get away?" Courtney asked.

"I was in Starbucks next door, on Broadway. I hid inside a cabinet. Others hid, too. I still don't know how I survived though. I came out after it was quiet. Every cabinet but mine had been smashed in. Hiding didn't work for anyone else."

Patty sat and took a bowl. "The same thing happened to all of us. Shane was a little different because they couldn't reach him, but we were all able to evade them in a way others couldn't. I don't think it was dumb luck."

Shane swallowed, frowning. "When I was in lockup, other guys were attacked before me. It was only a second or two lag but enough that I didn't get caught by surprise through the bars."

"Yeah," Bill said. "Shane's got what we've got, the zombie repellant or whatever. Otherwise, we would have had to ditch him to the mobs by now."

"I hear that."

"Maybe we don't smell great to the zombies," Jared said, pushing his glasses up his nose. "Or they may be like sharks. Sharks aren't interested in people unless you're surfing and look like a seal."

"So, you're thinking that for some reason we may not be their natural prey?" Bill asked. "We're different from other people?"

"No," Shane said, "they wanted to kill me. You guys, too."

"He's right." Courtney said, "I keep thinking they sense other people psychically or by smell. They don't sense us that way . . . but once they hear or see us, we're prey."

"But why us?" Patty asked. "Bill and I—I hope you don't mind me saying, Bill . . ."

"No problem."

"Bill and I do have something in common. We are both recovering alcoholics, addicts if you will."

"We're five survivors," Bill added. "Statistically, it seems odd that two of us are alcoholics. It could be more than a coincidence."

Jared got up and started pacing, anxiously, trying to think it through. "It could be something genetic affecting your scent in a way only a zombie would discern. It's like genetically modified crops that are unattractive to specific pests. But you're only two."

"Yeah, I've never had a problem with drugs or alcohol," Courtney said. "I can't see how that's a common thread."

Patty spoke. "Courtney, your father and mother were both addicts and alcoholics, right?"

"Me, too," Shane added before Courtney could answer. "Both my parents were addicts. They died of AIDS."

"Mine, too." Courtney took a deep, painful breath and spoke to Shane. "I mean, my mother died of AIDS. My father was clean and brought me up . . . but he started drinking when I was a teenager. He's been sober again for a few years."

"So," Patty thought out loud, "you could both have the addict or alcoholic gene if that's what it is. That makes four out of five survivors with that possible connection."

They all looked at Jared, who plopped into his chair. "Don't look at me. My parents were cool, and I don't have a problem."

Bill put a hand on his shoulder. "Fess up, dude."

Jared shot a hard look at Bill then shrugged. "I did go to rehab when I was sixteen. I was into Vicodin. But everything's been chill since then. Look at me: Ivy League, straight A's. Zombies are my only problem. They fucked up a great life."

"I still don't see it," Courtney said, peeved at the insinuation that her parents' addiction was somehow lurking inside her, even if it had saved her life.

"I don't know either," Shane said. "The whole world and definitely most of Manhattan drank and drugged. Did you ever check out the club scene? It could be totally random that we all ended up with some kind of common family history."

Bill sat at the table, unwilling to let go. "It's true the vast majority of people with the alcoholic gene didn't get as lucky as us, but a few of us must have something about us that gives us an upper hand . . . if we're careful."

"If you call being holed up surrounded by millions of zombies the upper hand," Shane said.

"Well, in a manner of speaking."

Shane mulled it over. "If it's mostly addicts that survived, we may have more than zombies to worry about. There may be some real thugs out there."

"You think they won't want to sing Kumbaya with us?" Patty said.

"Exactly."

"Okay, so I'm not convinced about the alcoholic connection." Courtney pushed back her bowl. "But if there's even possibly something genetic sparing us, I need to look for my father. How do we know others in our families haven't survived? You're talking about leaving the City? I can't do that without finding my father first."

"Where does your father live?" Jared asked.

"Inwood. North of Dyckman Street."

Shane calculated. "About four miles north of here."

"I don't think there's much chance they survived," Bill said, "but I have family, too."

"It's a huge risk," Jared said. "Looking for friends and family who are almost certain to be dead."

"I'm not going anywhere unless I look for my father first," Courtney said to Jared.

"Inwood is just north of the George Washington Bridge," Shane said. "We could check on Courtney's dad then circle back to the Bridge and get out of the City."

"Where are your parents?" Patty asked Bill.

"Montclair, New Jersey."

"I don't know if we'll live that long," Shane said, "but what goes around comes around, and you all saved my life. I don't mind looking for your families. I don't have anyone to look for myself, not to risk my life looking for anyway, but I'll look for yours."

"We need to be logical." Jared got up again, clomping around the table as if he had a pirate's peg leg, thinking about what they'd need for their journey. He thought back to all the zombie novels he'd read, the movies he'd seen, trying to envision how to manage the trip. "The logistics are complicated. It will be easier once we leave the city. We can stop at empty houses at night, ride during the day . . . Maybe Inwood *is* a good idea. I remember a bike store on Dyckman Street. The priest has an old bike here I can use for the trip there, but we could trade in for better bikes before we hit the Bridge."

"That store's only a couple of blocks from my father's house."

"That makes sense," Patty said, "Inwood then the bridge."

Jared kept pacing, warming up to the idea. "We can also see if they have child carriers to stash gear, the ones you attach to the back of a bike."

"I don't know about you," Shane said, his eyelids getting heavy now that he'd eaten, "but we need to get some guns with silencers before we head anywhere. First sleep. I haven't slept for three days and I can't do anything in the shape I'm in right now. Then we should try to get weapons that make some kind of sense."

"I'll take the first watch," Jared said, thoughtfully. "Someone should always be on guard."

CHAPTER 8

Shane, Courtney and Bill rode their bikes on the downhill stretch of Broadway that extended from 116th to 125th Street. Baseball bats stuck out of their backpacks. Each backpack also contained a flashlight, a bottle of water and bags of trail mix they'd lifted from the Starbucks near the church. In case they were trapped or forced to split up, they'd each have something to eat and drink. According to Jared's Zombie Survival Manual, that was the first rule even for short trips. But they had to travel light and leave room to fill their packs.

"It will be mostly downhill getting into Harlem," Shane warned before they left, "but it will be a bitch of a climb coming back, and we'll be weighed down with weapons and ammo if we're lucky."

They cycled between the Beaux-Arts buildings of Barnard and Columbia University, which lined both sides of Broadway. The thought occurred to Courtney that she would be truly buff if they kept up all this exercise. She smiled inwardly: The end of the world was a hell of a price to pay for the body of her dreams. Of course, such concerns were irrelevant now. What was important now was having a strong body for fighting and running. Her mind was still playing catch up with reality: Attracting a man was the opposite of what she'd been trying to do since the zombies struck. Luckily, none of the guys had hit on her.

Shane's dreadlocks flew behind him as he pedaled. There were no traffic jams in sight, except at the bottom of the half-mile hill. They picked up speed. If the wind held, it would be at their backs when they returned. He hoped for that. They would need all the help they could get.

A brick wall rose up at their left, splitting the street down the middle. The Number One subway train used to come out of its tunnel there, the tracks on top of the wall. The bottom of the three-story wall opened to allow the flow of crosstown traffic but much was hidden. They braced themselves for unseen zombies.

Shane pointed. A group of grisly undead rounded the corner onto Broadway. Still a block and a half downhill. Without a word, the three cyclists cut right, fast, sprinting east. Shane picked up his pace, all of them peddling furiously, deeper into the Harlem valley. They left the mob behind.

To the east, the early morning sun burst with blinding force from behind tenements turned gentrified condos turned tombs at the bottom of the hill. They squinted against the glare, trying to discern any movement before it was too late. A few seconds later, they turned uptown on Morningside Drive, its old trees stretching out overhead, and their eyesight returning. Shane had a hard time processing things now that he was back in his own neighborhood: The place was frozen, strollers empty on the sidewalk, cars halfway into parking spaces, building doors crashed in, glass and corpses everywhere. The enormity of loss slammed down on him but his feet kept peddling.

Morningside Drive became Convent Avenue when they passed a Catholic church and convent at 125th Street. Rats eating corpses were the only sign of life on normally busy 125th Street. A few blocks north, Shane pointed toward a six-story apartment building and spoke quietly, "We're here."

They dismounted.

"When I was a kid," Shane said, "they used to call this block the 'Wild, Wild West.' There was a rap song about it . . . we had no idea."

They balanced their bikes against a spike fence and pulled out their baseball bats, saving the guns they wore in their shoulder holsters for emergencies. They treaded lightly past aluminum trash bins lining a pathway to the building's service entrance. Shane carefully opened a black metal door. Feeling like prey entering the monster's den, he shone his flashlight inside.

The beam revealed a long, roughly plastered hallway. The smell of indoor-corpses hit him. He took an extra protective glance at Courtney before advancing inside, uncomfortable they'd taken the girl when she could have stayed behind. He'd been outvoted because three could carry more weapons than two. And he knew that was right. At least Courtney was tall and strong, and she'd already shown she could handle herself. He signaled he was going in. Courtney then Bill followed.

Inside the basement passageway, a dark maw opened to their left. Shane braced himself for vicious dead bursting out of darkness. But his flashlight beam revealed only a line of shiny washing machines, dense shadow beyond them. Silence.

"This way." He led the others further down the catacomb hallway.

In an alcove, a picked-clean body lay near two miniature-poodle corpses still tied to a chair leg. Shane glanced back to see that his companions were following then continued silently through a warren of hallways. Their flashlights lit up peeling plaster, piece-by-piece. Shane silently counted the seconds as they walked, his spine petrified in a vice-like grip. He'd heard how the others had walked a mile through subway tunnels, but he didn't know how they did it. He couldn't stand this fear much longer.

They turned a corner and came to an apartment door. He put his ear to it: no shrieks or moans.

The doorknob turned in his hand and they stepped inside an apartment hallway. Candlelight. Someone was there.

They breathed in thick chemical air just as they heard the click of a lighter and whoosh of a butane torch. Bill sucked in his breath reflexively, remembering the sound and smells from the days when he'd smoked crack. It filled him with a fast sense of familiarity, normality, even safety, compared to the zombie hell they were living in.

He shook his reaction off. He wasn't going to fucking die in a crack den. He wasn't going to die willingly. For an instant, taken by surprise, he'd almost been hypnotized by the idea of forgetting reality.

They rounded a corner into the living room. An emaciated woman sat on a sofa in front of a coffee table full of crack vials. Courtney peered at the woman: her prominent cheek bones stuck out as if poised to pierce through her thin dark skin. She was so skinny she could have been in a famine documentary. Hundreds of empty plastic vials were strewn around her on the low table, piled into dozens of skinny towers. The woman reared back on the couch, her protruding eyes opening wide when she saw them. But she didn't let the smoke out of her mouth. She held it until her lungs forced her to exhale.

Finally, she spoke smoke, "What the fuck?!"

Shane's voice was hard, "Anyone else here?"

"Nah." She leaned back, her hand patting her chest as if her heart were beating hard from the hit. "They all dead."

"How'd you survive?" Courtney asked.

The woman spoke to Shane, "What's she doing here?"

"The whole world is dead."

The woman giggled. "Yo, don't I know it? Everyone here got killed. Left behind little pieces of motherfuckers I'd been smoking with—feet, arms, bones. Smelled like shit." Jittery, talking fast, she nodded toward a dead TV. "I saw a news lady killed on the TV just when people started screaming and fucking shit up in here. *Fuck*." She shuddered. "I already knew where to hide fast. I shut myself in a closet and waited 'til it passed. I always look for the hiding places first thing when I come into a spot . . . just in case niggers decide to come in shooting."

"Do you want to come with us?" Bill asked. He didn't want her to come with them and she would probably get them killed, but he couldn't leave anyone behind.

"And leave this?" The woman cackled, her mouth half empty of teeth. She looked sad for a moment and waved her hand in front of her face as if swatting gnats. "I don't have nobody to find out there anyway . . . lost my kids to the System years ago. Don't even know where they live."

Courtney was about to say something to convince her, even though she was as reluctant to have her as Bill. But, moving fast, the woman took a vial from the top of one of her crack towers and opened it with her back teeth. "Look at all this shit. Good shit, too."

Bill had to look away.

The woman packed her pipe, staring at Shane challengingly, as if she had a special anger reserved for him, even though he'd never seen her before.

"I'm gonna smoke this shit 'til I die. And if I don't die, I'm gonna go to the crack house down the block and see what they got, then I'm gonna go to the next one. And ya know what, I'm gonna be fuckin' happy about it. And ya know why?" She looked at Courtney then back at Shane. "Because I don't have to suck no more fuckin' dick to get none of it. I have sucked my last dirty-ass, crackhead dick, that's why."

She pointed at one of the towers, her fingertips rubbed raw from flicking a lighter. "I have hit the fuckin' Lotto, that's why."

She was still clicking, exhaling and laughing while Shane led Courtney and Bill down a hallway to look for the dealer's stash of weapons. Face steeled, Shane felt compelled to explain, especially to Courtney. "I just came by this place from time to time. Business. This wasn't my scene."

Courtney imagined Shane and his drug dealer friends here. She'd heard the stories about the desperate girls being passed around and having sex for a two-dollar crack. She thought of her mother at the mercy of people like him. "Disgusting," she said to Shane.

Anger and shame burnt Shane's eyes. *What did Courtney know about his life?* "I didn't even play women like that. You think I needed to mess with skeezers? Crack whores?" He opened a door and spoke coldly, "Let's just get the guns."

Other than a massive flat screen TV, the bedroom they entered was monastery-plain with a bed, dresser and a couple of folding chairs.

"The guy who sold out of this spot talked a lot," Shane said to Bill, not looking at Courtney. "I knew him since we were kids, so dude felt comfortable talking. He was like most of the guys who stayed back in the hood, never went anywhere, never really grew up. Showed off guns like he used to show off Air Jordans in the school yard."

Shane signaled to Bill. "Help me move the bed."

The two lifted the end of the bed and pushed it aside.

Shane took a long look at the floor. "Lucky I wasn't the type to rip a person off or rat . . . not that it would matter now to a dead man."

Shane pulled wooden slats from the floor and put them to the side. Bill shone the flashlight from behind and beheld an arsenal. Nine millimeter handguns, AR-15 assault rifles. The barrels were long. Silencers were attached as if ready for a drug war. Shane passed the guns up to Bill and Courtney.

They filled their packs with the guns. Shane held up a box of 5.56

millimeter subsonic ammunition. "He said you need subsonic ammunition or the assault rifles create mini-sonic booms, even with silencers." Shane held a box. "We're gonna have to conserve the ammunition or the silencers will be useless."

They each carried a nine millimeter and made their way out of the building. They squinted, trying to get their vision back quickly in the bright sunshine. A sound emanated from deep in the narrow alley alongside the building. They rushed to get on their bikes, feeling the strain of their heavy packs. Shane saw an old dead woman in a house coat emerging from the shadows before they sped away and out of reach. For the first time in his life, he was glad that his grandmother had died young.

"WE SHOOT FOR shit," Courtney announced once Shane had bolted the rectory door behind them. They joined Patty and Jared on the second floor landing. "A few of them started to come after us while we were climbing the hill on Broadway. I didn't make a single head shot."

"We had to ditch our bikes on the hill," Bill added.

Shane shrugged off his pack. "Ran like hell."

No longer wearing his cast, Jared pulled a gun from a pack and looked it over, figuring out how to load it. "We need target practice. We can go on the roof."

They had to conserve their ammo, so their practice was limited to getting a feel for aiming, shooting and the kick, a few tries for each of them. Afterward, Courtney dragged out folded lawn chairs she'd found just inside the doorway to the roof. She grinned at the others, a rare smile. "Tar beach, guys."

Everyone took chairs from her and helped set them up in a rough semi-circle facing the sun. They had time to burn until Jared's leg got stronger, and they needed fresh air. The temperature was perfect, the sun baking them for only short spurts before ducking back behind clouds. Jared leaned his palms against the roof's waist-high wall, stretching the backs of his legs and looking out at Broadway. It was quiet down there for the moment, but since they'd been on the roof, they'd already heard a couple of mobs passing in mini-waves, going who-knew-where.

"We should all be stretching and exercising," Patty said. "We have a hard journey ahead of us."

Jared turned back from the wall. "She's right. We should be in training, getting stronger while we wait."

Patty clapped her hands playfully in a parody of Richard Simmons. "Get up, get up everyone."

The others followed Patty awkwardly through fifteen minutes of yoga stretches, then they took turns calling out exercises to each other. Sit-ups, pushups, jumping jacks. Jared sat out the jumping jacks, needing more time to heal. Patty went easy on the calisthenics, too. In recent years, she'd found she could injure a muscle or joint just by looking at it too long. Aging was difficult, and an injury now would be a game changer. But after an hour, she'd surprised herself with how much she was able to do.

"Just a few more days and I'll be ready," Jared said, rotating his ankle joint.

Bill passed around a gallon-sized bottle of water he'd brought from below.

"We're not exactly Marines," Shane said, sitting on a lawn chair, "but it could be a lot worse."

Shane looked over at Courtney. She hadn't said a word to him since the crack house. He'd been angry at her, too, for judging him, but he couldn't really blame her. He'd been living foul even if he hadn't taken advantage of the skeezers the way Courtney thought. He'd been raised better than to end up hustling drugs in the ghetto.

They all stayed on the roof for hours, feeling good about their workout. If it weren't for the shrieks of the zombies who owned the streets below and the memory of crack that kept popping back into Bill's head, they might have forgotten the insanity they were living through. It was almost evening when the wind shifted and turned the air into a smoky haze.

"Teachers College is burning," Jared said from the edge of the roof.

"I'll be glad to get out of here," Shane said, the smoke making his head ache. "This city is dead."

They went downstairs, prepared for another night of irritated throats and burning eyes. A depressed silence cloaked all of them. After dark, Courtney saw that Bill and Patty had gone across the hall from the residence into a twelve-step meeting room. She could recognize an AA meeting in her sleep. She heard Patty and Bill saying the serenity prayer, which catapulted her back to distant, safer memories. She had attended meetings with her father from the time she was five through middle school. On weekday evenings, she'd done her homework in church-basement meeting rooms. On weekends, she'd sat beside her father in a folding chair reading or helping serve the cookies. Her father had kept her close that way, and it had saved money on babysitters.

She heard Bill weeping. It wasn't a loud, desperate cry, rather the sound that men in AA made when they were fighting the good fight but the feelings overwhelmed them. She had heard her father cry like that in a meeting after her mother died, years after he had divorced her. Courtney turned away, wishing she had the kind of support that Bill and Patty had. She'd never felt more alone in her life.

CHAPTER 9

A week after Patty cut the cast off his leg, Jared announced he was "fired up and ready to go." He tried to sound enthusiastic but he was terrified. He held up a packing list he'd scribbled. "We need guns, ammunition, baseball bats, a couple of candles each, white-tipped matches, and enough food and water to get us through a short siege."

Bill smiled good-naturedly. He couldn't deny that Jared's encyclopedic knowledge of zombie fiction helped when it came to anticipating all the angles.

After a dawn breakfast, they cycled uptown on Riverside Drive, managing to stay well ahead of any zombies. The day before, Shane, Courtney and Bill had retrieved the bikes they'd ditched on Broadway, and Jared rode the priest's beat-up clunker. Now, just north of the George Washington Bridge, they rested at a stone-walled lookout with a view of the soaring cliffs and forests of the Palisades across the Hudson River, and the Henry Hudson Parkway below.

Courtney pointed toward the highway entrance a short block to their north. "That's the flattest and most direct route to Inwood."

The three lanes of the northbound highway passed between the woods of Fort Tryon Park and the Hudson River. They studied a frozen ten-car accident they'd have to pass on the winding road. There was enough room on the shoulder for them to ride through. They mounted their bikes.

The wind blowing off the river and park was cleaner than anything they'd breathed for days. Patty found herself inhaling deep whiffs of jasmine through her nose, savoring it, until the scent of zombie wafted from a semi-crushed car. Eviscerating any hint of normality, a trapped dead woman scrabbled to un-wedge herself but remained trapped, reaching for them as they rode by.

Courtney took point, leading them off the highway. They passed the woods and playground of Inwood Hill Park on the uptown side of Dyckman Street. Courtney had played there as a child and felt the pain of remembering.

On the downtown side of the street they passed parking garages topped with brick buildings the color of car exhaust. Many of the store signs were in Spanish, although the neighborhood still had several Irish bars from its past. In recent years, middle-class whites had returned, priced out of the downtown real estate market. Ahead, restaurants with sidewalk cafes lined the broad sidewalk, sandwiched between bodegas and *botánicas*. Patty pondered what archeologists would one day make of what they found here, if there would even be archeologists.

The smell of fire came in surges as the wind shifted. They could see columns of smoke here and there, some blocks burning and others not. They rode in the spaces between abandoned and parked cars. They saw the sign for Tread Bikes just as a dozen zombies spotted them and roared from behind the playground.

"Damn," Shane muttered as they picked up speed.

"The store has a glass front," Courtney called out, "We can't go in."

Bikes mostly blocked the view through the windows, but if the mob saw them go in, the glass wouldn't protect them long enough for the zombies to forget about them.

Without slowing, Bill pointed right toward the next corner. "We have to circle around to lose them and come back."

"More company!" Courtney called.

A new group of zombies came screeching around from the side

block where Bill had pointed. A dozen more had been wandering on Broadway and were moving their way now, too.

"We have to ditch the bikes, get inside!" Jared shouted from the back.

Courtney indicated the only open street. It ran north, alongside the woods of Inwood Hill Park. "My father's building. That way!"

They doubled around to the street. With too small a lead for comfort, they sped past a six-story apartment building then a row of three-story arts & crafts style houses, which overlooked the woods across the street. The narrow, one-way street sloped upward, the climb slowed them down. They could hear the zombies at their backs, keeping pace with them.

Catastrophe. Two males rounded a corner toward them. One was a teenager with bloody Mario Brothers boxers puffed up at his waist and his pants displaying the curve of his butt. That would normally have annoyed her, Patty thought, terror slowing down time for her. Then her eyes riveted on the other one, a man in a warm-up suit, his facial skin almost completely debrided. Even for the walking dead, he was disgusting.

Patty shouted, "We don't have time—"

They all knew what she meant. If they stopped to shoot at the two who blocked their path, the crowd behind them would catch up.

They heard barking from the cross street the two zombies had come from. Dogs. A pack of ten appeared. They were mutts and pure breeds, medium and large, all with leashes dragging behind them. A huge black German shepherd led the pack. The dogs ran from the cross street just out of reach of Faceless and Mario Brothers. They barked and yapped at the two zombies then jumped away when the two lunged at them. They scampered up a grassy hill into the wooded park, looking back, barking to make sure they were followed.

Behind the riders, a moan, it had to be from excitement, went up from the crowd of walking dead at the sight of running prey. It was as if someone had thrown a stick for the zombies to fetch. The entire mob—Faceless and Mario Brothers, too—shifted and turned in pursuit. But the dogs had the upper hand on the hill. Alternately barking and taunting the zombies, they dashed further uphill with the crowd slogging up after them.

It was Jared who started shooting first. Aiming for the backs of zombie heads, they all killed as many as they could to help the dogs.

Then they pedaled away, shocked and deeply grateful. Shane made a decision: when they got wherever they were going, he'd have a dog. He'd never been allowed to have one as a kid, not in his grandmother's house and definitely not in the group home. But if he lived long enough, a dog would be his reward.

They got off their bikes at the six-story building where Courtney had grown up. Its U-shaped brick wings embraced a courtyard entryway planted with cherry trees and flowers. They cased out the entrance with its shattered glass door, shining their flashlights inside to expose the dark corners of the lobby. Then they made their way inside and up a worn marble staircase.

Courtney's father lived five flights up. Fearful of what she would find, she felt the heat of impending tears. The smell of decayed bodies seeped out from behind broken apartment doors. Rats skittered away when human footsteps approached each landing. They walked through a dark puddle that covered the landing in front of apartment 5A. The door was battered and dented. Zombies had obviously worked at it, but it wasn't broken down. Hope flared, a physical shock that blossomed inside Courtney's chest. Shane heard her sharp intake of breath and looked at the dark shadow of her face. He hoped she'd get a good decision.

Courtney had to search for her keys within her backpack, something so normal it felt surreal. Her hand trembled. She chastised herself for not having her key ready. The others kept a jittery watch, staring down the dark corridor and up and down the staircases. Courtney found the right key and unlocked the door. It wouldn't budge when she turned the knob and tried to push in.

"The hinges are shot," Shane whispered beside her.

He put a shoulder into it and shoved inward. With a loud crack, the door opened. Light from the sunny apartment illuminated the hallway where they stood. Fetid air—the smell of a dead body—drifted out. Courtney held back tears.

The place was cluttered but homey. They entered the foyer and took in the sunken living room that overlooked the hilly park. The furniture was comfortably worn. Newspapers and DVDs lay in disorderly heaps on the couch and coffee table. The group stayed near Courtney, guns out, as she passed the kitchen with its dirty dishes still in the sink and the dishwasher open as if her father had been loading it. Courtney led the way down the hallway toward the bedrooms and bathroom.

The smell became overwhelming by the time they reached the bathroom door. Courtney reached for its old-fashioned beveled-glass doorknob.

Shane reached in front of her. "Let me check first."

She nodded.

He looked in for a second and reclosed the door. "If that's your father . . . I think he slit his wrists."

A cry welled out of Courtney and she moved to the door.

Shane stopped her again and spoke softly. "It's bad. You may not even recognize him."

"I have to see."

"Wait. Someone pass me a blanket," Shane said. They'd all seen how bad dead bodies looked—blackened and swollen—and this couldn't be any worse—but none of them had seen their families like that.

Jared brought Shane a blanket.

Shane took a breath, went back in and covered up the body to the neck. He left the swollen, sliced arm outside the blanket, draped over the edge of the claw-footed tub. Then he withdrew down the hall, leaving Courtney with Patty and Bill. He knew how Courtney felt about him after seeing the crack house. She would need Patty and Bill now.

When Courtney entered, she barely recognized her father's face but she made out the tattoo on the inside of his forearm, which had covered up 25-year-old track marks. He'd killed himself. She could understand why but she cried out, her legs melting under her. "You bailed on me, you bailed on me. Why couldn't you wait?"

Bill held her up, speaking to her softly and leading her out of the bathroom. "He killed himself before they got him, Courtney. He didn't bail on you. You saw the door. He wasn't . . . like us. They had his scent."

Courtney sank to her knees outside the bathroom, weeping. Patty kneeled next to her and stroked her hair. Courtney cried in the older woman's arms, feeling a dark hopelessness and abandonment, a bottomless pit of loss she'd been keeping at bay since Day One.

A GUST OF wind blew newspapers past them when they left the apartment building, no zombies in sight. But that didn't last long. After only a block of downhill riding, a woman with bare, pierced breasts and a gaping hole in her throat lunged at them from the space between two brick buildings. This time, Bill dismounted swiftly and shot her in the face.

"*Oye.*"

Five guns instantly aimed up. They all reared back. They'd nearly shot someone who talked.

A small woman, small and young enough to be mistaken for a teenager, beckoned to them from a fire escape. "*Oye, Rapido. Que vienen.*"

"She says more are coming!" Patty said.

"*¡Entran!*" The woman pointed to the building entrance. "*¡Ahi abajo!*"

They ran into a vestibule then the dim lobby of the building, then paused, unsure where to go. The woman barreled down a dark staircase toward them, waving them to follow. Her face was flushed.

They turned on flashlights and climbed two flights, past apartment doors that were mostly broken open. The woman led them through a door that was still in one piece. She locked it behind them, muffling the noise of zombies storming through the lobby doors below. They didn't know whether the woman had revealed herself and would be swarmed, meaning they'd all be swarmed. They waited, barely breathing, just inside the apartment door.

It sounded as if the undead were still downstairs but not coming closer.

"They don't have her scent," Jared whispered. "She's got what we've got."

The noise dissipated and the woman led them through a long hallway with small bedrooms on either side of it. Diffuse light entered alleyway windows, illuminating bunk beds with simple chairs and thrift-shop bureaus. Clothing on chair backs and open drawers—the way their owners had left them before heading off to work—belonged to both men and women. The living room was divided by plasterboard into two bedrooms. The woman sat down on a chair next to a window, where she had been watching the zombies that passed in packs and the fires that had still not reached her block.

She was small boned, four feet eleven inches, with almond-brown skin. Her dark hair and dark eyes, fine nose and full lips reminded Patty of her visits to Central Mexico as a teenage exchange student. The woman had braided her hair with a part in the middle and two braids down her back, the traditional way of the Mexican Indians there. She came from an ancient people, and her braided hair made the impression even stronger, despite her cut-off jeans and halter top.

Patty spoke to the woman in fluent Spanish that surprised everyone. She introduced their group.

The woman said her name was Ana. She took a look at each of them then back at her view, scanning for trouble. Jared joined her, watching out the window. Patty and Courtney sat on the bed while Shane and Bill leaned against a wall, all their faces set with anxiety. Jared could see the bike store on a cattycorner, a half block away. "There are still zombies hanging around near the bike store. It looks like there's one inside, too. There's movement in the doorway."

Ana answered questions about herself and waited for Patty to translate for the others.

"Ana worked the graveyard shift, cleaning up a bar," Patty explained to the others. "She was sleeping while all her apartment mates were at work. She heard screaming outside and . . . coming from the other apartments. She watched from her window . . . and on the TV before the broadcasts stopped."

"We're getting out of the City," Bill said and waited for Patty to translate. "There's too many of them here and we have to worry about the fires."

Ana stood and tried to reach under the cot where Courtney and Patty sat. "*Disculpe.*"

Courtney and Patty shoved over to give the woman space between them. Bill helped her pull out a small suitcase. Patty told Ana they were trying to get better bikes at the bike shop, then they'd travel to New Jersey and maybe south.

"*¡Híjole, por bicicleta!?*"

"What did she say?" Bill asked.

"Basically . . ." Patty said, "Oh jeez, by bicycle? I think she'd prefer a Hummer."

"Couldn't agree with you more but the highways are blocked," Shane said.

Jared turned from the window. "They drove a Hummer in *Zombieland*. Totally unrealistic. As if there wouldn't be a traffic jam in L.A."

Ana went to a bedroom that had belonged to a male day worker from Sinaloa, Mexico. She returned with a backpack and transferred her clothes from the suitcase. She had no doubt she was going with the group. She trusted her instincts: These people were far less frightening than the *coyotes* she'd entrusted her life to when she'd made the crossing into America. If they were headed south, there was no way she was staying behind.

CHAPTER 10

Bill approached the bike store, waving his arms. A dead guy, wearing skin tight logo bike pants and red cycling shoes, emerged from the store entryway. He headed for Bill, his face set in the now-familiar mask of starving-rage. Shane and Jared shot him in the head. Pieces of skull and brain splattered on the sidewalk.

"Damn, we're getting good at this," Jared exclaimed.

Inside, Patty found a new bike. Bill pulled out several for Ana to try from a line of bikes by the window, until they found one that was right for her size. He worried that she might not be much of a cyclist; she would have to get in shape fast. She didn't seem intimidated by the challenge.

Shane, Bill and Jared traded up to better bikes. They chose hybrids with tough mountain bike tires but greater speed than a mountain bike. Courtney already had a top-of-the-line hybrid.

"Yours is fine," Bill told her. She appeared understandably dazed, hanging on but obviously not up for any decision-making.

They found two aluminum-framed child trailers, which they hooked up to Bill and Shane's bikes, following directions that Patty read aloud. Each one would be able to pull one hundred pounds of supplies under a weather canopy meant to protect toddlers.

Patty handed out helmets. "With no doctors, we have enough to worry about without head injuries."

"Speaking of injuries," Jared said, "when we get out of the City, we have to stop at a drug store and pick up some antibiotics, bandages and painkillers. We need to have a full medic's kit."

Bill looked at him askance. The antibiotics were a good idea and pain killers in case anyone was badly hurt. Still, it wasn't a good sign that Jared was thinking about them. Bill hadn't forgotten what Jared had said about having to go to rehab for exactly that when he was a kid. They were under a lot of stress. It would be natural for Jared to want to medicate. Bill himself wasn't exempt from thoughts of taking the edge off somehow.

Shane tapped Bill's arm. "You ready?"

"As ever."

Shane and Bill ran the few yards to the gas station next door. While the others waited for them to return, Patty passed boxes of energy bars and drinks to Ana from behind the bike shop counter. Courtney and Jared had finished packing them and the knapsacks into the bike trailers by the time Shane and Bill returned with a map. They all kneeled together on the bike shop's tile floor, studying New Jersey.

"We have to build up our riding stamina gradually," Shane said. "It's been a long day already. We should get to New Jersey and find a place to hole up."

"I did grow up there," Bill said. "We should get across the river and head into Edgewater, the first town after the bridge." He pointed to a narrow sliver of land alongside the west bank of the Hudson. "I know that area pretty well. River Road runs south from the bridge, parallel to the Hudson. There's a Whole Foods a few miles south of the Bridge where we can get food. Even fruit."

Jared cut in, "Supermarkets are bad. Big glass windows, dead workers stuck inside."

"The Zombie Survival Guide?" Bill asked, sarcastically, suddenly tired of Jared's PhD in B-fiction.

"Well, yeah," Jared said dryly. *Results spoke for themselves and who the fuck was Bill anyway?* "Organic is not a priority."

Bill looked down at the map, biting his lip. "I didn't say that."

Courtney spoke, quietly, "I've been to Edgewater. On River Road there's townhouses and private homes. I agree with Jared and Shane. We should find a safe place to stay for the night. We'll find food in the empty houses."

Shane stood. "Sounds like a plan, let's just get out of this city."

Patty noticed Bill was miffed that the others had shot down his plan. "We're going to have to play it by ear anyway," she said in a conciliatory tone. "There's a lot we don't know between here and New Jersey."

The group looked at Bill for consensus. Bill knew everyone was worn out by the trauma of their last few hours, and his own nerves were sizzled. He wasn't usually so annoyed by Jared, who had been right more often than not. "Okay, let's do it. First priority: Find a safe house on the other side of the Bridge." Bill patted Jared on the back. "Sorry, dude. You just keep the information flowing. I'm behind you one hundred percent."

They made their way back the way they'd come, taking the Henry Hudson Parkway. Then they rode a long winding path up to the George Washington Bridge without serious incident. When the bridge leveled out at 600 feet above the water, they stopped and surveyed the Manhattan skyline. They could see all the way to the recently built World Trade Center.

Manhattan was still in flames. A cloud of smoke obliterated the tops of buildings as if it were a deep fog.

"Look at the Empire State Building." Courtney pointed at fire billowing out of the skyscraper, visible even through the haze of smoke.

Sections of New Jersey that bordered on the Hudson River were in flames, too. Yet, long stretches of the Jersey riverfront seemed untouched. Patty had a momentary vision of a military roadblock or some sign of law and order on the other side of the bridge, but she didn't hold out serious hope for that. New Jersey looked as dead as Manhattan.

Only a couple more hours until dusk, they mounted their bikes and rode. There was no way of knowing what lay ahead of them—or in wait for them—on the other side of the bridge. They cycled into the glare of the lowering sun, not daring to hope for the best.

CHAPTER 11

The riders swooped downhill from the GWB onto River Road. As Bill had told them, the two-lane road ran the length of the narrow strip of a town, sandwiched between the Hudson River and the towering Palisades cliffs only a few blocks to the west. On the river side of the road, developers had constructed malls and landfill condos that jutted out on the waterway. On the inland side, small stores and restaurants, interspersed with housing-bubble luxury homes, lined the road. Mostly modest homes, built before Edgewater had become fashionable, extended in straight lines inward from River Road to the bottom of the cliffs.

Riding with the wind at their backs, the cyclists kept ahead of stray undead that reached out from between homes and trees as they passed. A full block of stores had burnt down to embers and the rest were silent. They breathed in gusts of smoke when they passed a flaming condo development, turned into fingers of fire on water. Pushing past their emotional and physical exhaustion, they scanned the houses along the road for a resting place.

There was no sign of life in Edgewater. There would be no rescue team here. Bill remembered the traffic jams on the narrow road that used to piss him off when he'd come to the movie theater in one of the town's riverside malls. Riding second in the pack, Courtney pointed ahead toward a glass-faced home on the inland side of the road. It was perched high, up a small staircase, with a view past a marina to the river. It had a small yard on all four sides that could serve as a fire-break.

Shane spoke up from the back, "Let's check it out."

They all thought the house was a good choice. They'd seen enough action for one day. Bill was more than ready to get out of the fray, too. It had been a great accomplishment to make it this far. They could eat what they found in the house or go scouting for food, but they were overdue for the indoor safety and rest.

They dismounted. Bill gave a thumbs-up to Ana and she smiled. He thought she'd done well at keeping up with them. They parked their bikes next to the short staircase that led to the front door. The door was ajar as if someone had run out in a hurry, saving them from having to break in. Inside, they sniffed the air. In their short time in a zombie-dominated world, they already depended on their sense of smell in a way they never had before. It had become their early warning system: the distinct scent of rotten meat left in a refrigerator, a dead body or an undead one could foretell safety or danger. They didn't smell zombies this time, corpses either.

Guns out, they explored the sparsely decorated home with its blond-wood beams and earth-toned furniture. The temperature was comfortably cool, late in the day when all of Edgewater lay under the shadow of the cliffs. Courtney noticed that Ana seemed stricken when they peered into the empty child's bedroom then stepped inside. She felt teary herself, taking in the pink Dora the Explorer décor and a photograph of a little girl with her mother. Courtney had always assumed she'd have kids one day. When she won the Lotto, she'd engaged the fantasy of giving her to-be child all the things she herself had never received. Now, she was just relieved they didn't find this child's corpse.

"Pay dirt," Shane told Jared in the cookie-cutter, eat-in suburban kitchen. The house had an electric stove that wouldn't light, but Shane pulled out cans of tuna fish and an unopened jar of mayo. "At least it's not knockoff Welfare mayonnaise. No offense to the host, but I've had all the soup-kitchen meals I can take."

"Really?" Jared said. "I've never seen you leave food on your plate."

Shane chuckled. "It's amazing how three days of starvation can change a person."

They found bread, jam, dry cereal, kiddy boxes of Horizon organic chocolate milk and even apples for everyone. Shane took a huge bite of one.

"We will eat large tonight," Jared said to Ana, who walked in as they were scavenging.

She took down a bowl to make the tuna salad.

Patty was wet when she came in a few moments later after a cold shower. "Your turn," she told Ana in Spanish. The young woman disappeared as silently as she'd come in.

Patty picked up the chocolate milk container and read the label. "Expiration date: April 2014."

Jared's interest was piqued. "That stuff may keep us alive until we figure out how to grow things."

"Yeesh." Shane felt overwhelmed whenever he thought that far ahead. "How the hell are we going to live without electricity, gasoline, computers . . . *grocery stores?* And I used to think not having an iPad was a major problem."

"I miss my iPad." Jared flexed his thumbs. "I'm dying to tweet about finding tuna fish."

Patty sliced onions and put them in the bowl with the tuna. "It's still disorienting being so isolated without a news stream. Our world has shrunk down to just us."

Bill came in and sat at the granite breakfast bar. "Patty, has Ana told you her story? I wonder what her immunity basis might be . . . if there's any clue in her background about why we've survived."

"I mentioned it—gently. I didn't want to scare her that we were all addicts. I said we all had alcoholics in our family history. She said there's none of that in her family."

"What did I tell you?" Jared said. "That's the second person with no addict genes."

"Who's the first one?" Bill asked, wryly, amused that Jared could be in so much denial.

Jared shot him a 'don't start' look then shoved a kid's straw into his chocolate milk and sipped loudly.

"She's from a small town in Central Mexico, a few hours drive from Mexico City. There was some kind of trouble with gangs there. She needed to come to the States to make money," Patty said. "She had kids there."

Courtney spoke from the kitchen doorway, frowning, "She left her kids?"

Patty sensed judgment in Courtney's question. "Half the women who did our pedicures left their kids back home with relatives," Patty said. "They sent money back for food and clothes. It had to be the worst choice for a mother, being with her kids or leaving so they could eat. The women didn't see their kids for years."

"I had no idea," Courtney said.

"That's crazy," Shane said, "but not half as bad as them being dead now."

"I don't think she believes they're dead," Patty said.

The room fell silent as everyone pondered that.

They turned in for sleep right after dinner. They added Ana to the schedule for watch duty; everyone would do a three-hour shift in pairs. From the upstairs balcony, they could see miles of River Road, guard duty would be fairly easy from there.

The women slept in the master bedroom. Ana and Courtney lay on the king-sized bed in one bedroom, while Patty took her turn at watch. Sharing a room with the two women reminded Courtney of childhood sleepovers her father had let her have. Her friends had said she'd had the best father, and for ten years he was both mother and father to her. She wept in the dark, remembering him making fresh popcorn for her and her friends to eat while they watched movies. He'd done a great job with her . . . until he started drinking. Then, poof, she might as well have been *his* mother. She repressed a wave of tears, thinking of her father, her old friends and her old pain. Then an unbidden picture of his last moments flashed at her once again. She wept as silently as she could, not wanting to disturb Ana.

THE NEXT MORNING, they were all sore. It wasn't so much the distance they'd ridden. It was the death-defying uphill sprints with zombies in pursuit that had stressed their muscles. Only Ana had no complaints. She'd joined them after the sprints, but she assured Patty that riding a bicycle was nothing compared to the hard labor of her former cleaning job.

The group sat on the floor, stretching their sore muscles under orders from Patty, who said it would make them feel better and they'd avoid injury. Bill leaned into a hurdler's stretch, reaching his fingers toward his toes, his torso already firmer than it had been before Z-Day. "There are a half dozen mini-malls along the river if we head south. I can't see how we entirely avoid the risk." Bill tried not to come on as strong as he had at the bike store. He looked to Jared to see if he'd object. "We could get supplies and find another house, maybe ten or twenty miles down the road, depending on how things go."

"What we really need," Jared said, stretching out his gimpy leg with a grimace, "is a camping supply store, where we can get lanterns and a camping stove that doesn't need electricity. Camping lanterns are as good as sixty-watt bulbs."

Courtney sat up. "How are we supposed to find a store like that without the internet? Has anyone seen a Yellow Pages around here?"

Jared deadpanned, "What's a Yellow Pages?"

"Going mall to mall trying to find this stuff might be a suicide mission," Patty said.

"I guess we'll know soon enough how infested the malls are," Bill responded.

"Add binoculars to the shopping list," Shane said.

They left the house as they'd found it, taking only a bottle of Advil and a case of chocolate milk boxes in the trailers. Nearing the first mall, they could see an uptick in zombies in the distance, too many to challenge. Bill signaled with his right index finger toward a street running inland. The stretch appeared empty, surrounded by private homes where nothing stirred. They had to take a chance on going uphill for a few minutes.

Bill spoke to Courtney who rode next to him, "Up ahead, there's a road that runs parallel to River Road. Two blocks in. It's a better bet."

They all followed Bill, laboring on the uphill gradation past each house. As had become his habit, Shane rode at the back of the pack, making sure Ana and Patty didn't lag behind. Shane kept a special eye out for Patty, who rode just ahead of him. She was a trooper and had a calm head—probably worth several physically stronger people. Bill had told him that it was Patty who had killed all the cops at the police station. Shane never would have guessed it. But she was still small and less agile than the rest of them. They all kept an eye on her, although it would have upset her if she'd known.

A mile or so later they turned back downhill toward a small mall anchored by the Whole Foods Market. Shane thought he saw movement behind him. He noticed that Ana looked back, too. But by then they had crossed River Road to the driveway that ran alongside the brown brick side of Whole Foods. A crowd of two dozen zombies—mangy store employees and suburban housewives—surged on them from the riverside parking lot.

Everyone jumped off their bikes and ran to the side of the building, spraying the crowd with automatic gunfire. A couple of the zombies stayed down, but others unfolded themselves from the ground and got up.

"Single shot, keep your heads," Bill called out.

In unison, five quiet guns switched to single shots. They aimed for the head. Even Ana valiantly aimed and fired. Shane heard Courtney yell beside him and fire. A zombie had come from behind them. Wearing a green Whole Foods apron, the bellowing dead man moved faster than the others. Fat like a Romanian weightlifter, his thick neck gaped open and a piece of his jaw barely hung by a hinge where Courtney had shot him. But he was still coming.

Shane tried to grab Courtney's arm to move her out of reach and out of his own line of fire. No time.

The weightlifter grabbed Courtney's shoulder. Courtney grunted and aimed for his tonsils, pulled the trigger. She felt more than heard the gun click, the chamber empty. Her heart dropped.

Shane tried to free Courtney and reach around her to shoot at the same time.

A loud explosion rocked the air. Weightlifter hurtled sideways ending in a wet thump, his skull crashing into the building.

Released from the dead man's grip, Courtney went flying toward Shane, who swiftly put a second bullet through the guy's skull. They all used their bats to crush the skulls of any still-moving zombies remaining in the mob. Mission accomplished, they looked in the direction of the blast that had saved Courtney. A larger mob of zombies a block away had heard the explosion, too, and were headed their way.

Ahead of them, a middle-aged Japanese man with a rifle sprinted toward them. "You have silencers. Very useful." He spoke breathlessly. "Inside! Every time I shoot . . . it attracts a crowd. Follow me."

He led them to a metal door. They entered a dim corridor within the Whole Foods Market.

Shane caught Courtney when he saw her wobble.

She shook him off and regained her footing. "I'm okay. Thanks."

The man locked the door behind them. Surrounded by darkness, the stink of rancid meat was overpowering. The light of a battery-powered lantern perched on top of a carton filled the employee entryway where they stood.

"I cleared this place days ago, except for one zombie I locked in the meat freezer. The windows up front are broken, but I closed the metal gates before the electricity went out."

Banging started outside. They all turned toward the noise, ready to defend.

"Don't worry," he said. "It will hold. I've attracted a crowd before."

He led them down the hall, further from the noise.

"You got here right on time. Nice shot." Shane shook the man's hand, still assessing whether he would be friend or foe.

The man smiled to show friendliness. A tense battlefield smile. "I'm Kai."

Shane checked him out: Khaki pants, long-sleeve shirt, balding. He was dressed warmly in hot weather and that was strange. But he didn't project a thug vibe, which was a start. The jury was still out, though.

"Great shot," Courtney eked out the words. "Thank you."

"You had a fifty-fifty chance of being the victim," Kai said. "I'm a work in progress when it comes to shooting."

Courtney smiled queasily, not knowing whether to believe him. He seemed to be a damn good shot, and she preferred to believe that.

Bill shone the lantern at the darkness around them, not entirely trusting that the store was empty. "Are you alone?"

"You're the first people I've seen since Day One. With all the fires across the river and so many people in New York, I thought there would be many refugees. I've been watching but haven't seen anyone."

They were all silent for a moment, digesting that, the only sound the zombies banging outside. They hadn't seen anyone either, but they'd hoped a lot were still alive.

Kai took the lantern from Bill and led them forward. "There's a great deal of edible fruit in the store, and the root vegetables will last for months. They have soy products here in cans, falafel mixes, salmon, rice, beans. One can stay well nourished."

"Only the checkout is a bitch," Jared said.

Patty grunted, the smell overwhelming. "Maybe when we get into fresh air, we'll appreciate the thought of food."

Kai bowed slightly, apologetically, as if the store were his. He led them onto the main floor. "I couldn't clean out the store entirely—there are dead and the meat."

Bill spoke to the group, "Can't carry much anyway. We'll need to move fast to get out of here."

"There's another door behind the bakery section. If the zombies are wandering around where they saw us last, we'll be able to get out the other way."

"We'll need our bikes," Shane said.

"My house is only five blocks from here. We'll be safer getting there on foot and coming back for the bikes after the zombies leave. I have plenty of supplies there as well. I just came for fresh fruit and exercise. I promise you a good meal. My home is your home."

"Do you have any DVDs?" Jared quipped.

"Well, yes. I raided the Blockbuster a couple of days ago." Kai chuckled. "And we all thought Blockbuster had outlived its usefulness."

"Are you joking?" Bill asked. "You have electricity?"

"Pick out whatever groceries you want here and I'll show you. I was prepared for the unexpected. Unfortunately, as they say, 'I would rather have been happy than right.'"

Bill recognized that saying from the Rooms. *This guy is one of us, in recovery.* He patted Kai on the back. "It is good to meet you, buddy."

CHAPTER 12

They ran across River Road, feeling as scared on foot as crossing the wide avenues of Manhattan. Kai's Cape Cod-style house was located midway up a block of modest homes with no garages, built closely together. Short driveways separated each house from the next. They followed Kai alongside his home to a side door. From there, they could see a portable solar panel in the small backyard, aimed at the sun.

"There's one on the roof as well," Kai said.

Further into the yard, part of the lawn had been dug up. They saw a mound of dirt, a fresh grave.

"My family," Kai said, quietly, when his guests paused.

Despite all they'd witnessed, everyone felt a fresh jab of pain, their own losses mixing with their sadness for this man. They followed him silently up the back steps into the kitchen. It was dark inside. World War II-style blackout shades were pulled down over the kitchen windows. Kai closed the door behind them and flicked a switch. Light flooded the room.

"Yeah," Jared exclaimed. "I am liking this."

Everyone laughed, feeling saved for just a moment.

Kai took off his shoes and put on slippers that sat next to the door alongside a woman's and girl-sized pair. "We were in Fukashima when the March eleventh tsunami came. I lost my parents and we left because of the radiation. I was lucky to have a job opportunity here. I had been to the United States several times and my English is serviceable. After the tsunami, I decided to make our home green, but even more . . . I wanted to be ready for the next unthinkable event. As I said before, I would rather have been wrong. I wish I could have one day been an old grandfather, berating myself for wasting the money."

"We're grateful," Bill said.

Everyone took off their shoes and left them beside Kai's.

"Do you have hot water?" Courtney asked. Her skin was screaming for a hot shower.

"Yes. We—I mean, *I* have two bathrooms. I will show you the house. There's a cistern to collect rainwater from the roof for bathing and toilets, although I use bottled water for drinking. We can all be relatively comfortable here."

"Do you have computers?" Jared asked.

"Yes, but no internet. And the TV has only snow. I have a shortwave radio, but I haven't heard anything on it. I will show you and you can try."

Bill found himself in a hallway alone with Kai after the house tour. "Before you said, you would rather be happy than right. That's a familiar saying. Are you a Friend of Bill?" It was the code question twelve-steppers used to discreetly ask if others were in recovery.

Kai's face brightened. "Yes. Yes, I am, and Jimmy K. NA."

"Patty and I think something related to the addict or alcoholic gene makes us less attractive to zombies. We've been thinking it's like genetically modified plants that resist pests. The others aren't convinced."

Kai took in the new information. He paused. "My wife was a civilian, as we used to say. Not an addict. She turned into one of them. My daughter . . . I will never know." Kai choked up and turned away. "I will make dinner."

He prepared them a vegetarian meal made of canned seafood-flavored protein with a miso/wasabi sauce. He added roasted carrots, eggplant and squash. "The canned foods will last at least two years,"

Kai explained. "Canned meat will last longest, but most canned meats aren't healthy, very high in salt and fat. It will be important to stay healthy if we survive for the long term. None of you are doctors?"

"Wrong majors, all of us," Courtney said.

"Although Jared has an advanced degree in zombies," Bill added.

Kai's gaze snapped to Jared. "You know something about them?"

Jared raised his palms. "No. I just thought through a lot of the survival stuff . . . but you were way ahead of me."

Kai finished spooning out a portion of stew for himself. "It is very frustrating not knowing at least something about what happened to cause all this."

"None of us know anything," Bill said.

"I've wondered if perhaps it was the storm we had a few weeks ago," Kai said. "There are laboratories below sea level right in New York City . . . that were never mentioned after the storm. Who knows what viruses they were working on . . . whether the laboratories were breached."

Shane swallowed and took a sip of cold sparkling water. "It could have started anywhere,"

"You're right."

They ate in silence.

Patty put down her fork. "We don't need meat. The food couldn't taste better. You are a talented man, Kai."

"Thank you. I can't tell you what a pleasure it is to have company after so long without seeing another person."

"Canned food can actually last decades," Jared said. "I read once—they tested canned meat that was over a hundred years old. They fed it to a cat, and it was okay."

Shane grimaced. "I hope not to experience that."

Bill thought it through. "So, if we're never rescued by a government corps of agricultural experts—which I guess none of us really thinks is going to happen—we have time before we have to learn how to grow our own food." He paused. "We could even wait it out here for a while."

"What are you thinking?" Patty asked.

"I'm thinking . . . did any of you notice how the zombies looked? They're rotting. Not a lot, not fast, but they're rotting."

"So they may have a life expectancy," Jared pushed his glasses up his nose. "Or an unlife expectancy."

"Maybe we could just wait it out here—if you didn't mind," Bill said to Kai. 'It could be a matter of weeks, maybe months, even a couple of years? Jeez, I don't know. I'm just thinking . . ."

"There's a point to that," Courtney chipped in before Kai could respond. "Although it could be a long time. The one that grabbed me looked like shit, but he didn't seem any weaker for it."

"Not yet, but maybe they'll be weaker soon," Patty said, ready to grasp at any straw to keep up her own spirits. She translated the gist of the conversation for Ana.

Shane leaned back in his chair. "I never thought I'd say it, sharing a bedroom with a bunch of guys, but I kind of like this place. And we've got the best chef in the state. I know that's not saying much but—"

Kai interrupted. "Thank you."

"You'd think their brains would deteriorate if their bodies are decomposing," Jared said. "It's got to be just a matter of time."

Bill's mood lightened a notch. He envisioned zombie brains as compost. But a shot of survivor's guilt followed. "If we decide to stay here," he said almost to himself, "I still have to ride down to my parents' house."

No one disagreed, but no one volunteered to go with him. He pushed his plate away.

Shane's eyes met Bill's. "I'm still with you on that."

"Me, too," Courtney said, although her back clenched painfully as if every muscle in her body disagreed.

She was impressed Shane hadn't forgotten his promise to Bill. She remembered how the woman in the crack house had glared at him. The flesh and blood of that world had been far worse than the sanitized version she'd heard in AA meetings. She just couldn't wrap her mind around the two realities of Shane: a crack dealer and the stand-up guy they'd known. She was pretty sure he would have risked everything to save her at Whole Foods. She simply didn't understand him.

They cleared away dishes then sat down to the luxury of hot tea and coffee. For all of them, it was almost beyond belief that they were sitting in a room with lights on, civilized.

"We may want to spread out," Patty said. "Is there any chance, Kai, of our finding more solar panels and equipping multiple houses? If more survivors show up, we might end up with a small encampment here."

"The manufacturer I used was in Texas. I don't remember where its competitors were. I don't know . . . that this place will really be safe over time."

Patty had been so caught up in the conversation, she hadn't noticed how reserved Kai had been. He didn't like the idea of them staying with him.

Ana leaned over to Patty, speaking softly.

"Ana says she thought we were heading south," Patty told the group. "She wants to go south."

Ana's eyes were glittering, wet.

"*Porque?*" Bill asked.

"She wants to go to Mexico."

The table broke out in exclamations. "That's crazy," Bill said. "They not only have zombies, they have drug cartels. And it's thousands of miles away."

"*¡Pinche güero!*" Ana muttered angrily.

"What did she say?" Bill asked.

"Well," Patty said, "if my Spanish serves me right, she called you a fucking honkey."

Jared blurted out a laugh.

"Patty, yo," Shane said, laughing, too. "That honkey rolled off your tongue so naturally."

Patty patted his forearm. "I grew up in the Sixties." She glanced at Bill, who appeared to be taking the insult personally. "But, seriously, Ana wants to find her kids, just like you need to check on your parents, Bill. She had two children in Mexico, as you all know."

Heads dropped. Everyone registered the painful fact that Ana couldn't accept that her kids were dead. Who *would* accept such a thing without seeing for themselves?

Ana spoke up in accented English. "My kids are alive. I'd know if they were dead. I would feel it. I'll never give up until I find my children."

"You speak English?" Courtney voiced the surprise around the table. "You've been with us for days!"

"I've been listening!" Ana's face was ruddy with anger and panic that she'd never see her children again. "When you've been where I've been, you don't trust people so quickly. And now I know that maybe I was right not to trust you!"

"How can you say you don't trust us when we never even knew

what you wanted?" Bill asked.

"She may have a point about going south," Kai said. "This place is only a very temporary solution."

As if a punctuation mark, an alarm squawked from the far side of the living room. The sound sent shock waves through the quiet room.

Kai's face lost its color. He stood up.

Shane jumped up. "You have this place alarmed?"

Ana's chair fell backward with a thud. She crouched and took her gun from under her chair. They were all instantly standing and armed, ready.

Kai waved his hand with a downward motion toward the weapons, but he looked stricken. No one lowered their guns.

He crossed the room toward the sound and picked up a small black box from the window. "This is a Geiger counter. It's begun."

Patty's facial muscles went limp with realization. "Oh Jesus."

"We have to leave."

"You're not saying . . .?" Bill asked.

Kai stared down at the meter. "Do you remember how in Japan the nuclear plant operators said they'd never planned for both an earthquake *and* a tsunami? Well, it's been clear to me from the beginning that they never planned for . . . zombies. Nuclear plants have back-up generators that last only a couple of weeks after the electricity goes out, and there's human labor needed to maintain a plant.

"The readings aren't high yet. I had hoped it would take longer . . . but there's no telling how bad the situation is at Indian Point. And it's going to get worse."

"Ain't this a bitch," Shane said. "Indian Point is only thirty miles from here."

"There are other plants here in New Jersey as well. The northeast is full of nuclear plants likely to explode eventually if they haven't already. They will all be melting down in the next few days. This area will be a no-man's land. I've been delaying leaving, debating whether to . . . die here with my family. That's why I haven't left. But now that you're here, there's more reason to live."

Kai passed the Geiger counter to Jared. "The radiation is still low inside the house. So, there's time to leave after a night's rest."

Patty thought out loud, "We would never have known we were contaminated . . ."

"That's true."

"I guess we're headed south," Bill said. "We'll get you closer to Mexico, Ana. I don't know how far, but closer."

Ana was as frightened as the rest of them, but she waved her hand, acknowledging Bill. She did actually think she could trust him and the others, even if they didn't get her all the way home. She trusted her gut. These weren't bad people.

Kai went to the kitchen and returned to the group. No one was breathing easily anymore now that they knew the air was poison. Bill tried to chase away the feeling that his skin was being marinated. Kai held a medicine bottle in his hand.

"I have a general map of the plants that I downloaded before the internet went out. We need to head south and west, away from the coast. It will be challenging. We will be threading a needle between plants for as long as we're in the Northeast."

The room was totally silent.

"Nuclear power plants are built near water, so we'll need to be at least several hundred miles inland from the ocean but not too close to the large rivers or lakes." He opened the pill bottle. "I have a supply of iodine. We'll need to take it daily to help avoid thyroid cancer."

Patty put her head in her hands and felt Ana touch her back, comforting her. She should be the one comforting Ana, Patty thought. Thyroid cancer took at least ten years to develop. Ana and the others were younger and had more to worry about than she did . . . if any of them even survived long enough to die of cancer. She guessed they would all be lucky if that happened. But she didn't feel the least bit lucky now.

CHAPTER 13

Heavy rain ran in wide rivers down the windows of Kai's house. He entered the kitchen at 6:00 AM just before Bill and Patty wandered in. The younger members of the group were still asleep upstairs.

"Not a great day for a bike trip," Bill said.

"We'll have to wait here until the storm system passes. The rain would bring the contamination down on us in greater concentrations." Kai tried to convey calm rather than the worry he felt. "It will probably not affect us if we stay inside for several days. At least the level of radiation is still low."

"Without a weather forecast, we can't even predict when that will be," Patty said, feeling untethered by the layers of new reality. "It's so bizarre. I was the kind of person who checked the weather forecast twice a day before vacations. You can imagine how I'd want that in a mere nuclear disaster."

Kai smiled in commiseration. "Ah, but we do have coffee."

"I'll take it," Patty said at the same time as Jared, who walked in stretching his arms over his head.

While they waited for the rain to stop, Jared spent hours monitoring static on the shortwave radio. In the late afternoon, Kai joined Patty and Bill upstairs for a twelve-step meeting. They squeezed three chairs into Kai's small office. Patty and Bill voted good-naturedly on Kai being their speaker, looking forward to hearing his story after listening to each other for several days.

"I was a member of Narcotics Anonymous in Japan," Kai told them. "I didn't keep up well with meetings once I came to the United States. I didn't feel connected with the people who were so different from me here, and I needed to spend more time with my wife and daughter. My wife didn't speak English and it was an adjustment for both of them.

"I have eighteen years clean. I was a heroin and cocaine addict. As a young man, my life revolved around getting more . . . I did many things I'm not proud of. I shamed my family with a drug arrest before I got clean and went to college."

Patty and Bill would never have guessed that the mild-mannered, conservative man had been such a delinquent. They could identify with how bad it had been and how much he'd changed in the Program.

"It's good to be back in a meeting again, even if there are only three of us . . . in the whole world perhaps." Kai wrapped up, his eyes teary. "Twenty-four hours ago, as you can imagine, I never would have believed this would be happening in my home." He bowed his head, embarrassed by his emotion. "I don't know what it means, finding you, but for the first time since the attack I'm a little glad to be alive."

"I put my parents through hell, too," Bill said when Kai finished. "After all the effort to get there, college ended up being about keg parties, blackouts and absenteeism. My mom had a mild heart attack around that time, and my father was furious with me. He said the stress I caused made her blood pressure worse. He was trying to get me to stop, but it only made me hate myself more and I couldn't stop."

The wind splashed rain against the windows of the house.

"They're up having another meeting," Courtney said to Shane as they kept watch beside the living room window.

"What do they do in meetings?" Shane asked.

"Mostly, they tell their stories of how screwed up they were and how AA saved their lives."

"Do you know how that works? I can't believe the three of them were once like my parents."

"I haven't been to a meeting since I was fifteen, but it's something like this." Courtney counted off on her fingers. "They admit they can't handle the booze and drugs, which we all could have told them if they'd only listened. That's Step One. They realize they're stark-raving mad, which we also could have told them. Step Two. So, they turn to God or a higher power or the group or whatever helps them. Step Three. They pray and write about themselves and keep trying to get better every day because they're always a little crazy no matter how long they're sober . . . and so, of course, they have to say 'sorry' a lot. That would be Four through Ten." Courtney took a long breath. "Then they try to help other people when they're not praying and mediating and . . . that's about it, Steps Eleven and Twelve. I guess it really does work, at least for some people, some of the time."

"Deep."

"It's ironic we ended up with a bunch of addicts and alcoholics, except for Ana I guess. Who knows her story? She hasn't exactly been honest."

Shane shrugged. "Can you blame her? It doesn't seem as if she's trying to hurt anyone."

"I don't blame her, really. I was just surprised."

Shane chuckled, thinking about it. "It was actually pretty funny."

"Man, when she lit into Bill, I have to admit it was hysterical. There are things about Bill that remind me of my dad. He can be pretty annoying."

Shane agreed that Bill could be controlling. He seemed to think he was in charge of their group for some reason. The obvious reason was that he was a white man, but Shane gave Bill the benefit of the doubt on that. He meant well and Shane thought he felt responsible for the women and younger men, even though Kai was older than him. "I thought you were close to your pops."

"We were. But he could annoy the shit out of me. He was so bossy, even after all the stuff he put me through."

"I hear you. My father used to come around when I lived with my grandmother, his eyes bugged out on crack. He'd try to give me a talking to if my grandmother told him I'd been cutting school or staying out late." Shane paused. "I wished him dead sometimes when I was a kid, especially when my grandmother died and I had to go to a group home. I didn't see him much after that."

"You were in foster care?"

"Yeah. It was a mess. I stayed focused on school for two years, doing the right thing in my grandmother's memory. I was the only one in my house doing that . . . and it was really tough. For a lot of the kids, the group home was penitentiary training school. Their own parents had signed them into the System because they couldn't handle them. Try studying for the chemistry regents in a house full of kids nobody wants.

"Then in college it was a different kind of problem. I was surrounded by kids whose families wanted them. They called home when they were homesick . . . went home for the holidays. My father was out in the world somewhere and I hated him. But when I heard in my sophomore year that he'd died, it ripped me up."

"I couldn't believe my father started drinking," Courtney said. "For nine years we had a pretty normal life. Then, one day when I was fifteen, he came home bombed." Courtney snapped her fingers. "Poof, overnight, my whole life changed. He didn't start doing drugs like when I was little, thank God, but it was . . . terrifying. I was so scared he'd end up like my mother."

"Undead," Shane said.

A group of corpses walked down the middle of the street. Shane and Courtney went silent, motionless, watching. They were a strange crew: One hairy man in soaking wet shorts; a large woman in a sundress, which had gone nearly transparent in the rain; and a young boy of about twelve, his hair a sopping mop. Courtney and Shane studied them, hoping for signs of deterioration. The undead were perhaps seeping more from their wounds than before but it was hard to tell in the rain. The group passed without spotting them.

"That must have been rough on you when your dad changed like that. I was really embarrassed by my . . . situation. First my parents not being able to take care of me then going into foster care . . . as if it were my fault."

Courtney looked away from the window. "It was so embarrassing. I never knew what he'd do. I couldn't have friends over. He came to my school drunk."

Talking with Shane, Courtney knew he was the only one of their group who really understood what she'd been through. But what killed her was that he was the one she distrusted the most. In her old world, she'd prided herself on figuring people out fast and staying away from the ones who might harm her. But, nowadays, she second-guessed everything, even her most dependable instincts.

The next day, the rain stopped. Kai looked at the house next door through the kitchen window. "The husband was about six foot and his wife was about Patty's height. They were Russian immigrants. We never could talk much, just nodded and said good morning."

Kai wore boots and a rain poncho just in case it started raining again. Courtney and Jared wore knit caps and Kai's sweatpants, athletic socks pulled up to meet high-water cuffs. Kai felt a jab of pain when Ana walked in with his wife's sweats on, a baby blue hood pulled up. For a second, he almost deceived himself that the slight, almond-shaded woman was his wife, still alive. They all slipped plastic Pathmark bags over their sneakers and secured them with rubber bands at the ankle.

It was a warm June day but, no matter how uncomfortable, they would need to stay covered up until they escaped the contamination area. Before they left Edgewater, they would stop at a sporting goods store that Kai knew, a mile south. Everyone could get clothes that really fit, plus camp stoves, lanterns and rain ponchos. But they couldn't even make that short trip until everyone had long sleeves and long pants to cover them. That left Patty, Shane and Bill needing clothes, all of them unhappy that the others were going on the dangerous mission for them.

Kai and his crew of three shrugged on empty backpacks, their stomachs tight with anxiety: Going outside stripped away any veneer of safety. They headed into the muggy air and crossed the driveway to the house next door. Kai tried the knob. Locked. He put a crowbar to the crack between the frame and door, and jimmied it open as quietly as possible. They went inside and closed the door behind them, hoping the slight noise hadn't attracted attention.

It smelled clean. The Z-bomb, as Jared called it, had happened in the middle of the day when the neighbors should have been out working. They switched on flashlights to cut into the dimness of the house. Kai had never been inside the home before. A disparate hodgepodge of odd chachkas, large and small, cluttered the Russians' living room. Porcelain angels, Russian dolls, and classic Matchbox cars were displayed in ornate cabinets. The sweep of Kai's flashlight felt like an odd obituary of sorts for his neighbor. The beam of light landed on a life-sized plaster statue of Yoda beside an artificial palm tree. Kai's heart jumped and he nearly fired before he realized it was a statue.

Kai finished checking the first floor then made his way upstairs. The dosimeter he wore around his neck had been steadily rising. They needed to get out of the neighborhood as soon as possible. He met up with the others in the master bedroom and saw Jared flopping around on a king-sized water bed. "Dude, I've never seen one of these before. I hadda try it out."

With one arm full of clothes, Courtney pressed her free hand against the bed. She couldn't help herself. She flopped her butt down, laughing, bouncing up and down then falling backwards.

"Did you check out all the rooms up here?" Kai asked, sternly.

"Yessir, no walkers," Jared said with a Southern accent like a character in *The Walking Dead*.

Kai turned away. It was easy to forget that Courtney and Jared were still so young. He picked out a sweat suit from a mirrored black lacquer bureau with drawers, unfolded and checked it out, navy blue with gold stripes down the leg; a matching zippered jacket with a hood. Excellent for protecting the neck, and the thin fabric would fit under a bicycle helmet. He looked at Ana, who had started going through the woman's clothes at the other side of the room. She was probably as young as Jared, but she was all business. She'd obviously had to grow up a lot faster than him.

Kai kept his mind on business, too. He was now enduring his second nuclear evacuation and knew survival could be measured by seconds and minutes. He folded the garish sweat suit into his backpack then pulled a plainer pair of sweats from the drawer. At least they'd found clothing.

THEY ALL DRESSED early the next morning. When they distributed the clothes, Shane told Kai to give the glittery warm-up suit to "the white man."

"I don't want to bring any old stereotypes into the New World," he said.

Bill laughed, taking the remark lightly in the manner offered. Shane had been growing on him. He was a team player and it touched Bill that he was the first to volunteer to look for his parents. In fact, they'd been pretty lucky with everyone in their group. They were in ridiculously challenging circumstances that could bring out the worst in people, but everyone had shown up with their best game, acting with restraint and courtesy to each other. Even he and Courtney had ceased squabbling so much with each other.

Bill put on the sweat jacket. "Didn't you ever see *Saturday Night Fever?* This is right up my alley."

"I'd wear it," Jared said. "I'm not ashamed of my cultural heritage."

"Which is?" Bill asked.

"Mutt," Jared said. "Black/Irish/Italian with a little Cherokee. A true American. But we're all 'minorities' now. Zombies are the majority and they've got one hell of an affirmative action program."

"They did cut out a lot of bullshit," Shane said. "Like no more racial profiling."

Jared put on a long-sleeve shirt Kai had given him. "Can't say I miss the Stop-and-Frisk."

Bill put on his sneakers. "They just kill everyone now, no questions asked."

The group left Kai's house the way they'd come, walking to the mall to retrieve their bikes, the place preternaturally quiet. They filled bags from Whole Foods and loaded up the bike trailers before doubling back to Kai's house. They all reluctantly left the last house with electricity and hot water they expected to see for a very long time. Kai wept silently as he pedaled away, his second evacuation, this time alone. In his backpack, he carried a few family photographs, his wife's wedding ring, and a crayon drawing of their home made by his daughter.

They continued south on River Road. The day baked the overdressed cyclists, even their feet sweating in the plastic bags. Zombies only belatedly noticed the group wheeling past. Unable to match the speed of the bikes, the dead fell into a procession twenty yards behind them. The procession continued to grow, but eventually the back of the mob would peel off as the front expanded and obliterated the view from the back. As usual, the dead had a limited attention span when it came to this particular group.

Kai led the group to a sporting goods store in an L-shaped mall that backed onto the river. Out of sight of the first zombies who followed, they entered the store and ran at a crouch toward the cashier's stations.

The zombies arrived outside the storefront windows, filling up the sidewalk. Then the group heard the stirring of zombies from deep within the store. Bill looked beside him at Patty and Jared. He put his finger to his lip and then hand signaled: *wait for it . . . wait for it.* Barely breathing, they waited, counting on the zombie swarming instinct. Praying for it.

The shuffling and moaning within the store became loader. Dead employees and customers moved forward, migrating toward the sound of the zombies outside. The outside ones—having lost sight of their prey—loitered on the far side of the glass as if they'd forgotten why they'd come.

The zombie sounds and smells intensified as the store zombies funneled through the cashier stations, heading toward the windows. When all of them had passed, their heads exploded with the force of silenced bullets. As fast as the battle had started, it was over. The shooters dove back down behind the cashier station counters, unseen by the zombies outside.

Bill crouched for a few moments, hearing nothing inside the store. "Let's move," he whispered.

Staying low, they all ran toward the center of the store and re-grouped out of sight and earshot of the dead outside.

"At the end of each day in a contaminated zone, we will need to throw out the clothes we've ridden in before we go inside for the night," Kai said. "Everyone must get several changes of clothing, double bag them and pack them into the bike carts."

After they'd found clothes and supplies, it was a half hour's wait until the zombies outside had mostly wandered off.

"Lucky thing the undead are idiots," Jared quipped.

They didn't want to jinx themselves by saying it aloud, but they were all starting to envision surviving the zombies. They hoped Kai was right that they would also get out of the radiation zone before permanent damage. When only a sprinkling of dawdling undead remained in the parking lot, the group went out and put them down.

BILL'S HOMETOWN LAY forty miles to the southwest. They'd decided to go together. Bill dreaded what lay ahead but almost equally feared feeling hopeful. He tried to shut out the thoughts of a happy reunion with immune parents. He hadn't been that kind of lucky, ever, and despite being one of the few people left alive, his recent experiences—a zombie and nuclear apocalypse—had not increased his optimism.

It was nearly dusk before they crossed the train tracks on the outskirts of Montclair, a quaint edge city, where many of the residents had commuted an hour by train to Manhattan. Its main street was mostly a string of burnt stores now. They took a right turn away from its charred boutiques, Starbucks and New York Sports Club, and entered a tree-lined residential area.

"My parents were retired school teachers," Bill told Courtney, who rode beside him. "There was a good chance they were home when the zombie attack started."

She didn't say anything. What could she say?

Bill felt his blood pounding in his ears when they entered the streets where he'd grown up. He led the pack. Much like Edgewater, the houses on the side streets sat close together in the part of town where he'd lived. But the homes were older. Mature trees with massive roots shaded small Tudors and Victorians with their covered front porches. Bill's block could have been a squeezed together Norman Rockwell portrait.

Bill stopped in front of the blue house where he'd lived from the age of ten until he'd left home at nineteen. The windows were dark behind the front porch, no flickers of candles or other sign of life. Bill repeated the litany that had prepared him for the worst: His parents weren't addicts or alcoholics; they weren't children of addicts. Their group hadn't been able to agree about what it meant, but they hadn't seen anyone alive who wasn't an addict or child of an addict . . . except Ana. They didn't know why she was "immune," which was why despite himself he hoped. *Damn.* He didn't know why he kept doing that to himself, going over and over the puzzle, always coming back to the Ana question when he thought of his parents.

He reached for the doorknob. His parents rarely locked up during the day. With his friends gathered behind him, he opened the door. They all raised their guns. Bill stepped into the shadowy hallway when suddenly the distorted face of his mother reared up in front of him.

"Mom!" He lifted his hand out to her.

She gripped his hand.

He felt himself thrown off his feet to the left. Jared had shoved him aside. Two muffled pops, sparks of indoor lightning filled the hall. Bill's mother flew backward and crumpled to the floor. Behind her, the half-eaten face of Bill's father appeared and splattered, Jared's second bullet hitting him squarely. Bill let out a howl of shock and despair.

Shane caught Bill by the arm. They all rushed inside, packed into the maggot-stinking, blood-sprayed hallway. They had to stay inside long enough to make sure any zombie trailers had lost sight of them.

Bill straightened up, quickly, embarrassed. He swiped away tears with the back of a hand. "I'm sorry. I'm sorry. Thank you . . . Jared."

"I'm sorry, too," Jared said, both proud and in pain.

After a moment, Kai spoke softly. "Is there anything you need here, Bill, before we go? I'm sorry, we can't wait. We have to get out of these clothes and stop for the night." He glanced toward the corpses. "Not here."

"No. I'm ready to go," Bill said, in shock. He didn't want to pass his parents' corpses to walk further into the house. He knew he would never forget his mother and father's faces right before they exploded. The grip of his mother's hand. It had been worse than his worst fear, indelibly branded on him.

CHAPTER 14

Moments later, they were back on their bikes. Bill took the lead, his brain feeling thick and slow. He was the one who knew the neighborhood and he had to guide the others to a place to settle down for the night. He looked for a home that held no memory for him, not wanting to find any of his old friends or their parents if he picked a familiar home. They settled on a large house at the center of a generous lawn in Upper Montclair, the wealthier part of town, breaking in by using the crowbar that Kai had brought. Nobody was home.

They wheeled their bikes inside the garage then wiped them down with rags they found next to an old Corvette. In a mudroom off the garage, which they agreed they wouldn't enter again, first the women then the men stripped off their clothes and put on new ones.

Jared and Kai set up the lanterns, which lit up the living room as bright as a light bulb, as promised.

"We won't have hot food here," Kai said. "Electric stove."

"What about the camp stove?" Patty asked.

"Camp stoves emit carbon monoxide and we can't open windows."

So, they were back to eating from cans, but no one was complaining. Jared unpacked the shortwave radio, which had become his own. He set it up on a desk where the deceased owner of the house must have sat to pay bills. A stack of bills waited. The radio's white-noise crackled alongside the dusk-birdsong coming from cherry trees outside the living room window. Jared played with the radio knobs, trying to keep himself from pacing. Nervous energy traveled like electric jolts through him after killing Bill's parents.

Bill sat in the adjacent living room, motionless. Everyone left him alone, knowing there was nothing they could do for him. But he looked up as Ana approached.

Her hair was parted in the middle and tied back in a long pony tail. "I found this." She handed him a five by seven-inch photograph. "It was on the refrigerator door at your parents' house."

Bill saw the two of them, smiling, tanned, on vacation in the Caribbean. He swiped away a tear, blown away that Ana had thought to bring it, in the midst of everything, and that he had overlooked it.

He gripped her hand for a moment, for support, as if she was a visitor and he was sitting shivah. "Thank you, really, thank you. I'll always be grateful for this."

Before they all turned in for the night, Kai spread a piece of printer paper on the coffee table. "This is the Nuclear Regulatory Commission map. I downloaded before the internet went down."

The others leaned forward to get a better look at the map of the United States. Black dots represented nuclear plants. There were a lot of black dots.

"Before we escape the Northeast, we'll come even closer to nuclear power plants than we've been." Kai pointed to the map. "There are two plants ahead in Pennsylvania and one in Ohio."

"Then why are we going that way?" Courtney asked.

Kai ran his finger down an alternate route. "It is worse in southern Pennsylvania and New Jersey. Heading west before south avoids a more concentrated cluster of plants near the main roads there. But, even our way, I'm afraid the radiation will get worse before it gets better if the plants are already melting down."

In the morning, Bill led the others to I-80. It was barely seven AM and they were already dressed too warmly for the day. At the top of the ramp, with no followers, they paused to check out their surroundings. They beheld a surreal multicar crash of thousands of cars. Piled and crushed, one on top of the next, the cars had become a metal snake with block-long charred pit marks where fire had eaten into it. Even standing on the guardrail, they couldn't see where it began or ended.

They cycled beside the crash, only occasionally having to dismount to squeeze through. They rode single file with ample space between riders to avoid collision if a rider had to avoid a zombie. The formation also gave the person farther back a chance to shoot if needed. The road became increasingly rural as they traveled. Woods surrounded the highway, and the white of houses became smudges between the trees. They rode with all their senses on edge, fearful of what might emerge from the crumpled metal. Patty only hoped no one would get hurt out on the highway. There would be no way to get to safety if one of them couldn't ride.

Kai worried, too. They had to find a clear roadway and needed a vehicle. They were traveling too slowly, exposed to radiation. But all they could do now was focus on getting past the crash.

After miles with few shots fired—most of the undead had burnt to cinders or must have walked off to find live prey—they reached the beginning of the accident. A car had been rear ended. An old man drooled inside, watching them. It must have been 110 degrees inside the car.

"They decompose faster when hot," Jared observed when they stopped for a water break. The geezer still looked capable of taking a big bite out of them, so none of them felt all that reassured by the observation.

With the sun blazing down, they stared out at the first stretch of unblocked highway they'd seen. It was an obstacle course of crashed and skidded cars but it was passable. Patty panted, dying to peel off her super-heated cycle-wear. She looked around at the flushed faces of the group. "How is everyone?"

"I don't know how long we can ride like this," Shane said. "Are you okay?"

Patty was still catching her breath. "All that 'hot yoga' is finally paying off. Can you believe I used to pay for this kind of experience?"

Jared walked to the guard rail and climbed up to get a better view ahead.

"Should we try to start one of those cars?" Bill asked. "We'd have to do a lot of weaving but we could get through."

Jared jumped down. "We can't give up our bikes in case the road gets blocked again."

"Right."

"The radiation has been going down as we travel," Kai said.

Courtney shaded her eyes, peering ahead. "That's great."

"Only a temporary reprieve. It would be better if we could just get through the next two hundred miles fast with the protection of a car. Ninety miles ahead, we'll pass very close to the first Pennsylvania plant. Then we'll be close to two more plants, one after the next. In a car, we could drive two hundred miles past the plants, with minimal exposure. But on bikes ... we have to stop for rest out of range of the plants behind us but before the ones ahead. We may have to do that between each plant." Kai rubbed the bridge of his nose. "I'm sorry I don't exactly know where the safe places will be if we travel that slowly. In Japan, even with equipment and weather forecasts, the radiation blew in unexpected ways."

"So, bottom line, we need a car," Bill said, "or we stretch out the torture of riding in Hazmat suits and sleeping in a radiation zone, maybe for days." He paused. "Of course, if our car gets stuck without bikes, we could be in worse shape."

Shane's eyes snapped to the side. "There's movement in the trees."

They all headed for their bikes.

"How about a pickup?" Courtney asked as she mounted her bike. "We could put the bikes in the back and ditch the truck if the roads get blocked up."

"That would be perfect, wouldn't it?" Patty said.

"Yeah." Bill took point as they started to pedal. "The trick will be to find one."

After a few miles they spotted a relatively new, bright blue pickup truck that hadn't crashed into anything. It might as well have been gift wrapped, the way it appeared—pristine, shiny, promising. It had two rows of seats inside, the equivalent of a car, plus room in the back for their bikes and gear. The truck was boxed in by cars and the guard rail on three sides, but there was only one car, a Honda, in front of it.

They approached the truck carefully. There was no one inside and the door was open, as if the driver had tried to make a run for it. The passenger and back windows were cracked but not shattered.

They heard a moan. Swollen dead-heads popped up in the back windshield of the Honda. All guns instantly aimed at two dead brunettes with bouffant hairdos. They weaved their heads, their mouths up against the glass, as if trying to eat their way out. After nearly jumping through her skin, Patty said, "Zombie bobble-heads."

The others chuckled.

Bill slid into the driver's side of the pickup and felt for the key. The driver had actually turned the car off before escaping, which meant there would still be gas. Bill turned the key. A weak engine-whine. He pumped the gas and turned it again. The engine came to life. Bill looked at the fuel gauge. "Pay dirt, guys! Almost a full tank."

Ana crossed herself. "*Gracias a Dios.*"

Jared glanced at her out of the corner of his eye. "You still believe that shit?"

Ana had no chance to respond before Jared marched off, anger in his steps.

"What's eating him?" Courtney asked Ana.

Ana shrugged again. "Maybe his life . . . how do you say? Sucks."

"True."

Jared fell in next to Shane and Kai, pushing the Honda from behind. The bobble-head sisters let out high-pitched shrieks of excitement. They flailed at the window, each exposing bloody finger stumps, what was left after two weeks of mindless clawing. Courtney joined the pushing, wanting to get the hell out of there.

The Honda moved easily, and they pushed it out of the way. Bill drove the truck forward, and the men began passing bikes onto the truck bed. Standing on top, Courtney positioned the bikes close together to make room for the load. "Pass me your backpacks, guys. There won't be room for them inside."

Kai put his hand up. "If we're ready to get in, we need to change. We can't be in close quarters for hours with contaminated clothing."

Patty looked in the cab. "There's only room for six in there. I won't change. I'll ride with the bikes."

"No," Bill said.

"I'm the oldest and have the least to worry about long-term. I'll cover myself with tarps."

Shane took Patty's arm. "This is bullshit, Patty. We can be uncomfortable for a few hours or one of us can get radiation poisoning. What makes you think that's a choice?"

"Seven people in a car is not," Ana struggled with the word, "discomfort. You should see how I came to this country."

Kai ushered everyone to get their clothes changed. "Discuss in the car."

The men and women split up on opposite ends of the truck with their backpacks, leaving their contaminated clothes on the highway pavement. With fresh clothes on, they wedged their backpacks between and under the weight of the bikes then covered the bikes with a tarp and roped it down.

Four in the back, three up front. It was a tight squeeze. In back, Ana sat perched on Shane's knee as chastely as possible. Although he knew Ana would put his legs to sleep after a while, he was glad to be inside.

The cab filled with the scent of seven sweaty bodies. "Phew," Courtney reached toward the air conditioning. "We're ripe."

Bill drove, weaving around cars and scanning the road for surprises. His sense of responsibility weighed on him. He didn't know why he felt as if he had an extra responsibility for everyone, and not just when he was driving. He was always scared he'd screw it up. He'd actually shared about it in one of his meetings with Patty and Kai. Patty had laughed, sympathetically. "It's just like an alcoholic to think he's doing the Zombie Apocalypse wrong."

She'd hit it on the head. That was just what he'd thought, and it was what he'd thought when he'd struggled during his first semester of college and after 9/11, too. That morning before the towers fell, he'd obeyed the cops, walking north instead of helping a single soul. It wasn't as if he'd seen anyone he could have helped when he'd walked away from rather than toward the disaster. He told himself afterward that the police weren't allowing civilians close to the buildings, and he would have been killed, buried by the North Tower if he'd disobeyed them. But, still, he'd thought he should have done more. And, now, despite the irrationality of it, the not-so-nice voice in his head (his own) was telling him that he could have done more for his parents, too. He'd given them eleven worry-free years after he'd gotten sober, he'd become a model son, but he hadn't been able to save them in the end.

He accelerated, telling himself not to be such an idiot. Deep in his heart, he knew he'd been doing his best during this endless disaster. No one expected him to be perfect. No one had ever expected him to be perfect, other than him. He sighed, staring intently ahead, navigating around a car crash. He only hoped he didn't make a bad call and somehow lead others to catastrophe. But, for now, his task was simple: he needed to focus on not blowing a tire on the debris-strewn highway.

In the front passenger seat next to Courtney, Jared opened the glove compartment. "Hey, a GPS." He plugged it into the lighter socket.

Courtney couldn't restrain her fingers when she saw the map come onto the screen. She pressed Points of Interest. "There's a diner, guys. Only two exits away. What I would give for a cheeseburger and fries."

Jared leaned forward and entered Denver, Colorado, thinking that would be a nice place to live . . . or it would have once been a nice place. Others called out their destinations.

From the back, Ana said, "Mexico, please."

The car went painfully silent. Everyone knew she wasn't joking.

Jared spoke kindly, "This isn't loaded with Mexican maps. I'll do San Antonio, Texas. I think that's close to the border." They waited as the map loaded. "Arrival time . . . twenty-nine hours," Jared said. "I don't think that takes into account the walking dead in the road."

Bill groaned. He didn't want Jared encouraging Ana about heading toward Mexico. She didn't say much but he already knew she wanted to find her kids. He could imagine her walking off alone into a desert to find them.

After that, no one spoke more than a few words. The Interstate began wending its way toward the Pocono Mountains. Jared looked out the window at a tall forest. Out of nowhere, his mood had taken a hairpin turn. In a post-adrenaline crash that rivaled the hangover after a night of cocaine, he was suddenly exhausted and desperately sad. There was nothing for him ahead. No Denver. No California. Nothing. He'd spent half his life working to get into an Ivy League school. He had thought he would be a filmmaker. He'd networked, landed the right internships, done a shitload of hard work. He'd scared the hell out of his parents when he'd veered off course for one summer of teenage drug taking, but since then, he'd made them proud.

When Jared thought of his parents, he hiccuped back a cry before he could prevent it. He thought everyone in the group wept in private, except maybe Bill. You could hear it once in a while, passing a closed bathroom or bedroom door, but they had an unspoken rule not to bring each other down. Jared melted into his seat, into a pit of shame made worse by the heavy silence in the car. There was no feeling he hated more than embarrassment.

By the time they neared the Delaware Water Gap, Jared, staring out the window, saw nothing.

Kai checked his Geiger counter. "We're down to almost normal levels."

At a narrow bridge high over the Delaware River, Bill stopped behind a car that was stuck in the toll lane. "We've gotta move it."

Everyone piled out of the pickup. It was the first time they'd had to stop. The noise of their motor had attracted the walking grotesque. This time, the predators were three highway construction workers with orange vests. The women shot the construction workers as they came into range, while the men ran to the car that was blocking the lane. Shane steered while the others pushed.

A family group on a camping trip from hell climbed over the embankment onto the road behind the pickup.

"Just leave them," Bill called. "We've used way too many bullets already."

Everyone threw themselves inside the truck. Shane took the driver's seat and hit the accelerator.

"We're about sixty miles now from the next plant," Kai said after his breathing had calmed. "The highway will pass ten miles south of it. That is much closer than we've been. We just need to keep moving."

They rode silently through the mountains. The Geiger counter needle gradually rose then spiked as Kai predicted.

"We're ten miles north of the plant now."

Bill felt himself getting claustrophobic the way he'd felt when he'd taken an MRI. He imagined himself riding in a moving tomb, buried alive in zombie air. It made him want to jump out of the car.

Ana spoke softly to him, "Are you all right?"

"Just getting a little freaked out. I'm okay."

The road ahead became straight and clear. Shane got them as far as he could as fast as he could.

"The readings are going down," Kai said after a while. "I'm not an expert, but I think all we received was the equivalent of an X-ray. We are fine for now. But we need to get away from the Northeast before it gets worse."

The Geiger counter went up again slightly when they passed the next plants Kai had told them about, but they were located fifty miles from the highway, so it wasn't as bad. After six hours stuffed into the pickup, Kai pronounced the air clean. They had passed through the nuclear gauntlet. "We're done. That was the worst I expect."

Courtney and Patty applauded the way people did when a plane made a safe landing after a rough trip.

CHAPTER 15

The sun was free falling toward the tops of the mountains. It was time to find a safe place for the night. They all noticed how oddly silent Jared remained when they exited the highway and started house shopping. He was the one who'd predicted they could find homes with generators in rural areas. They'd expected him to be spouting generator factoids by now.

"What should we be looking for?" Patty asked, trying to draw him out.

Jared looked at her morosely, the glint gone from his eyes. "A rectangular metal box at the side or back of the house." He went quiet again.

They skirted the main street of an early twentieth-century industrial town with its low-rise, sepia storefronts, wide sidewalks and zombies. At the outskirts, they began to see homes spaced widely apart and flanked by woods.

"We should look for an isolated place without a car," Bill said.

"No car probably means no one was home."

They pulled onto a random lane and approached a pristinely maintained cedar-sided home, with a two-week growth of lawn. It was in the middle of a clearing on a small hill, surrounded on three sides by woods.

"No car," Courtney said, thinking a place like this might have been a nice second home if she'd ever gotten her Lotto winnings. *She would have wanted it next to a lake or river, but*— She cut off her thoughts. She couldn't afford the crash and burn back to reality after indulging in fantasy.

They stopped the pickup, crickets and birdsong the only sounds. Guns out, Shane and Bill went to check the place out while the others covered them from a few paces back. Courtney shoved over into the driver's seat, the getaway driver, just in case.

"It has a generator," Bill announced when he returned and they regrouped near the car. "No movement inside. The side door is unlocked."

When they entered the home's kitchen, they stood for a minute, letting their eyes adjust to the dimness but mostly smelling the air. Country mildew and rotting meat from the fridge. Nothing else. With flashlights, they searched to make sure they were alone, and tried a wall switch that might turn on the generator. Each time they came to a likely switch, nothing happened.

"Many generators turn on automatically in a blackout," Kai said. "A generator like that would have run out of gas a long time ago. We need a house with a generator that switches on manually."

Courtney was the first to say that it didn't matter. "We should just stay here. I've had all the excitement I can take for one day."

Everyone agreed, relieved to be inside. The rotten meat smell dissipated once they retrieved what they needed from the kitchen and closed the door. The camping lanterns lit up the living room enough to make things feel close to normal. They would use flashlights to enter bedrooms and bathrooms. They settled in for the night.

Jared didn't eat much of the dinner Kai, Patty and Ana prepared from cans. The birds singing outside might as well have been a broken car alarm, making him want to jump out of his skin. The dense scent of the forest, which the others seemed to like, only reminded him of the camping trips he would never again take with his brother and father. Reality had crashed down on him: Right here, right now was as good as life was going to get, and he hated every second of it.

He followed the beam of his flashlight down a pine-paneled hallway, knowing he would never be able to sleep. The thought of being awake all night in the middle of a pitch-black zombie-infested forest was too much to bear, so he explored the medicine cabinet in the master bathroom. He found a bottle of Ambien sleeping pills. Behind it was Vicodin, the good stuff. He shoved the Ambien into the front pocket of his shorts. Then, without giving himself time to think, he opened the Vicodin bottle and popped one of the pills into his mouth, swallowing it dry just like the "good old days." It surprised him how, after all the years since his last time, it was so easy to do it. He took out a second pill and swallowed that one, too. He might as well enjoy himself.

He felt better knowing he'd feel better soon, and went to the living room to set up the shortwave radio. He sat, listening to static, while he waited for the pills to hit. When he started to feel his muscles relax and his mood lightening, he stood. "Going to bed."

His chair flew backward with a dull thump on the carpet before he could stop it. Everyone looked up from their quiet conversations, watching Jared fumble to right the chair then weave out of the room. Bill and Patty exchanged distressed looks, neither of them that surprised. They both knew it was only a matter of time for the stress and depression to start taking its toll on Jared, an addict without a program.

Courtney and Shane also exchanged knowing glances, remembering the chaos addicts had always caused in their lives.

"Jared, yo," Shane called, following him. "This is totally out of order. You can't get fucking sloppy on us."

"What are you talking about?"

"I'm not getting killed because you decided to get fucked up. How are we supposed to depend on you when a zombie's coming? You have totally fucked up."

"Dunno what you're talking about, yo." Jared wobbled away, his voice slow. "I'm just tired and took an Ambien. I'm going to bed."

Shane returned to the living room. "Now the motherfucker can't even take a turn on watch. We'll never be able to trust our backs to him. Just when I thought things couldn't get worse."

"Okay, let's stay calm," Patty said.

"Maybe he really did take an Ambien and he'll be fine in the morning," Courtney added.

"You believed that?" Shane's angry expression faded. He looked at Courtney, sympathetically but in disbelief. She'd probably bought a whole lot of excuses from her father and even made up a bunch for him, too. "I've got a bridge to sell you, Courtney. Actually, a whole city."

"We just tell him he has to stay clean or he's out," Courtney said.

"Can we?" Patty asked. "Then what happens the first time he picks up again. Are we going to vote him out and leave him to die like in the *Lord of the Flies?* I agree this is a shitty no-win situation within a shitty no-win situation, but panicking about it and making threats we're not prepared to keep, won't make things better."

"I think Patty's right," Kai said. "Let him sleep it off. We can talk to him tomorrow. Hopefully, we will get someplace safe before his addiction has a chance to get worse."

"Okay, we'll table this until tomorrow." Bill ran a hand through his hair, worried and angry at Jared, too, the same as Shane. But after years in AA, he knew that talking to people didn't work unless the person was ready to stop. If Jared was medicating depression—understandable, really—the boomerang effect of the drugs would make him even more depressed tomorrow. Then he'd have to medicate again, probably at progressively higher doses. Bill also had little faith in Kai's idea of getting someplace safe. There wasn't going to be a rehab facility waiting for them at the end of the street. They were living in hell, and there was nowhere to ship drunks and addicts. Jared was their problem and he would stay that way, putting all of them at risk.

NOT LONG AFTER nightfall, the men and women split up into separate bedrooms. The women shared one room more out of a desire for safety in numbers than because of a lack of additional space. Patty and Ana shared one queen-sized bed. Courtney could stretch out in the other. They all fell asleep quickly, their minds and bodies exhausted.

They awoke with a start. The room remained as pitch black to their searching eyes as it had been with their eyes closed. A mix of howls and barks filled the black air, loud enough to have been broadcast from a boom box in back of a low rider. The amplified, primitive voices sounded in unison, like a mediaeval drum circle, seeming to come from everywhere.

"What the hell is that?" Courtney asked.

From the darkness, Ana responded in Spanish, *"Coyote."*

They could all sense now that they were hearing a pack of animals circling prey. The howl-barks went on for several minutes until they heard the distressing high-pitched scream of the victim. It sounded like a dog but it might have been deer, dying in terror and pain.

"I had hoped they were hunting zombies," Patty said. "But zombies don't scream."

"The animals are taking back their world," Ana said quietly, a disembodied voice in the darkness.

Courtney lay back down, shuddering, imagining a stone-age future where animals ruled the Earth. Nothing in her life had prepared her for this, even if their world were one day miraculously free of zombies.

She felt she'd only been asleep again for a moment when Bill came to wake her for watch duty. She shared watch with Shane, as usual. Kai had been keeping track of the watch roster since their time at his house, and the teams hadn't changed since then. At first, Courtney had resented being paired up with Shane but she had come to enjoy their watches.

Courtney and Shane talked quietly now about Jared, their old lives, and how maybe animals would inherit the Earth.

When it was nearly dawn, Shane said, "Why do you have so much shit for AA?"

"What are you talking about? I don't have anything against AA."

Shane laughed. "You're always sniping at Bill about it."

"Get out of here."

"Was it because of your mom and that boyfriend she had?"

"*No.*"

"Fess up. The whole Twelve Step thing pisses you off."

Courtney looked outside. The moon had lit up the silhouette of the trees at the edge of the front yard. "It's not really about my mother. Honestly, she never gave the Program a chance to work for her. The guy who picked her up there was just an excuse for her to start using again. Truthfully, the guys in AA were really good to me when I was a kid. They were like uncles . . . or I thought they were, but a lot of good it did . . .

"I barely noticed at first when my father stopped making meetings. In my last year of middle school, we started doing other things together, watching TV at home, walking around the neighborhood on summer nights, going to my soccer practices together . . . instead of spending our nights in meetings and eating in the diner with his friends afterward. Really . . . I wanted him to stop, even though I was used to meetings. I remember begging him to take me home when he picked me up from after-school. I wanted him to myself and I wanted to be able to come home at night and relax."

Courtney went silent for a moment, really thinking that through for the first time. Her voice caught in her throat. "I had no idea what I was doing. He'd been sober for almost as long as I could remember. I didn't know that it was so . . . fragile."

"You were only a kid. It was his decision."

"I always blamed his friends in the Program for not stopping him and then for not saving us when we were drowning . . . do you know what I mean?"

"Yeah."

They sat quietly, listening to the forest sounds.

Shane spoke up after a while, "At least he got it together in the end."

"I was long gone by then, in college."

They listened to the trees rustling in the breeze, the cicadas buzzing in time with them. Courtney rested the side of her arm against Shane's, needing the comfort of physical touch with another human being.

Shane felt the touch burn. He forced himself to leave his arm side-by-side with Courtney's. He knew what Courtney's body language would normally mean and he couldn't lie to himself about how much better the apocalypse would be if he were sleeping with Courtney instead of in a room with Bill (who snored by the way). But these were new times and all the rules were new. He wasn't going to push up on Courtney so fast. He resisted his impulse to put his arm around her to comfort her. He knew she'd run scared if he did. She was as skittish as a doe, and he could understand that.

They sat there silently until it was Ana and Kai's turn to take watch. They didn't have to wake the two. Ana had already woken up and roused Kai moments before their designated duty time.

IN THE MORNING, they were packed and ready to move out shortly after dawn. Jared was among them and ready to go as if nothing had happened the night before. A mist hugged the forest, which the rising sun dissolved, sweeping away the moisture as if it were a wide paintbrush. It was an idyllic summer morning and they let the wind blow into the pickup cab as they rode down I-80, which was only a two-lane highway now.

"It will be a couple of hundred miles before we reach the Ohio plants," Kai said.

"We don't have enough gas to get that far," Shane, the driver, said.

Jared spoke from the back seat, "There's a way to dismantle a pump and retrieve the gas manually, but we can't count on enough zombie-free time for that."

"We should look for a new truck with a full tank before we hit the radiation zone," Courtney commented.

Riding shotgun, Bill kept his eyes peeled for a new pickup. "We'll give it two hours and if we don't see a new truck, we'll get off the highway and start looking in the towns."

Not long after, Shane stopped. "I guess we'll be riding bikes."

A car accident had completely blocked the road. They loaded the bike trailers with their backpacks and supplies, and reluctantly parted with what had been a perfect vehicle.

After a while, if it hadn't been for their worries (what would come next, where would they get a truck, how would they get through another day?), they might have believed they were on an incredible mountain cycling trip. Dressed for summer without plastic bags on their feet, cycling through mountains on a pitch-perfect day was actually pleasant.

Kai chose to forget his concerns for a while, focusing on the peaceful sounds of the birds. As a young man, often sniffing coke as dawn light filtered through Venetian blinds, he had hated the sound of birds. Their song had been a reminder that real life was passing him by while he was trapped in an endless night. But after he'd begun to recover and established a dawn meditation practice, he had found their song the most soothing call of the spirit. He hadn't lost that, thankfully. Even the zombies hadn't stolen that.

Patty felt the blood burn in her thighs as they made their way up one of many hills. She didn't mind the effort. She was damn proud of herself for keeping up with kids half her age. All of them were becoming strong, thriving on the long workouts.

With Shane on point, they came upon another car accident. This one was smaller than the last, just a couple of cars. Ready to draw their weapons if needed, they passed close by the front car.

"Look ahead," Shane said. "A landslide."

Rocks and mud covered half the road. With no work crews around to clean things up, Patty reflected that not just the animals but the Earth itself would take back the world now.

They rode slowly past a ragged pile of boulders half as tall as men. The space between the rocks and guard rail was less than a lane wide. Beyond the end of the ragtag wall of rocks, they saw what looked like a pile of clothes on the ground.

Pedaling closer, within ten yards of it, Shane registered two bodies sprawled there, one on top of the other. Even from a distance, he could tell the corpses weren't blackened and swollen yet. Relatively fresh kill.

Shots slammed through the air, as loud as a direct hit of lightning. Strobe-light flashes cracked and echoed against the surrounding mountains.

"GET DOWN!" Shane shouted.

Bikes clattered to pavement. More shots split the air. Everyone dove and crawled toward the guardrail.

"Is everyone here? Everyone here?" Shane called out, lying flat on the down-slope at the far side of the guardrail. More shots rang out. He covered his head. The others rolled toward him.

Jared spoke at Shane's side, ruminating aloud about his zombie novels. "There's always guys who take advantage . . . the ones who wanted to rape and murder even before the zombies."

"Hey, you, motherfu-u-ckers," a voice called out from above. "Hey, you fucking, motherfu-uckers," shouted a quavering redneck voice.

A rattle of automatic weaponry blasted above.

"No one passes here!"

Bill spoke, "Fuck. We're trapped."

Shane yelled up at the voice, "We're not zombies! Hold your fire."

The voice yelled back, "I don't give a fuck. At least zombies don't fuckin' rat you out. They don't say you can't get the shit on credit even when they made it in a motherfuckin' bathtub." The voice dissolved into giggles. "I got all the shit now."

"He's out of his mind," Shane said.

Bill took a quick look up. Rapid fire cracked the air again. It kicked dirt in front of him and pinged the metal guardrail.

"I won't be voting for him to join our group," Bill said through gritted teeth, the side of his face pressed against grass.

Courtney took aim and shot as the man came into view on the slope above them. Heavy machinegun fire returned. Kai put a steadying hand on Courtney's arm. "Don't waste your bullets."

Shane tried to survey for possible escape routes. The ground they lay on sloped gradually downward into a forested valley, but they would have to expose themselves before they could get downhill out of range.

"Ana's gone," Patty said in a whisper from the end of the line of prone bodies.

Bill's face reddened with panic. "Goddamnit."

Then they heard a pop of a silenced bullet followed by a high-pitched human yelp.

The shooter rose up, fully visible for the first time. His wasted-away face was little more than a skull with acne stretched tautly over it. He took an uncertain step, pointed his assault rifle. Then they heard another muffled shot and the man's brains flew out the side of his head. He fell sideways to the ground, his body catching up to his brain. Then silence.

"Don't shoot." A woman's voice. Spanish accent. Ana appeared on the slope near where the shooter had been. Her hair had come loose from its ponytail. She was streaked with mud and grass stains, her knees and elbows bloodied.

"Take cover," Bill shouted. "Is he alone?"

"He's alone," she called back.

Shane and Courtney ran toward the bodies on the road. A dead woman lay on top of a child of about twelve. They lay in a dry stain of blood. Neither of them had been shot through the head.

"Immune," Courtney murmured, tearing up. "He was killing regular people."

They climbed up the hill to the dead shooter, fanning out to make certain no one was hiding nearby. Then they regrouped and stood next to a recently extinguished campfire, shaded by tall evergreens. Bloody hypodermic needles were strewn around. A freezer-bag full of white powder lay near a pair of muddy hiking boots.

"Meth," Shane said.

They all turned to Ana.

She met their gaze, her face muddy and her eyes clear and hard.

"No time for thinking. If we didn't kill him, he'd kill other good people."

She pulled her hair back into a scrunchy she took from her pocket. Everyone stared at her. Killing a living person was somehow different from killing zombies. She was the first one to do that. They took in the new information about their travel companion.

Then they heard leaves crunching and the cries of approaching zombies. The sound of the assassin's shooting had attracted an audience.

CHAPTER 16

They dispensed with a couple of wayward mountain zombies who shambled down the hill toward them. One wore jeans and a t-shirt, the other a checkered hunting shirt, plastered wet against his rotting body. The dead hunter's eyeball had fallen out of its socket and swung like a pendulum on wet gristle. It fell off as he walked, trampled by his partner's oblivious hiking boots. When they came into range, Kai picked them off with two shots. The sniper's shooting had obviously attracted zombies before. The two zombies crumpled and joined a circle of corpses, all with their brains blown out, a gruesome border around the campsite at the range of a handgun—an insane addict's version of a gated community.

The group gathered up the dead shooter's weapons and ammunition. They found an arsenal, including some guns with silencers, even subsonic bullets for the assault rifles. It was a wonder the crazy sniper had opted not to use a silencer. He must have enjoyed attracting the undead. Shane knelt and opened a wooden box he found nestled amongst the roots of a pine tree. His heart beat faster. Grenades. Luckily, the sniper hadn't been lobbing these, and Ana had finished him off before he switched weapons. Shane placed the box inside his bike trailer.

They cycled up a long hill through the quiet forest. The pavement rose and fell under the wheels, their thighs burning then sighing with relief. None of them would be lulled into enjoying the day as they had before. On top of zombies, they were now afraid of humans, and people were faster, smarter and apparently crazier than zombies.

Zombies had an instinct they followed consistently, Kai thought as he rode. Humans had always been crazy, as the Buddhists and Toltec had said. Who knew what sorts of human maniacs they'd run into?

Even Bill had to admit that as much as he'd viewed recovering alcoholics as something akin to God's chosen people—doing the work of saving other alcoholics—they could also be some of the most unstable people around. Even sober, if you placed an addict under stress, it was a crapshoot whether his best or worst would come out. That was why Bill had shared in meetings that alcoholics and addicts needed to work steps and make meetings even after long-term sobriety. Jared was a case in point. Although nothing like the assassin they'd run into, he was definitely coming apart.

Bill caught up to Ana. Wow, she'd impressed him. She was full of surprises. She looked over at him and smiled.

"So, how'd you do it?" he had to ask, even though she was so damn unapproachable it took courage to probe.

"For a minute . . . I could see he was looking only at the front of the group, so I ran the other way behind a rock. Then up the hill . . . on my stomach behind him."

"You could have been a Navy Seal."

"I guess they're all dead now. I am lucky."

"Or blessed . . . You're the only one who's not an addict."

She had no answer to the question of blessed or lucky. "When my husband and I came to this country, things were very bad in my town. We had to leave. We were lucky at first and made it into this country. Only then, we were stopped by *los traficantes*. They wanted money and we had nothing . . . They locked us up. There were forty of us in two rooms, only tortillas to eat for many days. By the end, they killed my husband because our families had no money to send."

She rode silently. Bill rode alongside, not daring to utter a word, not wanting to spook her now that she was opening up.

"They let me go." She glanced at Bill then back at the road. "I paid in other ways than money. I don't know much . . . about luck or blessings."

Bill took in her quiet anguish that required no response. "Whatever it is, I'm glad you're with us."

With no suitable vehicle in sight, they took an exit off the highway and entered a small town in the hopes of finding a pickup. They cycled on a four-lane road lined with gas stations and big-box stores, riding down the yellow center line, afraid the area would be congested with undead shoppers.

"Look there," Patty pointed toward a gas station.

They all saw it: A pickup at a gas pump. A dead attendant walked toward them when they neared.

"This is self-service, buddy," Shane said and crushed the skull of the attendant with his baseball bat.

On Z-Day, the owner of the truck had been in the midst of filling up. The gas nozzle was still sticking out of the truck's tank. The door was wide open and the engine had been turned off.

Courtney checked out the gauge on the pump. "He's got twenty-three gallons in there!"

Patty took the nozzle out of the tank.

Bill slid into the driver's seat and the engine turned over without a hitch. "Let's load up."

"We better hurry." Shane looked across the road. "I think we're the Walmart Value Deal."

Several former shoppers loped toward them from the big box's driveway across the road. The men lifted the bikes into the truck bed. The women methodically aimed and shot. Then they all jumped in the truck and drove away. They drank warm bottles of water and ate canned chicken salad on crackers they'd found in the house that morning. They passed around a jar of sour dill pickles, while Bill gave a talk on the relative merits of sour, half-sour and gherkins.

Shane sat in the front passenger seat and studied a map of Ohio he found in the glove compartment. After a while, the Pennsylvania hills gave way to a flat highway. A sign welcomed them to Ohio. The Geiger counter started to go wild.

"We're coming near the Ohio plant," Kai said from the back.

Tension heightened in the car. Jared couldn't take his eyes off the

Geiger counter needle. They all prayed for clear roads until they were out of range of the Ohio plants. They rode into the sun, which curt-seyed toward the horizon in front of them.

In the driver's seat, Patty followed the GPS's directions toward San Antonio. Even though none of them had actually agreed to go that far, it would set them away from nuclear plants and toward more tem-perate winters. The highway signs eventually directed them toward Cleveland/Columbus. The Geiger readings went down.

Jared leaned back in his seat, exhausted, his anxiety building rather than waning. He wasn't good with fear or inactivity, but especially not a one-two punch of it. Add in a dose of hopelessness brought on by the sniper attack, and he felt as if he were a Molotov cocktail waiting for a match.

"Jeez," he said, trying to brighten his own mood. "I can't remem-ber a single time when I ever wanted to visit Cleveland or Columbus, not even BZ."

"BZ?" Patty frowned. "Oh ... Before Zombies." She laughed. "I'd have to agree. I can't remember ever thinking: I'm tired of Man-hattan, maybe I should move to Cleveland."

"I would *so* take Cleveland now," Courtney said. "I'd live happily if we could just have the old Cleveland back, not that I've ever been there."

"Maybe that should be our new mantra," Kai said. "When we fail to appreciate the good moments, we should tell ourselves: 'Remember Cleveland.'"

Shane shrugged. "No offense to Cleveland, but I'm worried that this highway's going straight to the city. Too dangerous. The mobs." Shane pointed his finger to a line on the map with Kai watching over his shoulder. "We can go on this route southwest. It's a local road but it goes a long way. We'd have to pass through more towns but we'd skirt the cities."

Bill spoke from the back, "If we bypass the cities, we may miss any groups of people that might have survived somewhere. I know it doesn't seem like it, but what if there actually is some piece of the mil-itary or government left somewhere?"

"Even President Bush was an alcoholic and probably an addict," Patty said, "Obama did drugs, too, although he didn't seem—"

"Yo, don't talk about Barak," Shane said, feigning offense.

Jared sounded irritated. "If there were any civilization, we'd have heard something on the shortwave. And based on what we've just seen, I don't think humans are necessarily our friends."

Shane cut in before Jared and Bill could get into it. "Face it, Bill, you're probably the highest ranking government official left. . ." He shook his head. "The Lotto P.R. guy."

Bill laughed. "That's chilling, I admit it."

Patty drove on the two-lane state road Shane had suggested. Just before dark, she began to drive more slowly through the outskirts of a small town. They scoped out locations until they came across an old colonial house—what real estate agents used to call 'gracious'—on an acre of lawn.

"Stop," Courtney said. "That's a generator on the side of it."

Patty backed into the driveway, best for quick escape. She stopped in front of an attached garage. They jimmied into the front door and piled into the entryway. The place passed the stink test. Bill pointed a metal camping lantern in front of them to get a look into the shadows. The light revealed an impressive center hallway and a polished mahogany staircase to the second floor. No zombies.

Jared, last one in the door, reached inside the change pocket of his jeans, took a pill and popped it into his mouth. He was ready to relax after another day in hell. He looked forward to chilling, listening to the shortwave and then a long sleep after dinner. Bill looked back just in time to see Jared's hand going to his mouth. He handed off the light to Ana, who filed inside with the others, leaving him in shadow.

Bill holstered his gun just as Jared was about to pass him. He grabbed the younger man's collar and slammed him against the wall. Bill's grip held him up.

"Listen," Bill growled quietly in Jared's face so the others wouldn't overhear. "You can't fuckin' do this. You can't check out on us."

"What are you talking about?"

"Don't play fucking stupid. I saw you."

Bill stayed close, their faces only inches apart. Jared put a hand on Bill's chest, pushing him away. "Look, dude," he spit out the words. "I know you're used to sponsoring people, but I'm not your sponsee. I lost my whole family and everything else. I'm depressed. I feel like I'm gonna bust out of my skin if I don't take something to calm down. There's no doctor here, so I've got to prescribe for myself. I need medication or I'm gonna freak out. That's all it is. I'm all right."

Bill gave Jared a little more space. Maybe he'd overacted. "An addict is the last person who should prescribe to himself. Maybe you can let us hold the meds for you. We could figure out the right dosage and give it to you. Not me—I'm an addict, too—but maybe Courtney or Shane." Bill smiled. "Or Ana. If you give her a hard time, she can just kill you."

"I'm not doing that." Jared's face went hard. "I don't need Ana and I don't need your AA bullshit either. You know, you're like a fucking Jehovah's Witness. An AA fundamentalist and you want me to be an AA jihad warrior." Jared laughed bitterly, perversely enjoying the pain in Bill's face. "Get this, Bill, I don't want what you have to offer, not someone dishing out pills to me, and not going to any meetings. You can stop trying to Twelve Step me, you can stop trying to be my father or my sponsor or whatever the fuck you're trying to be. I'm not interested in what you have to offer and I'm not going upstairs to hold hands and pray with Patty and Kai either. A lot of good your fucking higher power has done us. Get off your holy horse. Look around, motherfucker. I can't even believe you bother."

Jared elbowed his way past Bill, who took in a breath, trying to calm down. His grasp on any kind of faith was pretty fragile right now. He'd lost his family, too. He missed his sponsor, sponsees and all of his friends in the Fellowship. He felt as if he were walking around 24/7 with a fist punching into his gut. And he was jealous that he had to feel every second of it while Jared got to check out with a "happy hour" pill. But Bill knew, if he chose oblivion like Jared, he would have to take the whole bottle and end all the fucking pain and fear fast, not on a fucking installment plan. There could be no half measures for him when it came to drugs and alcohol.

Dusk brought deep shadows that enveloped the entryway where Bill stood alone. He heard the generator kick in with a surprisingly loud hum then the exclamations of his friends as the lights flashed on. He quickly found the hallway light switch and turned it off. He walked into the living room, which fit a grand piano with room to spare, and closed the drapes before turning on the lights there. He headed across the center hallway toward voices in the kitchen.

He heard banging . . . at the back of the house. He swung around toward the noise, pulling his pistol from his shoulder holster. He looked back toward the living room, banging there, too. *Jeez.*

Shane ran in. "It's the generator! They must have heard the generator. I'll turn it off."

Fevered crowd noises gathered outside. The neighbors were anxious to welcome them.

Kai ran in from the kitchen, gun in hand, Patty following. "Let's go."

The place went black and quiet, the generator off again. The zombie shrieks intensified. Everybody moved toward the entry foyer. Courtney and Ana ran down the staircase, backpacks on, guns out.

"Where's Jared?!" Patty asked.

"Fucking Christ!" Bill started running, pulling open doors. "Jared! Jared!"

"A little help!" Shane called from the dim dining room.

Jared was passed out at the table with the shortwave in front of him. Bill shook him. Jared opened his eyes and tried to stand, wobbling like a newborn calf. Shane and Bill each took an arm and ran with him draped over their shoulders. Ana grabbed the shortwave.

Kai had the car keys. "We can make a run for it. They're not in front of the house yet."

"Choose your plants!" Jared slurred.

Shane recognized the battle cry from a zombie video game. *Fool.* He had half a mind to drop Jared's ass and leave him.

The zombies continued to bang. Glass shattered.

"Everybody ready?" Kai whispered, his hand on the doorknob.

"I'm sorry," Jared slurred, his eyes slit. "I'm sorry."

"Shh," Shane said.

They all ran toward the pickup.

Before they could reach it, the first zombies—a group of obese males and females—rounded the corner of the house. Courtney and Patty turned, aimed and fired. Behind them, Ana threw open the doors to the truck, while Kai brought the engine to life. With the first group of attackers down, a next line of zombies appeared. Rolls of All-American fat jiggled on their rotting legs and bellies as they lurched toward the live group. The women continued to pick them off.

Bill and Shane shoved Jared into the back seat then helped with the shooting.

"Too much McDonalds." Jared giggled from inside the truck. "Too much McPeoples!" he announced before he closed his eyes again.

Patty and Courtney scurried inside the car. Ana leapt onto Jared's ragdoll lap and pulled the car door shut behind her. Bill and Shane slammed the last doors shut and the truck jetted out. Jared woke up enough to look out the back window and see the zombies following, as if it were the first time he noticed them. He giggled again, taking in the sight of a dead guy with a hat that said "Cedar Rapid Kernels." It was confusing. He thought he'd read a book about zombies in Ohio. A zombie had a hat like that. He fell into a deep sleep, still puzzling over what was real and what wasn't. He smiled in his sleep. The last few weeks had just been the best zombie book he'd ever read.

CHAPTER 17

Their car hurtled into the night, everyone silent. As his heartbeat slowed, Kai let up on the accelerator, wary of obstructions. He knew none of them was up for exploring another house in the dead of night. They would find a safe place in the morning.

A pall of desolation descended. Jared began to snore.

"That's just salt in my fucking wounds," Shane said. "How did we get caught up with a guy like that?"

"He's not a bad guy," Patty said.

"You could have fooled me. He could've gotten us killed."

"Maybe we need a memorial service," Kai said, "to put our families to rest. I did that for mine. I will always be sad, but Jared's spirit is unsettled."

Everyone contemplated that. Kai knew a lot about handling loss.

"Who could believe in God, now?" Bill blurted out, even though no one had said anything about God.

"Or who could not believe in God? It's a miracle we're alive," said

Courtney, her face glowing orange from the dashboard indicator lights.

"We obviously can't settle that question," Patty said. "There's a lot of ways you can look at it."

"I'm not thinking about it at all," Shane said. "God never did anything for me, and I didn't sign on to any religion."

Everyone sat quietly with their own thoughts. Shane peered out into dark Ohio farmland. There wasn't a lit-up house anywhere. He should have been used to that by now, he thought, but it was still scary. And he knew God wasn't going to turn on any lights to make it less so, not until dawn at least. If that was God's doing, it was no big favor.

"After the tsunami, most of us Japanese focused on revering our dead and moving on with life. We tried not to focus on why, which would never be answered. Since then, I've prayed for patience, perseverance, and self-sacrifice . . . for the good of all beings."

Bill inhaled deeply, comforted by Kai's view, although there were a lot fewer beings left to sacrifice for.

"I was living on Columbus Avenue and 106th Street during the early nineties," Patty said. "In a tenement over a check-cashing place that doubled as a crack spot. Addicts used to run up and down the blocks there all night long. It was insane."

"You've gotta be kidding," Shane said. "Columbus and 106th was the hood back then."

"Ahh, there's much you don't know about me, Shane." Patty smiled, unseen in the dark. "Anyway, one night, it must have been two in the morning, I heard yelling in the street. People were shouting 'fire!' I looked out my window across Columbus Avenue. There was a woman with three really little kids on a fire escape. The flames were shooting from her window. She and the kids were huddled on the outside corner of the fire escape. Each time the wind blew, the flames got closer. They were screaming. I started crying, watching it. It was horrendous.

"But, you know what? It was the dope fiends who ran into the building, shouting 'fire,' waking up the tenants and trying to reach the family. The same guys I tried to get past as fast as I could when I came home from work. They were the ones who risked their lives to rescue people."

She stared through the windshield from her place in the back seat. A drizzle was falling on the glass, too fine to require wiping. Everyone waited for her to finish her story.

"Addicts need the sense that their lives are worthwhile and that only comes from being valuable to others. Self-sacrifice. Active addicts were the first ones to try to save lives because doing that gave them a reason for being alive just for that moment. Nothing has really changed about that. It may not pay to ask why."

They rode silently again, Ana noticing shadowy movements in a field they rode past. She couldn't tell whether they were animal or zombie, but they were no threat at the moment. She thought about her children and how she would have felt on that fire escape with them. Not much different from the way she felt now, every moment of every day.

"What happened to the family?" Courtney asked. "The one on the fire escape." She realized it was a meaningless question. They were all dead now. She had been so wrapped up in the story, she forgot.

"The fire department arrived. They rescued them with a tower ladder and bucket. The whole family was saved."

"All for nothing then," said Bill.

"The addicts risking their lives? Maybe one of those addicts learned that his life was worth living. It's hard to know what the effect is of any event. Watching what they did definitely affected me. I've remembered it for over twenty years. Maybe that was the divine purpose . . . just so I could share it with you now."

"God or no God," Shane said after a while, "if Jared keeps this up, we're gonna have to ditch him. If he gets us killed, none of us will be serving a divine purpose."

Patty exhaled. "That would be a death sentence."

They traveled through the night, Shane riding shotgun with a map spread on his lap and Courtney in charge of the GPS next to him. They drove a meandering southwestern route on back roads, aiming to miss the big cities and nuclear power plants that Kai talked about while he drove. "There are three to the South in the Tennessee Valley. They should be far enough east not to affect us. Perhaps within months, half the country will be a dead zone if all the plants melt down, but for now we'll have a few clear states for travel."

Past midnight, Bill pulled into a rickety gas station in a tiny town. It had stopped raining and the night sky was clear. The station was surrounded by trees. They could hear the flow of a small river behind it. There was a pickup parked out front, as if the driver had just pulled into the convenience store for a newspaper or cigarettes. A compact Chevy sat at the pump, its driver's door open. With guns and flashlights out, the women approached the doors of the store, headed for their second bathroom break of the night.

Inside, Courtney almost tripped over the Hindu Patel store clerk. She jumped back, gasping in surprise. Off balance, Patty and Ana nearly toppled behind her. The store clerk had lost his legs from the knees down as if he'd been surfing a Great White. He snarled and lunged on his stumps, rearing up at them. Courtney shot him, successfully avoiding the splash of zombie brains on her clothes. The last thing she needed was to stink like a zombie in a packed car. Ana's flashlight illuminated a co-ed bathroom sign, and they lined up just like old times.

Outside, the men put their guns back in their holsters, knowing by the quiet that the women had handled whatever had caused the commotion. They checked out the new pickup. The driver's door was locked. Bill swept his flashlight beam on the pavement, illuminating the path the driver would have walked between the truck and convenience store doors. He saw a ring of keys off to the side as if they'd flown from the owner's hands. Some things were predictable even in their upside-down world. Bill picked the keys up and tossed them to Kai. Kai opened the door and tried the ignition. "Battery's dead."

They clamped on booster cables between the pickups. The new truck came loudly to life and the men looked around quickly. No unwanted company.

Shane went to the compact Chevy. He tried the ignition. It worked. He returned to Bill and Kai. "Now we just have to get *that* guy out of the truck." He pointed his thumb toward Jared, who still slept with his face plastered against the back window of the old pickup.

Bill opened the door; Jared spilled into his arms. "Wake up, come on. Wake up."

Kai took Jared's other arm and, with Jared awake enough to weave forward, they pitched him into the back seat of the Chevy.

None of them was comfortable splitting up into two cars but the new pickup had only one row of seats. At least they'd be physically comfortable now.

Courtney returned with a grocery bag from the convenience store. She took the wheel of the Chevy. "My turn."

"I'll ride shotgun," Shane said nonchalantly, but he was clear that he wanted to ride with Courtney.

Driving point, Courtney sipped warm Mountain Dew and talked with Shane, making sure she stayed alert with the roads so dark. When the sunrise overtook them, she pulled up at a farmhouse and they all got out. The farmhouse was set back from the road and cleared of trees for acres around it. They decided to take a break until the next day, get some sleep, and eat three meals if supplies were sufficient. Only Ana wished they weren't taking an extra day, but even she was too tired to really mind.

ANA WAS ALREADY outside in the early afternoon, a few yards from the back of the house. There were a couple of shade trees there and an outdoor kitchen with an aluminum overhang. The area was a working part of the farm, with a tool shed, bales of hay and odd pieces of farm equipment lying around in loose hay. Ana fed chickens from a bag of feed she'd found in the shed.

Bill and Kai walked out at the same time

"I wonder if all chickens survived or just some, like us," Bill said.

"It is interesting."

The air was comfortably warm and breezy. Acres of fields separated them from the farm's perimeter where the woods started.

Kai scanned the line of trees with binoculars. "Seems clear."

Then he walked away, around the other side of the house to take a look at the woods from the front. Everything was quiet except for the sound of a few clucking chickens coming to eat and the distant cooing of a dove. Bill stood still, the visibility provided by the empty expanse of the farm making him feel uncharacteristically safe.

The wind picked up for a moment, blowing the grass flat toward them with a rustling whisper. It carried a rotten smell. Bill looked toward the barn. "I'm no expert on barns, but it smells like a lot of dead animals in there."

"Yes," Ana said.

She had a propane stove working. A large pot of hot water was simmering on it. She wore a long apron that came down below her knees.

Bill sat on a wooden bench with his back to a low wall made of bales of hay. He let himself enjoy the breeze, which had now shifted to blow the pleasant scents from the forest toward them. He knew not to even ask Ana what she was doing. There was something about her that told him to wait for things to become clear. He enjoyed her quiet company.

Ana turned and took a few running steps, with a quick movement that shot Bill to his feet. She closed in on a squawking chicken and lunged. She held the chicken up by its ankles. "*Pollo Guisado* today. Chicken stew. A feast."

She sat with the chicken grasped between her legs. She held a small knife that Bill hadn't even noticed before. She petted the chicken and spoke softly in Spanish, feeling behind its beak for its jugular. She swiftly sliced it then broke the neck. The chicken struggled for a moment then went still. She let the blood drip out until it stopped.

Bill felt a momentary twinge. Funny how he could still feel anything after all they'd seen, but life seemed even more precious amidst so much death.

Ana pulled out feathers in large clumps. "My people were good farmers until loggers came to steal our forests. They joined with a drug cartel that tried to starve us to make us give up our land. That is why I left, to send back money."

"She's pretty handy," Jared said from the back door as Ana went after the next chicken. He'd woken up at dawn when the car had stopped and the engine went quiet. He'd stayed awake long enough to find a bed inside the house then passed out again. He felt a little bleary now but rested.

Jared watched Ana kill the second chicken, not flinching the way Bill had. Bill would have felt better if Jared had apologized, but it wasn't clear that he even remembered their argument or being carried out of the other house.

Jared spoke without looking at Bill. "I know I can't keep doing that, what I did last night. I'm going to stop."

"Okay, bro. I'm here for you if you need me. But, just so you know, people aren't going to keep risking their lives to save you. You're going to get booted if you don't get it together."

Jared's eyes opened wide, betraying his fear. "Okay, Bill."

Ana turned to both men, appraising them. "There's vegetables in the garden. We can pick them."

Bill patted Jared on the arm. "Come on."

WHEN IT WAS time to leave the next morning, Patty woke up sneezing and coughing. Courtney insisted on finding her a thermometer, which read just over 100. Everyone agreed to wait another day or two at the farm until she got better. They didn't know when they'd have to ride their bikes for extended periods of time, which might be too much for her. And there was more chance of everyone getting sick if they rode together in a closed car. Ana made chicken soup for her.

"You must want to move on," Patty said.

"We'll never get there if any of us are sick. You need to get your strength back."

Patty was surprised at the warmth in the girl's voice. She wasn't sure where the "there" was that they were supposed to get to but she believed it was a small town in Central Mexico.

After Patty napped, Courtney came in. The sun was setting and she lit a candle. It was a hot night and she brought a bottle of water along with a plate of cut-up peaches they had picked.

Patty could tell Courtney had something on her mind. "So, what's up?"

Courtney pulled a chair from the desk at the side of the room. Biology and political science textbooks were stacked on the desk. This had been a young adult's room.

"I've been thinking about . . . Shane."

"Really?" Patty suppressed a smile. No surprise there.

"I really like him . . . I mean I *really* like him, and I think he likes me."

"I can tell."

"Really? But after what I saw at the crack spot, who he was . . . I just can't get over that. I keep coming back to it."

"I can understand that," Patty said.

"I haven't seen any sign of that person in who he is now. I mean, we've all been together nonstop for weeks and he's been the best . . . I feel safe with him. Not just safe . . . I want to be near him all the time. But if he's a bad person, I'm just not gonna give in to it. No way. There's no room for that kind of mistake."

Patty looked at Courtney, feeling warmth for her with all her childhood terrors crashing up against her new ones. "Are you asking me whether I think Shane is a good person?"

"Yes."

"I think he's a wonderful person. He has baggage, like all of us, maybe even more because of his rough childhood. But look at how he's showed up for all of us." Patty paused. "I think he just needed a burning building to run into. The zombies did that for him. You're doing that for him, too. And we are all the beneficiaries."

"You think?"

"I think."

Courtney leaned back. "Thank you."

Throughout the night Patty slept fitfully, hearing muffled shots and seeing the light flashes through the window curtains as the others took turns firing at the zombies who seemed to be wandering toward them with increasing frequency. She wondered whether they were drawn to the bit of light that seeped out from the farmhouse. As dawn began to whittle away at the Ohio darkness, ibuprofen finally broke Patty's fever. She walked downstairs. She couldn't stand another day of lying in bed.

It was already hot and humid. Kai was on watch, sweat dampening his face and hair. Patty wiped a cobweb off a rocking chair and came to sit next to him on the front porch. They listened to the birds, the knocking of woodpeckers, and humming cicadas. Pink streaks announced the new day, then a hot sun blasted out from behind the forest.

"Ready to go this morning?" Kai asked.

"Ready as ever," Patty replied.

CHAPTER 18

They chose air conditioning over gas mileage on the sweltering day and rode with the windows up. The sky was heavy with humidity but clear of even a wisp of cloud. A sign said they were entering Kentucky. They drove past big-box towns and stately horse farms. White rail fences surrounded empty pastures, and oaks lined long driveways that led to Forrest Gump homes.

"Look!" Jared exclaimed, as they came upon horses grazing in a meadow. They'd seen only carcasses until now. "Stop. We have to let them out."

They pulled the Chevy onto the long driveway. The pickup followed behind. When they reached the pasture gate, Ana went into the back of the truck and took out some carrots, calling to the horses. It was a relief for all of them to pet the neck and nose of the stallion that approached them. He was a huge creature, whose ribs poked out—more like the Mexican horses Ana knew than a Kentucky thoroughbred. A couple of other horses sidled up to the humans, obviously glad to see them.

Bill opened the gates to the pasture. Kai opened the stable door with Shane covering him in case of living-dead farmhands.

"They'll have grain, hay and some protection from the weather if they can come in and out of the stable," Kai said. "Maybe it will help them transition to the wild."

Shane and Jared cut up huge bags of feed with box cutters then left the doors open and the horses eating.

They resumed their drive, watching the pastures now for more horses to save, and passed through the center of a one-traffic-light town. There was a gas station on each side of the road at the intersection. A quarter acre of grass at their right separated one of the gas stations from a tiny church. Courtney and Shane saw a figure ahead on the road.

Courtney grimaced. "I hate when they're kids. "

"Yeah, it really sucks." Shane was holding Courtney's hand while he drove. He couldn't believe how happy that made him. In his old life, the holding hands stage would have lasted five minutes, at most.

The child in the road looked to be four or five. She wore a filthy green sundress stained with dried blood and walked barefoot down the center of the road, dazed like all the undead. Shane noted the space around her. He wasn't in the mood for getting out and killing a kid zombie, but he didn't want to hit her and possibly damage the car.

The girl lifted her eyes toward the oncoming car and darted off the road.

"Shit!" Shane said.

The girl crawled under a skinny log fence that separated the church from a weathered house with a small yard.

Shane hit the brakes, the pickup nearly back-ending him.

Courtney shot out of the car door. "Hey! It's okay!" She ran and climbed over the fence, not thinking a thing about whether zombies might be nearby. "Honey, it's okay."

The girl stopped and peered from behind a tree. Her face was caked with dirt, deeply furrowed by long-dry tears.

Courtney walked slowly toward her. Shane and the others stayed a few yards behind.

"Hi. Where do you live?" Courtney asked, approaching the girl gradually.

The girl shrugged.

Courtney's eyes tore up at the sight of her. *They'd actually found a child. A living child.* Courtney crouched, making herself almost as small as the girl. "Come here."

The child allowed herself to be enveloped in Courtney's arms. She put her head against Courtney's chest, closed her eyes, and put her thumb in her mouth.

"We're going to take care of you now." Courtney lifted the little girl and carried her back to the car. "Are you all alone?"

The little girl nodded.

"What's your name?"

She whispered incomprehensibly.

"What?"

"Beth."

"Well Beth, you can be a part of our family now."

The others couldn't take their eyes off Beth, all wanting to touch her but afraid they'd scare her. Courtney put her in the back seat and got in after her. Beth pulled herself tight under Courtney's arm. Courtney smelled urine. The child had become almost feral. It broke her heart to think of what she must have been through.

Jared passed back an apple and a bottle of water. "Feed her slowly in case she hasn't eaten for a while."

But Beth had fallen asleep. She didn't wake up even when Courtney bathed her face with bottled water or when they stopped to get her clean clothes.

Courtney and Patty remained in the car, parked in a shady back corner of a mall parking lot. Patty was still feeling ill, so they all agreed it would be best if she acted as lookout while Courtney babysat the girl. The rest ventured forth toward the mall, the sun beating down furiously as they walked.

Inside a small department store, their flashlights attracted every dead salesperson.

"I always wished for this kind of service when I shopped," Bill told Shane, spraying automatic fire at an approaching group of undead.

Shane ran forward with a bat and crushed the skulls of those who tried to get up. "I hate to say it, bro'," he took a breath between swings, "but the sales people always followed me. It was called Shopping While Black."

Bill lowered his AR-15 and wiped the sweat from his brow. "Those days are done now."

"Yeah, zombies are the New Black." Shane scanned the pile of corpses. "But who knows who it'll be if they actually die off one day."

Ana and Kai did the shopping for Beth, picking out sneakers, shirts and shorts in her size. In case of radiation, Kai chose long pants and a sweatshirt, too, finding a pink one that he knew his daughter would have liked. He noted how seriously Ana was contemplating which items to pick out. It seemed as if their entire group had received an energy boost when they'd found the child.

Bill picked up some walkie-talkies from the electronics section. "We're going to need these now that we're traveling in two cars."

He acted as lookout while Jared chose a new bike trailer for the girl. Bill felt good about a kid riding in one of their carts, even though it was going to be a lot more complex caring for a child and keeping her quiet in times of danger. His mind gnawed on the possible scenarios that could jeopardize Beth and all of them now that they had her with them.

They chose a sprawling horse farm to spend the rest of the day and night. Ana and Shane helped heat water to make a warm bath. Courtney sponged off weeks of grime from the girl then dressed her. For the rest of the afternoon, Beth followed Courtney around, mostly under Courtney's arm with her hand wrapped tightly around her hips. Beth hadn't uttered a word since she'd said her name, but her large brown eyes tracked everything that went on around her.

As dusk approached, she fell asleep on a couch with her head on Courtney's lap. Now that the sun had lowered, a cross breeze cooled them through the open windows. Kai, Bill and Ana were preparing dinner and Patty was taking a nap upstairs, still tired out from her cold. Jared listened to the shortwave then left the room, sick of the white noise. When he returned, he carried a coffee mug. Shane noticed a perky bop to his walk. It wasn't long before Jared started participating in conversation.

Shane pointed toward the cup, irked that Jared would think they hadn't noticed. "Don't hit the booze too hard. The shit could hit the fan any minute."

"Did you know we're on the Bourbon Trail?" Jared smiled at Shane. "The home of fine Kentucky liquor. Don't worry about me. I've never had a problem with booze. As long as I stay away from the dry goods, I'm cool."

He turned back to fiddle with the knobs.

"Motherhood suits you," Shane said quietly to Courtney, trying to forget about Jared.

"Get out." Courtney swatted at Shane playfully. But she had to admit that holding Beth had calmed an intense skin hunger that had gnawed at her since Z-Day. It was as if the child's embrace had filled a huge vacuum.

"I don't know," Courtney confided. "Just when I'd started to get used to things the way they were . . . it's scary. It's been hard enough taking care of ourselves." She glanced at Jared and her face went hard. "And now we're teamed up with a drunk. Bill told me he had a talk with him but it didn't take him long to hit the booze."

Jared glanced over at the two of them sitting on the couch and took another sip of bourbon, then a longer drink. He would have liked someone for himself, too, not to be in this bitch of a world all by himself. He fiddled with the radio knobs. Its static crackled loudly for a moment then morphed into words: "Hello. This is the Southeastern Group Settlement. Hello, this is the Southeastern Group Settlement. Is anyone out there?"

"Holy crap!" Jared yelled.

Shane launched to his feet. Courtney lifted Beth's head off her lap.

Jared leaned over, his words slurring, "We hear you. We are in Kentucky."

"My God, it's good to hear from you," the voice said. "My name is Mark. We are a settlement of sixty-eight people."

Bill, Patty and Kai came rushing in.

"I'm Jared. We're seven, traveling from New York and New Jersey, plus one from Kentucky."

"We're located fifty miles outside of Memphis in a gated community," Mark said.

"We're not so far. Kentucky. Did you say sixty-eight people?"

"On Z-Day, there was an AA convention in Memphis, and a group of us got out. A few others have wandered in over the weeks. We're trying to establish civilization and we're happy to have more joiners. We have plenty of room."

Bill took the mic from Jared. "Did you say you're all from AA?"

"The original group. The rest who've come since, well, they had . . . the *symptoms* when they arrived . . . or their parents were alcoholics."

"I rest my case," Bill whispered to Patty. "It's genetic. Something about our genes makes it harder for the zombies to sense us. The stats don't lie."

Jared raised his glass in a halfway toast and celebrated with a deep swig of bourbon.

Courtney envisioned Jared getting them all killed when they were almost to safety. She took a stride toward Jared and smacked the glass out of his hand. It flew across the wall and crashed against a framed Bluegrass festival poster. "There's a kid at stake now," Courtney growled. "Are you fucking crazy?"

Shane stepped between Courtney and Jared, just in case. But Jared only retreated blearily, as wide-eyed with shock as a drunk could be.

"Is everything okay, there?" Mark said when Bill returned to the radio.

"We're fine. Sorry."

Mark chuckled. "Don't want to lose you guys now . . . There was another group that said they were coming, never heard from them again."

Everyone calmed down and, other than Jared, regrouped next to the shortwave. Courtney's face had reddened from adrenaline, not so different from how she looked when she fought zombies.

Bill pressed the talk button. "It was nothing, thanks."

Everyone listened as Bill and Mark traded AA pedigrees, how many years sober, and reminiscences about the AA lost.

"You gotta come out and join us. We're a sober community," Mark said. "You'll be right at home and we need more guys with double-digit sobriety." He gave them directions that Patty wrote down and signed off.

Bill assured everyone that this guy was the real thing. Patty and Kai agreed.

Jared slurred a warning from a chair in the corner, an index finger wagging in the air: "Jim Jones motherfuckers will have you drinking Kool-Aid if you don't stay in line. There's not a single zombie apocalypse without human beings fucking things up."

Courtney glared at him, but Patty laughed, surprised at the unpleasant thought. She wasn't entirely comfortable herself. It sounded as if they were running a treatment program there—not exactly her idea of how she wanted to live her life after 25 years sober. Yet, she was beyond excited by the idea of a community.

Kai unfolded his nuclear map. "The settlement is well west of the

Tennessee nuclear plants. It is not optimal for long term because we don't know how far the radiation will spread when every plant melts down. I would rather be five hundred miles further west, but we can think positively." He folded up his deeply creased paper. "We can always move later if needed. That's what Geiger counters are for."

It took little discussion for their group to decide. They would head for the Settlement in the morning. Everyone went on with the evening as normal, although Jared stayed warily out of range of Courtney, and Shane could be heard chuckling from time to time. They all went to sleep that night, envisioning the possibility that tomorrow would be the start of a new life. Only Ana was clear that her visit to the Settlement would be a limited one, even if she had to walk by herself to Mexico.

THEY WOKE UP the next morning to another steaming hot day. Jared ran to a bathroom and threw up. Then he staggered toward the medicine cabinet for Tylenol. He couldn't find any, so he settled on one of his stashed Percocets to take away the pain of the hangover. After all, Percocet had Tylenol in it. He wasn't planning to get high or not too high at least. He definitely didn't want to appear high when they reached the settlement. So, he bit off a bitter half-pill and put the unused half back in the bottle.

Ana sat in the back seat of the car with Courtney and Beth. As they traveled, she tried to draw Beth out with a doll she'd dug up at the house they'd slept in. Beth took the doll and held it, but she wouldn't talk to Ana.

"Look, Beth." Courtney pointed to a Tennessee mountain range on the horizon. Their car climbed to impressive heights then descended on the far side of a mountain.

The girl watched, silently.

"So, Ana," Shane said from the driver's seat, feeling lonely with Jared snoring beside him rather than Courtney holding his hand. "Are you Mayan or Aztec?"

"Neither. I'm P'urephecha. I come from a town in Michoacán, in the mountains . . . west of Mexico City."

"A small town?"

"Yes, but you may have heard of the town where my people came from originally. Paricutin, it had to be abandoned. A volcano grew in a cornfield there overnight."

"I remember a book about that in elementary school," Shane said. They rode for a few moments then Shane added, "We're going to have to teach Beth to read. Maybe I'll do it."

"I think she's old enough," Courtney said. She gave Beth a squeeze. "I just wish she'd talk."

The cars stopped at the foot of a truss bridge, blocked by a jack-knifed tractor-trailer. They opened their doors to a kiln-like blast of heat. They pulled the bikes from the back of the pickup, but they would have to push their bikes up the steep incline. Courtney spoke softly to Beth, cajoling her to get into the cart that was attached to Shane's bike. She couldn't hold her hand and push a bike up the hill at the same time, she explained.

The slope over the bridge was too steep to see what lay on the other side. Bill and Kai took point, the others spacing themselves behind. Bill climbed the hill, frustrated and worried, sweat pouring off him under the unrelenting sun. They'd been super lucky up to now. But how long could that last? Here they were almost to a settlement and he was sure that, as Murphy's Law would have it, a swarm of zombies would be right over the crest of the hill.

He relaxed as he remembered how Ana had grasped his hand and squeezed it, saying, "*Buena suerte*" before he and Kai started up the hill. He looked back and saw that she was watching him now as she pushed her bike, her deep-set eyes so serious but somehow encouraging. Bill thought she was a lot more capable than he was, but she had been cleaning a nightclub for a living in a world that was totally unknown to him. In a million years they never would have met if the world hadn't turned upside down.

Just short of the crest, Bill gripped the handle of his gun. But no zombies waited for them. Instead, he beheld a killing field. As far as the eye could see, hundreds of mutilated bodies lay on the road. Kai signaled to the others to come up.

They rode silently, watchfully, past blackened, picked-over corpses. Vultures nearly obscured a stretch of road ahead. Fresh kill. The huge birds glared at the cyclists, daring them to challenge for their kill. Through the gaps in their huge black wings: human bodies were visible, ripped apart. What remained of the bodies had bloated but not turned black yet.

All registered that it was the group Mark had spoken about, the ones that never arrived.

Courtney cycled past, ready for anything. Riding alongside Beth in Shane's cart, she put her finger to her mouth. "Shh."

The road overlooked a valley. A small town, little more than a row of wooden stores, bordered one side of a lake. They could make out some sort of distribution plant with delivery trucks and pickups in its parking lot. None of them fooled themselves into thinking the town was as empty as it looked.

"We either go for one of those trucks," Bill whispered when they stopped, "or we ride the bikes out that way." He pointed toward the steep uphill road leading out the other side of town.

Everyone groaned.

A moment later, they were cycling down the hill toward the distribution plant. They scanned the woods as they went. No movement. At the side of the building, they jumped off their bikes. The men ran toward the trucks, looking for open doors and keys in ignitions.

Crouched next to the building, weapon ready, Courtney watched Beth carefully. Every inch of her intuition told her they'd never get out of this town without a fight. If Beth screamed, it would be like a noon whistle at a Chinese iPhone plant.

The dead appeared, shambling down the hill. Courtney counted eight. Beth watched stoically, silently, as the women aimed and fired.

Bill pulled the door handle on the first truck. Locked. The second one, also locked. His heart beat harder with each try. Their strategy was all or nothing. They had no real backup plan. He saw the other men going truck to truck, too, without luck.

On the third try, Bill found one. It had been abandoned in a hurry, keys in the ignition. When he turned it on, he cringed at the noise of the engine. The townspeople heard it, too. Preternatural voices echoed through the wooded hills. A lot of voices.

Bill backed the truck up toward the women. Jared opened its back gate with a screech of rusted metal that sent a second wave of excited zombie-wails through the hills . . . coming closer now.

Courtney grabbed Beth from the bike cart. Shane and Kai lifted her bike into the truck bed. They loaded the bikes attached to trailers first. If they were going to run out of time and lose bikes, they didn't want to lose supplies and weapons, too.

A second wave of dead stormed down from the hillside. Dozens of them. Ammunition clips fell to Courtney's feet as she emptied her gun into dead skulls and reloaded, Beth hiding behind her. "They're coming. Come on! Too many."

"Only two more bikes," Kai grunted, as they kept loading. "Hold them off."

The men lifted the last of the bikes into the rear of the truck just as hundreds of zombies emerged from the tree line.

"It's now or never. Let's go!" Patty called.

Courtney dove in after Beth. The mob was almost to the road now.

"Let's bail!" Shane called, but he was the last one standing outside. He hit the side of the truck. "Get moving! I'll catch up."

"No!" Courtney yelled, ready to climb over Jared and Patty to get out.

Shane turned and ran behind the truck. Bill slowly steered toward the parking lot exit, not planning to go anywhere without Shane.

"Shane!" Courtney screamed, hyperventilating at the sight of a score of zombies on the road ahead, boxing them in.

Shane took two long strides, grenade to mouth. He hurled it into the approaching pack. He threw a second grenade—a hail Mary pass—into the group that was just coming from the hillside. The one-two explosions sent zombie pieces flying, the closest ones obliterated.

The mob seemed to lose its instinctive organization, some zombies attracted to the sound, others to the prey. The road was momentarily clear enough for the truck to pass through. Shane ran after the truck.

"Come on! Come on!" They all shouted.

He leapt into the open door, falling on top of the others in the back seat. Patty closed the door behind him and Bill floored the accelerator.

CHAPTER 19

It took another day to reach the settlement. When sober, Jared had warned that the GPS might gradually become less accurate without human beings on the ground to calibrate readings from the satellite. So, Bill double-checked the GPS screen against the directions Mark had given them. Shane steered the pickup down a back road. The GPS picture showed them headed toward a lake.

"Look!" Courtney pointed to a sign that read Lake Kensington Active Adult Community. "It's one of those fifty-and-over complexes."

The truck filled with exclamations of relief and joy when they saw two armed guards at the entry gate. They had found other people! A man and a woman, both carrying automatic rifles and sweating in shorts and t-shirts, watched the truck approach. Their faces were tense with hollow-eyed shock. Patty wondered whether their own little group would look like that to others. They'd been lucky, no one hurt or killed among them.

Jared opened one eye. "Where's the Somalian girl-soldiers with the mini-skirts?" Obviously one of his zombie novels again—no one bothered to ask.

Lucky in almost every way, Patty thought. She couldn't blame Courtney for her outburst. Patty was furious at Jared, too, despite knowing that addiction was a disease. Worst of all, it frightened her that they might have to decide whether Jared lived or died. The thought of it was almost too much to bear. She'd come to view the young ones—Courtney, Shane, Ana and even Jared in the weeks before he'd picked up—as the children she'd never had.

They drove slowly toward the entry gate. As they approached the guards, Shane rolled down the driver's side window to the pickup, momentarily nervous. He was in the South and he was Black. Without any government, would this be the New South or the old one?

The two guards smiled, their grim sun-scorched faces transforming for a moment. They reached into the window to shake hands. "Welcome. Welcome. Mark told us to expect y'all," the woman said. "He's up at the clubhouse, take a right and you can't miss it."

The group of survivors exhaled nearly as one. They had found civilization, and it was friendly.

With effort, Jared roused himself and tried to shake off his drowsiness. He was as happy as everyone else, even happier, to have found the settlement. Maybe he could get himself together if they settled down in one place. He hated himself more than any of them could imagine, even more than Courtney hated him. He downed a tepid Pepsi for the caffeine and looked out at their new home.

The senior development was built around a golf course and abutted a lake at its far end. Cul-de-sacs of attached townhouses branched off outside the drive. Between tall trees in the distance, sunlight glittered on blue water. They passed a couple of cul-de-sacs and tennis courts on their right before they came to a building on the inside of the loop, which had a carved wooden sign out front: Clubhouse. They parked on blacktop.

A large man was just coming out of the building when they pulled up. He was easily six feet, four inches, stocky with bad skin. He grinned when he saw them.

"Hey!" Kai said, excitedly, as they all left the truck and stretched the kinks out of their cramped legs. "You're Dale James. You used to play for the Braves!"

"Yeah, that's me," Dale said. "The last famous man." He mimed batting a ball. "I got a heck of a zombie-crushing swing now."

They each shook his huge hand, although Beth remained firmly planted behind Courtney's leg.

Bill was beaming, feeling as if he'd come home. "You're an alcoholic?"

"Yeah. Got three years. No way I would have stayed sober through all this if I hadn't met Mark and helped him start this community. If I had picked up instead," he ran his index finger dramatically across his neck, "there's no doubt what would've happened to me."

"This is an incredible place," Shane said.

"Yup, they say God speaks through people but, I tell you, he speaks with a megaphone through Mark. Mark was the glue that held us together. He brought us here from the depths of hell, if you know what I mean."

"We know the place," Patty said.

"Has there been any sign of government or police?" Courtney asked.

"If government means the slimy politicians that used to run things, we haven't seen hide nor hair of them. And, I'll tell you, I don't think a cop could have survived the way things rolled out. It was their job to run *to* trouble. We had off-duty cops at the AA convention, we always did, but the wrath was just too big a piece of trouble and came too quick to confront head on. Probably the best of us died on Zombie Day trying to save others. The only ones who survived had the good sense and cowardliness to run and hide. Dumb luck is what saved me, although we say here that luck was just God's way of staying anonymous."

He slapped Bill's shoulder affectionately. "Go inside and meet Mark. Everyone's excited your group is here. I used to love New York ... didn't much love the fans." He winked at Kai. "But I'm sure you guys are all right."

Inside the expansive common room of the clubhouse, floor-to-ceiling windows looked out on the lake on one side and the golf course on the other. Light from the windows cut through particles of dust in the air and revealed comfortable couches and folding chairs pulled into a large circle. A stone fireplace on one wall under the chalet ceiling completed the look of a ski lodge, but it was cool inside with a breeze through the tall, screened windows.

The man they presumed to be Mark sat on one of the couches with a young man of about twenty, who was talking earnestly to him with a thick AA Big Book on his lap.

Mark stood when they approached. "Welcome to our world."

Mark was about six feet tall with strong features, dark hair and hazel eyes. They introduced themselves then Mark described the birth of the settlement. "Out of the thirty thousand people at the AA convention, just our group escaped and made it to this place. My father and stepmother had lived here. No one was alive when we arrived. The few alcoholics that joined us here later weren't sober anymore, if they ever had been. Some of our original group relapsed, too, and they're counting days again. That's to be expected under the circumstances."

His eyes zeroed in on Jared. "We have a halfway house set up that will be perfect for you."

Jared's free hand fluttered to his sternum. "Me?"

"Listen, buddy, even running from a pack of zombies doesn't make a guy look like that."

Shane and Bill smiled, amused. But Shane still watched Mark closely, trying to get a read on whether they could trust him. He felt protective of his adopted family and he didn't know how they would fit in with Mark's operation—if it really was Mark's. It sure seemed to be.

"We're not all alcoholics," Courtney said.

Mark turned to her. "Really? ACOA?"

"What?" Shane asked.

"Adult Child of an Alcoholic," Courtney told him.

Mark walked with his protégé toward the front door, the group following with them. "We have some here. They have their own Al-Anon meetings. They're not quite as diligent as us alcoholics. Even before Z-Day, most family members of alcoholics looked at their meetings as optional, not a matter of life and death. But we have two AA meetings a day. Folks make one or two a day, depending on their work rotation." Mark turned to Bill. "We'll be happy to hear some new drunk-a-logs. We've already heard everyone here with enough sober time to 'qualify.'"

He turned back to Courtney. "We only insist that you abstain from drugs and alcohol. We've gotten rid of every bottle of booze. It's not that the Program doesn't work when the stuff is around, but we don't see any reason to keep it. When we cleared the zombies out of each house, we cleared out the booze, too."

"Just as well," Shane said.

"Speaking of which, you can choose a house or split up. Lately, we haven't had much trouble with zombies making it here, but just in case, people don't live completely alone." They all walked outside the clubhouse. Mark pointed. "We've filled up that cul-de-sac and that one." He pointed to another. "Over there is our halfway house for the day counters. If you have a year or more of sobriety and have worked the steps, you can staff the place as one of your work duties. We also have guard duty, sanitation, hunting, and foraging trips to the towns outside. Once you get settled, we'll figure out what special skills you have."

"Jared can stay with us," Patty said, "if he wants to." She felt queasy making that call for everyone, but turning him over to strangers so quickly made her uncomfortable.

No one objected. Courtney shrugged. *What harm could he do here?*

Mark raised an eyebrow in disapproval. "We don't recommend it . . . but suit yourself." He looked back at Jared for an answer.

Jared stammered, "I don't know. Can I think about it?"

"Sure."

"Do you have electricity?" Kai asked.

"We have backup generators. Fuel is a problem we're always working on. We put the generators on for two hours a night. During that time, half of us get to bathe and the other half kill the zombies who come out of the woods, attracted to the noise. We've pretty much fenced and barb-wired the complex near the generator. They come into a gauntlet and we pick them off."

"Nice," Bill said.

"There's less of them. Our clean perimeter is getting wider, so fewer zombies are wandering within earshot. But one of our long-range projects is to enclose the entire perimeter. That takes a lot of fence."

"Have you been making trips to the library? Do you know where to get solar power panels?" Kai asked, wondering what it would take to make the complex more sustainable.

"No." Mark smiled, condescendingly. "We're just trying to make sure we have everything we need to prepare for winter. The winters are mild here compared to New York, but we've been doing a lot of for-aging to stockpile canned foods and supplies."

"There is a lot to learn but we don't have to go back to the Middle Ages," Kai continued, enthusiastically. "The books exist already. Many of us will be able to teach ourselves the engineering, medicine, agricultural and other skills needed to sustain us at a comfortable level. We should also bring back animals that will not survive winter without our help. Have you noticed that some of the animals—we've seen chickens, goats, horses—weren't killed by the zombies? We don't have to limit ourselves to canned goods and hunting. There's enough animal feed to last for years."

Mark cut him off with a hand up. "We stay sober and everything else takes a number. First things first."

Kai's mouth snapped shut. It had never occurred to him that they couldn't do both. He exchanged a worried glance with Patty.

Bill seemed oblivious to any concerns, as did Jared, who wandered along with them, trying to think through his living arrangements. But Shane was still thinking about what Mark had said about the "Al-Anonics." He remembered Jared's drunken comment about Jim Jones and wondered whether the New Black might be the people who didn't go to AA meetings.

Beth slipped one hand in Shane's, another in Courtney's. She jumped, swinging her feet off the ground. It was the first time Beth had done anything like that. Everyone laughed, the tension breaking.

"She's the first child we've seen. Is she yours?" Mark asked.

"Yes," Courtney said, perhaps too quickly, surprising herself with her answer. But she had the strongest feeling that she would lose Beth if she didn't claim her. "I'd hoped there would be other children for her to play with."

"No, I'm sorry." Mark frowned. "In fact, we've never seen third-generation immunity . . . someone whose parents weren't at least alcoholics. Her father was an alcoholic?"

Courtney was flustered by the unexpected questions. "No."

"She must have the alcoholic gene herself. I guess that could prove the question about whether alcoholics are born or made. Unless—" He assessed Courtney. "Are you sure you've never had a problem?"

"I was never even a shop-a-holic," Courtney said, testily.

He shrugged then turned down the path to a townhouse. "See if you like this one. It's one of our biggest. Four bedrooms."

Patty put her hand on Mark's arm. "Are you saying you haven't found a single person alive who isn't an addict or child of an addict?"

"Alcoholics and, by extension, their children are apparently God's chosen people. There's not many of us." Mark looked into the distance. "No one knows why any of this has happened . . . but we're all that's left, probably in the world."

He resumed walking up the path.

"Except Ana," Shane said. "She doesn't have the gene."

"Ana?" Mark followed everyone's gaze to the Mexican, walking beside Jared. Mark paused. "Interesting . . . I guess more will be revealed."

Ana frowned, not understanding. Patty recognized the saying from the Rooms. Mark doubted Ana's honesty—he thought they'd find out Ana's *real* story in time. Disturbing, Patty reflected.

As they waited for Mark to open the door to their new home, Courtney leaned over Beth and whispered in Shane's ear. Her heart beat wildly. "Can Beth and I share a room with you?"

Shane tried to keep from grinning like an idiot. "Do you think she can protect you?"

"For a while."

After everyone went inside, Bill went back to the clubhouse with Mark to get the pickup.

"The meeting is at seven PM," Mark told Bill. "You'll like it."

Bill drove the pickup back to their new home, taking it all in, whistling. He'd missed going to real meetings. He couldn't wait.

THEY FIGURED OUT the sleeping arrangements in the townhouse and Kai began scraping together food in the kitchen, pleased with the large, modern space. "We still have vegetables and potatoes to put in the soup," he announced.

He pulled out canned soups from an overhead cabinet.

Ana opened the refrigerator door. "They cleaned out the bad food. This is the first house that's smelled good."

The unaccustomed trill of the doorbell launched them toward their weapons. It was a sound from another life, spooky.

Everyone came out to the two-story entryway, holstering their guns and laughing at themselves. Zombies didn't ring doorbells. Jared let in a woman carrying a plate with a dozen slices of roast venison.

"My boyfriend got lucky and snagged a deer this morning," she said, smiling warmly at everyone. "The only problem is that, after the gunshot, it took a bunch of us to fight off the dead guys that showed up. Every deer has to stretch a long way but we share it all out the same day. We're still trying to figure out how to preserve meat."

Moments later, a couple of young men—one short, one tall and skinny—came bearing bread they'd baked during the last "Light Hour." Patty was so happy to see fresh bread she hugged them. The two men greeted everyone then shook Jared's hand, enthusiastically. "We heard about you. You're the new guy who's thinking about joining the rehab?"

"Yes."

"I live there. It's great," the short one said. He signaled to the tall, skinny man. "I'll move into Keith's house when I get ninety days. Keith is my sponsor."

"I sponsor a couple of guys," Keith said, "but I have time for one more. If you want, we can talk about it . . . whenever you're ready."

After the young men left, Patty took Jared's arm. He seem elated. "You have a real chance here, Jared."

"So far, so good."

Two young women came along next with a plate of grilled catfish. "We won't stay long. We just had to come and see y'all," one of them said. She scanned the living room, which overlooked the woods out back. Ana thought she was checking for any good-looking men in their group. She instinctively moved closer to Bill.

Bill asked, "The lake's good for fishing?"

"Oh, yes. We have all sorts of fish in there." She flashed a flirtatious smile. "We're so blessed."

Both Ana and Patty felt a familiar sensation of being invisible, Ana the Mexican and Patty the older woman. Civilization was a mixed blessing, Patty thought, but she was still damn happy to be there.

When they had eaten, the New York group, as they were clearly going to be called, sat on a screened-in porch facing a copse of woods. There were enough wicker couches and cushiony lounge chairs for each to relax in the shade.

"I can't believe how calm I feel to be in a cleared settlement," Bill said.

"Did you see the people running the Loop with an iPod?" Courtney said. "A group of girls stopped and said 'hi.' They told me they charge them during 'Light Hour.' They share an iPod since they can't download new music. They were pretty happy when I told them I still have mine. That's like a thousand new songs."

When it was time for the meeting, Bill and Patty stood.

Kai got up, too. "I'm looking forward to meeting our new neighbors."

Jared lowered his legs from a desert-colored ottoman. "I'm going."

Beth had fallen asleep on the wicker couch with her head on Courtney's lap. Ana looked at Courtney and Shane sitting beside her, joy on their faces. She certainly wasn't staying behind with them. "Can I come?"

"Sure," Bill said. "Mark said it's an open meeting. Anyone can come."

"We better stay here with Beth." Shane leaned over to pick up the sleeping child. "I'll put her in bed." He winked at Courtney, who blushed.

Everyone headed out for the two-block walk to the Clubhouse.

"We should find them a *padre*," Ana said to Bill.

"For confession?"

"To marry them." Ana paused. "One thing about Black and Latino men I think. More times, they will let a woman know they want her. *Los blancitos* . . . maybe too shy."

In the distance, they heard a shot. The guards were keeping the perimeter clean. No one from the settlement seemed particularly concerned. A stream of people entering the Clubhouse stopped to greet the new arrivals.

CHAPTER 20

The clubhouse was steamy with so many people milling inside. A breeze from the lake occasionally cooled their perspiration. It appeared as if everyone in the settlement was there. They welcomed the New York group, who looked around, amazed at seeing so many people. Some wore guns in holsters, or had left them on their seats as place-savers. Others had rifles. But many were unarmed. The New Yorkers had come armed but felt safe.

Patty was stunned that many of the people were dressed up. Every woman wore a dress. Some of the men wore suit jackets and others had on crisp shirts and khakis. It reminded her of vacationers dressed up for a resort dining room, although some of the young women looked as if they were headed out to a New York nightclub. She wondered how they'd managed to get the clothes. Had there been a girls-day-out-raid at the mall?

She watched how the woman interacted with men and realized she was witnessing an elaborate mating ritual. Survival of the fittest—A.Z., as Jared had coined it. The quote from the AA step book—"girl meets boy on AA's campus"—had come to life. Patty suddenly felt grimy in the bike shorts and t-shirt she'd worn for days, but she would not be in this particular game anyway. It looked as if she was the oldest survivor, and of course well beyond child-bearing age. She marveled at how the instinct for survival of the species had kicked into overdrive so quickly.

Everyone wanted to shake the New Yorkers' hands. Some seemed shell-shocked and, Patty thought, were perhaps mentally ill. Without making eye contact, the shy ones dutifully lined up to shake hands anyway. A super-energetic gaggle of girls just out of their teens introduced themselves to Patty. "This is my sponsee, Mara," one dark-haired girl said, "and this is my grand-sponsee. And this is my sober-sister, Debbie. Tina is our sponsor."

The girls fawned over each other. Patty wondered who was crazier under the circumstances, the ones who were shell-shocked or the ones who acted as if they were at a sorority party. She tried to suspend judgment and focused instead on everyone's kindness.

A group of guys had gravitated toward Jared, who was still standing. After he'd said he was a newcomer to the Program, young men surrounded him, speaking encouragingly to him about getting sober. They told him getting sober was the most important thing, especially in a zombie-dominated world. Jared felt the warmth of their welcome as if the weight of his loneliness had been lifted off his shoulders.

"Hi, everyone." A pretty Bangladeshi woman with a British accent stood up to quiet the crowd. She was in her early 30s, wearing a pink lace dress. "Welcome to the Southeastern group of Alcoholics Anonymous."

The crowd quieted. Mark sat beside the woman. He seemed to have a personal air conditioner that kept him from sweating in his buttoned up collar and tie.

"Tonight is a beginners meeting," the woman said. "I've picked out a section to read from the Big Book. Then Amber here," she nodded toward a young woman in a black dress and heels. "will share her experience, strength and hope. Then we'll go to the secretary's break and a show of hands."

The woman in pink read a page from the Big Book about the history of Bill and Bob's first meeting. Then Amber told a routine story of drunk driving, underachievement, and embarrassing behavior. Kai pondered the black hole in her story: There hadn't been a single reference to zombies or the loss of everyone she'd ever loved. In his meetings with Patty and Bill, they sometimes talked about the loss of their families and friends. They often talked about the anxiety of living in a zombie-infested world. He couldn't imagine not talking about it.

After Amber finished, everyone in the room took turns and said their name, sober date, name of their sponsor and what step they were working on. Perky young women popped up from their seats as if they were a happy whack-a-mole game. The young men recited similar information with a James Dean sort of swagger. The men seemed young to Patty, as if they were playing dress-up as zombie killers. Patty noticed that many of the men and women were very new to recovery, too, and were already on their fourth step. She wondered what it would be like to still be detoxing from drugs and alcohol, killing zombies by day, then writing about their deepest selves at night. It struck her as odd timing.

When Jared said he was working on his first day sober, the crowd erupted in cheers and love-of-Jesus smiles. Again, Patty tried not to judge the meeting. The energy was positive, and she saw how Jared was soaking up the warm reception. Meetings were different everywhere and, even though something about this one made her uncomfortable, it was going to be her "home group" for a long time.

Everyone clapped enthusiastically when Bill stood, said he was an alcoholic and recited the date when he'd gotten sober eleven years ago. When he rose, Patty noticed how tan and muscular he'd become in their weeks together. He looked like a different person.

Mark commented from up front, "Here's a new potential sponsor!"

They actually oohed and aahed when Patty said she was an alcoholic with 25 years sober, so far the longest in the group.

Kai stood when it was his turn. "Hello. I am Kai. I am a member of AA. I am very glad to be here. My clean date is September 23, 1995. I am presently focused on Steps Three and Eleven."

Mark asked from up front, "Are you an alcoholic?"

"I am a member of AA."

Mark's smile stiffened. "Are you an *alcoholic?*"

Kai froze. He was an addict from NA, originally. But he had always been welcome in AA. Three quarters of the people who called themselves alcoholics were drug addicts and a lot of them had way more problems with drugs than alcohol. Alcohol was just a drug anyway. He stammered, "I am an addict. I am a member of AA."

"This is AA," Mark told him. "We are alcoholics and we deal with alcohol."

Around the room, a patronizing sing-song echoed Mark's sentiments: "Keep coming, Kai."

Kai sat back in his seat, crushed. He didn't think he would be making meetings during the zombie apocalypse. These people were AA fundamentalists, the type who became upset when you talked about drugs—even when they'd done drugs themselves. At the end of the world, he just couldn't believe they'd stick to that conservatism.

Ana stood when it was her turn and tried not to stammer. She'd chosen and mentally rehearsed her words. "I'm Ana. I'm not an alcoholic. I'm just new here."

There were frowns around the room as if her statement were confusing. Mark spoke to the group, "We have a few new members for Al-Anon."

Ana sat down, quietly, and Bill held her hand in support. She thought maybe he had finally gotten her hint about being too shy. It had been more like beating him over the head than a hint. She wondered why she would be a member of Al-Anon, though, since she wasn't a child of an alcoholic or addict like Courtney and Shane.

When they walked home, Patty walked next to Kai. "I think we should keep having our own meetings in the house."

Kai scowled. "We couldn't have found a more close-minded group. Did you notice that no one said a word about zombies? Do they think that's an 'outside issue'?"

"Hard to imagine . . . but these are extreme times. In the early days of AIDS, some people didn't want discussion about that in meetings either. Eventually common sense and compassion won out over prejudice and fear. I guess we should just wait and see, but I have to believe they're only trying to keep zombies from being *all* they talk about. Hopefully, the wrinkles will fall out over time."

Bill caught up with them, a huge smile on his face. "It feels good to be back in a meeting."

No sooner had they reached the house when the lights went on. It was time to take hot showers. Mark had said they shouldn't work their first night, so they could all have a chance to shower and sleep.

Bill walked into the kitchen with a pile of towels. They could hear shooting out in the woods: the gauntlet near the generator.

"I guess they change out of their party dress," Ana said, dryly, taking a towel from Bill.

Kai and Patty laughed.

"You didn't like the meeting much," Bill said.

"It reminded me of the churches with lots of rules."

"Not all meetings are like that. In Manhattan, there was a nut for every screw. If you liked a meeting, you went to it. If you didn't, you went to another. I don't know how it will work now."

"We can always start a new meeting," Patty said. "We can call it a New York-style meeting."

Kai liked the idea. But he had a bad feeling that it wouldn't be that simple.

THEY FELL INTO the community's routines, picking up garbage and driving to the nearby town to bring in supplies and canned goods. Each morning after the AA step meeting, there was an 8:30 AM "Roundup," where everyone gathered to make sure work details were in place for the day.

"We're going to set up a farm," Mark announced a week after Kai's suggestion. "It will mean a longer trip outside the settlement to pick up animals, feed and hay, so we'll only do a couple of trips a week. Kai will lead the crew."

Mark patted Kai on the back after the meeting broke. "I'm giving you good people. Don't let me down."

"I'm relieved that Mark and the others came around," Kai told Bill, Jared and Shane before they headed off to their separate jobs. "I would have liked to add trips to the library. It would help with more than just farming if we had books."

"Bring me back some science fiction—skip the zombie novels," Jared quipped. "But no way I can add any extra trips outside. I'm already out there more than I want. You know how they used to say to stay away from 'people, places and things'? Zombies are definitely a 'thing'."

"I'm booked up at work every day," Bill said. "Don't have a spare minute."

Shane carried a gun in a shoulder holster and an assault rifle over his broad shoulder, ready for his own trip to the mall. "They don't like independent trips outside the Settlement anyway. If I see any good mechanical engineering books at Target, I'll bring them back."

Bill chuckled. "Fat chance."

A small group of men and women waited for Kai in the parking area. It made him a bit nervous to suddenly be in charge. "I'd feel more comfortable if you guys were with me."

"I know the feeling," Shane said. "But at least the folks who survived this long have a good fighting instinct. We can trust our backs to them in a crunch."

KAI BROUGHT CHICKENS on his first few trips outside, and Ana became a busy chicken farmer. Courtney and Beth arrived at the shady spot behind the tennis courts where a work crew had built a corral. They crossed paths with two women on garbage pick-up duty. Beth let go of Courtney's hand and ran down the slope to where Ana stood. Courtney felt comfortable walking in the Settlement alone with Beth, even though she was always armed and watchful. She'd only once seen a zombie incursion. The lone stalker had been surrounded and killed long before he'd posed a threat. But that was more than enough to stop her from letting down her guard.

Courtney and Beth helped Ana out for a while each day. Courtney had made sure that she and Beth had jobs they could do together to contribute to the community. Courtney and Patty were the only ones in their group who didn't have to work off site at least a few days each week. It was actually surreal to have a halfway normal life while the others were coming home with stories of the infested world.

"Good morning," Courtney called out to Ana.

"¡Hola!" She grinned. "We have eggs today. *Huevos.*"

Courtney appreciated Ana's efforts to teach Beth Spanish even though Beth still pretty much refused to speak English. "What's up?" Courtney asked, wondering why Ana had seemed unhappy when they'd approached.

"Those two who picked up garbage asked questions about my family. When I said that my father was just a farmer and my mother helped him sell fruit and vegetables at the market—they were angry. I could tell."

"They probably think you're in denial about your life."

"Yes, they said I was an alcoholic or child of an alcoholic but wouldn't admit it."

"That's totally out of line," Courtney said as they walked toward the supply shed they'd turned into a chicken coop. "Actually, out of line seems to be a specialty here. I can't tell you how many people have tried to pry into my life history to figure Beth out."

Ana was glad to have Courtney to confide in. "Like you say: 'Whatever.' At least it's nice that Bill is happy here working at the rehab . . . but I miss him. Last night they held all-night meetings."

"They do keep him busy. We hardly see Jared either," Courtney said. "He goes to the rehab for Big Book study and therapy groups on top of his regular meetings and work assignments. It doesn't seem like either of them sleep. But Jared is so much better, thank God."

"It's been very good for him here. He even apologized to me for the time we had to carry him from that house."

"Me, too." Courtney laughed. "He practically apologized for me having to hit him. That wasn't one of my best moments."

Ana took a pail from a hook she'd hammered into the shed wall and handed it to Beth. "It's lonelier now than it was with just the eight of us."

Courtney stopped. "You think?"

"I am mostly invisible here the way I was to the *gringos* in New York. But here I think it is mostly that I am not an alcoholic." Ana signaled to Beth to follow her to the chicken nests on shelves Kai's crew had installed. "Maybe it is best anyway."

"Why?"

Ana reached under a chicken and pulled out an egg. "I don't want to become too . . . happy here. I can't stay here forever, never knowing what happened to my children."

"But what about Bill? You guys have gotten so close."

Ana bit her lip. "I don't know. Maybe I made a big mistake."

A DRY WIND blew dust into a swirl around Patty, cycling to the lake on a path between balding lawns. She'd been assigned to the easy job of fishing along with a group of young women, "sober sisters" and their sponsor. The women were already waiting for her when she arrived. In side-by-side rowboats, Patty enjoyed the beauty of the tree-lined lake. Tennessee was actually more beautiful than Patty would have imagined, although the bone-dry summer had tinged the trees gray.

The all-girl fishing crew behaved as if they were on their senior trip. In between catches, they giggled and gossiped and wrote gratitude lists, which they shared aloud. Patty thought it was helpful. "I'm grateful for my health, a beautiful day and that there were no zombies in the water," Patty offered.

The girls agreed.

"I am so grateful for my sponsor," a young woman said, "for my sober sisters, and for," she spoke breathlessly, "my God, the steps. I would be dead without the steps."

It had become a mini-meeting, and the girls treated Patty as both irrelevant grandmother and wise elder. She often felt as if she were the unpopular girl in high school who didn't quite get the inside jokes. Then they'd turn earnestly to her and ask what she thought about a recovery issue.

The sponsor of the group was a woman named Kerry. She was in her early twenties, three years sober. The others were so newly sober their pores practically oozed booze and coke.

"Prayer is everything," Kerry told the group. "I pray my way through every day."

"I so identify," one girl said. "I would never have hit my knees before. Oh my God, I've been wearing out my knees."

"After Z-Day, I finally came to believe that I needed to get down on my knees and pray to God to help me find his path," Kerry affirmed. "I don't care where I am or what's going on, I hit my knees."

The youngest girl quipped, uncomfortably, "Except if there's like zombies coming?"

Kerry looked at her. "You know, Fiona, if you don't surrender, you'll die, with or without zombies." Kerry stared out at the horizon. "Maybe you need to move back to the rehab. There's such a thing as emotional relapse."

Patty felt sorry for Fiona. "I tend to pray in a lotus position and definitely," Patty chuckled. "while running from zombies. The Program is broad enough for all of us, even those who don't pray on their knees or don't pray at all."

Conversation over. They fished in total silence, hearing nothing but the distant caw of crows for an impossible twenty minutes before the women resumed their chatter as if nothing had happened.

By mid-afternoon, they docked their boats and brought their catch toward a boathouse. Fiona lagged behind to speak to Patty. "Thank you for standing up to them . . ." She whispered, "There have been suicides here. People who couldn't fit in."

Patty put a reassuring hand on Fiona's back. "Are you okay?"

Fiona spoke almost too softly to hear, "They're talking about exiling people who don't follow suggestions."

"What? That can't be true. The rumor mill is ridiculous here."

"First you get the bad job assignments if you don't take suggestions: the Gauntlet, extra trips outside. If your sponsor fires you, none of your sober sisters will speak to you. Then they send you back to the rehab where they watch everything you do . . . until you stop sassing and change your ways. Then what?

"I'm not even drinking or drugging, but they keep saying they're disappointed in me." Fiona's dark eyes were sunken within her sockets. Tears welled up. "I miss my parents so much, and my sisters and brother. Everyone here keeps telling me they're my family now. But they're not."

Patty held Fiona, who quickly wiped her eyes.

"I don't want them to see me crying. They say I'm not living up to my potential. They say we should talk about our feelings but when I do they say stuff like, 'poor me, pour me a drink.' Self-pity is a character defect, right?" Fiona hunched her shoulders. "I don't want to go back to the rehab. I'm afraid all the time . . . I know I can't make it here. I couldn't even make it through high school."

CHAPTER 21

Kai felt as if he were Noah, hauling back skinny goats and cows with the help of three men and two women. They'd found horse trailers and attached them to the two pickups they used, which allowed them to transport large animals. Kai's crew had begun cleaning out the former caretaker's house, transforming it into a barn. Cat, one of the women in the crew, hammered fencing onto posts, expanding the corral they'd built for the goats. Kai noticed the strong muscles of Cat's leg as she crouched, her khaki shorts riding up to the top of her thighs. She had a small tattoo of a kitten there and tiny blue stars on her wrist. Her short dark hair framed her tanned and freckled face. She smiled at Kai as if she could sense him watching her. Kai realized how badly he wanted companionship and . . . sex.

"I'm glad we're inside the Settlement today," Kai said to a young man assigned to his crew.

The kid smelled of tobacco from a cigarette break he and the others had taken. "Yeah, dude, it's deeply stressful out there."

Kai's eyes wandered back to Cat.

The kid followed Kai's gaze. "I'm glad it's not all about me anymore. It's a lot of work doing Higher Power's will and letting go of mine."

Kai picked up a burlap bag of feed from the back of the pickup and put it on his shoulder. "Life is challenging."

The young man picked up another bag and walked alongside Kai toward the garage. "I didn't have a clue before about honestly relating to another human being. It took a lot to shake me out of my self-centeredness . . . zombies and the end of the world to be exact. Now, it's all about the work, exactly the way Bill and Bob did it. All twelve steps fast, a spiritual awakening and service. That's my life now."

Kai threw down his bag in a corner of the garage. Six months ago, the kid had been sticking up gas stations for drugs. His sponsor had no more than a year clean himself. "In the old days, some people went slower, some faster. It's helpful to remember that spiritual development comes over time as we face life. Many years of meditation deepened my understanding of myself and couldn't be rushed."

The kid grunted when he threw down his bag. "The old days and old people are dead now. We were the ones chosen."

Kai paused, blindsided once again by the things people believed here. Was he not alive? Did anything else matter?

"Here, everyone rushes to work the steps because they want to date," Cat said with a laugh. "It's an amazing incentive."

Kai turned, surprised. He hadn't realized that Cat had come in, pushing feed in a wheelbarrow. "What do you mean?"

"Before zombies, you know the old slogan about not getting into a relationship in the first year? Well, I was in the same group as Mark before Z-Day, and we took that suggestion seriously. They said newcomers got distracted and screwed up when they dated. In our group, sponsors even fired you sometimes for dating in your first year. But out here, people want a warm body next to them more than just about anything, and the guys can't sneak off to hookers when their sponsors aren't looking." Cat gave the kid a knowing look. He shrugged and looked away as if he weren't listening anymore. "So, Mark bent the rule for our circumstances. If you have less than a year, you have to get through all the steps before dating and your sponsor has to okay it."

Kai tried not to stare at her, wondering why she'd decided to run down the dating rules for him. "I didn't know that," he said.

"Yeah, that's the deal."

The young man watched Cat leave. "From what I hear, she's on Step Nine now," he told Kai. "She's writing letters to all the dead people she owes amends to."

Kai felt his face heating up. "I'm that obvious."

"Dude, she's a hot girl. There are a lot of guys wanting her to finish the steps. No telling who the lucky guy will be but, for what it's worth, she seems interested in you."

COURTNEY HAD NEVER before experienced such extremes of mixed emotion—the anxiety and unfathomable loss of their post-zombie lives, the discomfort she felt with some of the people in the settlement, alongside mad love with Shane and the deep satisfaction of suddenly having a child. Before the zombies she'd felt orphaned, but now she had a family. She had an extended family, too. Patty had become her surrogate mother. She felt as if she'd known Kai, Bill and Ana her entire life. Even Jared had become a kid brother. He was so much happier and had over a month clean.

Courtney held Beth's hand as they walked the Loop toward Kai's farm, now brimming with animals to see and feed. Kai's crew had finished retrofitting the caretaker's house into a barn and had a sizeable herd of goats in the new corral. In the distance, cows grazed on the far side of the overgrown golf course near the caretaker's house. Courtney worried about Beth—she was still barely speaking. She had lost some of her skittishness, staying peacefully with the others in their group if Courtney were out of sight for a few moments. But she still spoke no more than a few words a day, "yes" and "no" normally the extent of it.

Beth seemed to be in a good mood, letting go of Courtney's hand and skipping ahead of her.

"Hey, Beth," Courtney tapped her on the shoulder. "You're it."

Courtney back-pedaled away from her, taking a couple of steps, gauging Beth's reaction.

Beth squealed and chased Courtney, who ran backward a few more steps, feeling the shift from hard pavement to the grass of the golf course. Beth was fast and Courtney feigned great effort to get away before allowing herself to be tagged. "Oh, you got me! Now I'm gonna get you!"

The little girl turned and ran, laughing with her whole body. She ran up onto the golf course hill nearest the clubhouse. Courtney tagged her then turned to run away.

"I'm gonna git you!" Beth called.

Courtney couldn't believe it—Beth had spoken a full sentence. She hugged the girl. "I'm so proud of you."

Courtney took off her bulky shoulder holster. "Now, try this!"

She showed Beth how to roll down the hill. The ground bit into Courtney's joints, but Beth shrieked with glee. At the bottom, Courtney looked up dizzily. A huge figure was coming at them. The sun beamed into Courtney's eyes, shrouding all but a male's blurred outline. Beth scurried behind Courtney as they both launched to their feet. Courtney grabbed Beth's forearm and pivoted to make a run for it up the hill to where she'd left her gun, but no way they'd make it in time. She looked back and took in the measured gait of a man. *Oh.* She exhaled. Not a zombie.

"Hey, hey, it's me," Dale said, his eyes hard to see under a baseball cap. The clubhouse shimmered in the sun behind him.

Courtney caught her breath. "I thought—"

"I'm mistaken for a zombie more than you know. What are you all up to out here?"

Courtney put her hand behind her back for Beth to hold. "Children need to play."

"I guess that's right." Dale scratched his pockmarked cheek. "I heard her talking just now. That's real nice. We've been speaking about her, too. That's why I came out when I saw y'all."

"Really?"

"Yeah, we think she should be in school. We have a teacher here, who could make sure she gets a proper education."

Courtney shaded her eyes with her hand. "Shane and I are teaching Beth for now. Everyone is welcome to help."

Dale looked doubtfully at Courtney. "I'm not sure that will be acceptable."

Courtney returned his look with a steely glare. "What is that supposed to mean?"

"There will be more children after her. We already have one pregnancy. We want the children in one school."

"Look, I understand the long-range planning, but she's not even five and she's traumatized. She's barely speaking." Courtney looked up at the huge man, her anger compensating for their size difference. "I'm not letting her out of my sight. So, forget it."

Dale twitched. "Suit yourself."

He walked away.

For the rest of the afternoon, Courtney sequestered herself and Beth on the back porch of the house. Too upset to hide how she felt, she'd wanted to stay away from the probing eyes and concerned questioning of her neighbors. It was funny that she hadn't met a single person here who she trusted to take into her confidence.

"What's wrong?" Bill said, coming out on the porch.

Courtney's jaw was hard set with anger. "Dale talked to me about school for Beth. Did you know anything about that?"

Bill sat down. "I heard something about it earlier today. Planning for the next generation and all that."

"Really?" She spit. "And who put Mark and his minions in charge of my next generation? I've got more sober time than all of them. I've *never* had a drink. Why should he be telling me what to do?"

"You've gotta be kidding. I didn't know that."

"That is not the point." Courtney leaned forward with her forearms on her thighs. "Why should we want to live like this?"

Bill was glad she was mad at someone other than him. "Come on. It's just that people respect Mark. You have to admit he's worked a miracle organizing this settlement. A lot of the people here are too new to sobriety to make healthy decisions, and Mark, Dale and the few others with sober time are trying to make sure we have 'good orderly direction.'"

"Hah." Courtney calmed her tone. "These guys are Moonies, Bill."

"Bullshit."

"I know you have a lot of hopes wrapped up in this place—"

"Face it, Courtney, you have a resentment against AA and it's coloring the way you're looking at things."

Courtney crossed her arms. "I do not."

"Oh, yes you do."

"Say I do?" she challenged him.

"I've been meaning to talk to you about it, although it wasn't our most pressing issue when we were fighting zombies day and night. You've got a resentment against AA, but the sad truth is that AA doesn't save everyone, never did. Your father got cocky about the disease after a long time sober, and relapsed. That happened a lot in the old days. The disease—alcoholism, addiction—is a bitch. That's what you should be mad at: the disease. AA gave you a childhood. It was the disease that took it away, not AA."

"I can't believe you went there." Courtney felt stunned, vulnerable, hearing Bill—AA poster boy—talking about this. She fought the urge to run. "You're right. I have little faith in AA guys ... present company excluded. But you're wrong—I do kind of understand the thing about my father. What gets me, though, is why no one came to help *me?* I was fifteen years old and living with a drunk ... There was a whole group that knew me from the time I was five. I was taught to look at them like family. But no one helped me."

Bill grimaced, understanding now. "Listen ... people in AA know how to get drunks sober. They don't have any expertise in helping their kids. The only way they know to help the kid is to help the parent. But if the parent isn't ready ... there's not much to do. Besides, you said yourself that your father had isolated from his friends long before he relapsed. They probably didn't know how bad it was until too late. Then what should they have done? Call the authorities? You would have ended up in a group home like Shane."

"The thought occurred when I heard Shane's story." Courtney considered his point out loud. "They left messages for my dad, and I remember his sponsor visiting. My father put on the great 'happy family' act."

"Alcoholics are good at that."

Bill took a swig of orange juice, feeling the tang on his tongue. He and Courtney sat with their own thoughts for a while. "There is one thing I wasn't completely honest with you about though. I didn't think you'd understand and we were dealing with more pressing matters at the time."

"What?"

"I did Thirteenth Step a girl once."

Courtney laughed. "You've gotta be kidding. Not you?"

"It's not always how you think, guys being predators. In my case, a girl came to the meeting. Everyone was attracted to her, and she seemed like she had it really together for a newcomer. I only had a couple of years sober then and I couldn't resist. But she wasn't anywhere near ready to stay sober. I ended up with an active-addict girlfriend. I was totally obsessed with saving her. She lied, cheated, stole from me, you name it."

"Wow. That's rough."

"I shouldn't have gotten involved with her, but I was human." He lifted up his thumb and index finger like pincers. "I was this close to relapsing . . . all that pain I was in and her practically using in front of me. I might have fallen if her family hadn't taken her away. I never saw her again . . . although she friended me on Facebook a few years ago."

"An interesting story," Courtney said, "but is there a moral?"

"Yes. We're all human. Everyone here is basically devastated after losing everyone they ever loved. It's the Walking Wounded versus the Walking Dead. The people here are doing the best they can under unbelievably shitty circumstances. You could cut them some slack."

Courtney joined Beth on the floor, feeling less angry. She picked up some Legos. "What if their 'best' is to turn into Moonies?"

Bill laughed. "It would take more than Moonies to get you down."

KAI WAS WAITING on his bike for Patty when she returned after a day of fishing. Despite herself, Patty had begun to think of her crew of sober sisters as the psycho sisters. Except poor Fiona, who had mostly retreated into silence while the others chattered.

"I thought I'd take a ride with you," Kai said, his expression pensive. "I could use the exercise."

"Sure." Patty had become accustomed to members of their group riding alongside her during her exercise sessions on the Loop, especially when something was bothering them. Jared did it a lot, although he was on a recovery pink cloud lately and just wanted to pepper her with questions about the Twelve Steps. Fine with her.

Kai and Patty rode silently for a time.

"I desperately miss my wife," Kai said, eventually.

"Of course."

"The pain is still almost too much to carry. But at the same time, it's as if I'm looking through a long telescope at my old life, as if that is someone else's life. The two lives, before and after are so . . . separate." Kai paused. "I want to move on. I'm interested in Cat. We've been talking a lot over the last few weeks."

Patty picked up the speed. "She's a nice girl. Bright."

"But I can't stand the meetings. I talk to you guys about my feelings, we have our meetings in the house, and I'm surrounded with recovery talk with the work crew. But I don't go to the official meetings."

"I've noticed."

"When I do go, I never share. The meetings make me uncomfortable."

"They make me uncomfortable, too. But you seem to be doing fine under the circumstances."

"I am doing okay. But apparently Cat's sponsor, grand-sponsor, and whoever else they consult—Mark in the end, I guess—don't think I'm a good candidate for her to date."

"You're kidding!"

"Cat needs her sponsor's permission to date me. So would almost any other woman here. But her sponsor told her I'm not 'doing the work.' She won't okay it unless I make their meetings and work the steps out of the Big Book with one of the guys here for my sponsor. The Big Book is great, I've read it many times, but I'm happy with the way I work the Program. My parents and home were destroyed by a tsunami; I moved halfway across the world; my wife and child were destroyed by zombies; but I've stayed clean and relatively sane. I haven't hurt anyone or myself. I believe I've been doing fairly well. I'd like to go to more official meetings but . . ."

Patty found her anger building again, the way it did when Fiona talked to her about her tortuous relationship with the psycho sisters. "I've never met a more solid person than you, Kai, from the first moment we laid eyes on you." Patty rode silently for a few moments. "We need to start a new 'official' meeting . . . so we can have choices and more people attending, so it's not just us. Everyone needs to have choices."

"I'd like that."

"What did Cat say?" Patty asked.

"About dating me? She's not going to oppose everyone in the world she cares about. Why should she? We've just started to get to know each other and there are many other men who would be in better standing."

"You could *convert*," Patty said, sarcastically.

"No, Patty, I really could not. There's a saying they had in NA: 'If you don't stand for something, you'll fall for anything.' I couldn't do that."

THE NEXT DAY, Patty posted a sign on the clubhouse bulletin board for their New York-style meeting. She decided to schedule it for early evening before the big meeting, to avoid conflict. She knew it would make trouble but felt it was time to take a stand and offer an alternative. People had always been able to choose the kind of meeting that worked for them.

Mark had the sign in his hand when he ran into Bill a few hours after she'd posted it. Both men wore shorts and t-shirts, wrinkled after a sweltering day. Mark put a heavy arm around Bill's already hot shoulder. "How are you, buddy?"

"Okay, okay," Bill said. "Busy day at the rehab. Good service."

"Great," Mark said, distractedly, taking his arm back. "Ya know, I've gotta talk to you about some of your group. Things seem to be going in a . . . bad direction."

"Really?"

"Well, yeah. Maybe it's a New York thing, being contrary and the like. I don't know. But you've got the Japanese guy who hardly makes our meetings. Then he goes out with his crew, talking about how we need to get better radiation-measuring equipment even though we're hundreds of miles from the nearest plant. You have Patty telling the girls that it's okay not to believe in God. The Mexican one makes believe she can't speak English . . . and we all know she does. She's a stubborn one. The only one who seems to be fitting in is you and, well, Jared, who's doing pretty well now that he's decided to move into the rehab full time."

"Oh, really. He didn't tell me that."

"Yeah, we talked about it today." They walked a moment in silence in the direction of the New York House, as it had come to be known. "God protects fools and drunks. We're the drunks and the Al-Anonics are the fools. The children of alcoholics have been a handful to deal with, whining and puling all the time. Luckily, there haven't been too many of them and most of them are meek housewife types. Of course, they want to run things their way, and they're none too happy about being at the end of the world with a bunch of drunks. But now we've nearly doubled their number with the three from your group.

"Everyone is talking: The New Yorkers are so high and mighty. Especially Courtney and Shane." Mark grimaced in disgust. "Do you think Shane could take that ring out of his nose? My God, he's even growing a beard. We're trying to set a certain standard of decorum here. Otherwise, this whole place will go straight to shit."

Bill felt as if his body was vibrating with the shock of hearing

Mark's negative assessment of his group. "I don't know what to say."

"Well maybe you can say something to your friends about the Traditions. We run this place by AA Traditions. Tradition One says that our common welfare should come first, personal recovery depends on our unity. Maybe you can remind them. Everyone should be making meetings, Shane, Kai and even Ana. *Our* meetings are the common thread that binds us together." He handed Bill the New York-Style Meeting announcement, thrusting it at him just roughly enough to punctuate his message. "And maybe you can give this back to them. Two meetings a day is more than enough. People have work to do. And we have to leave time for one-on-one step work, guided meditation, book study, you know the drill . . . or the newcomers will never stay sober. Frankly, Bill, you should think about moving out of that house. You've got great potential, but they're dragging you down."

CHAPTER 22

Shane walked from the bathroom adjacent to the master bedroom he shared with Courtney and Beth. It was Light Hour. Beth played on her mattress, which they'd pushed against a wall. A clothesline draped with sheets separated her space at night, but the sheets were pulled to the side now.

"Let's go, Shorty," Shane told her. "I brought you new bath toys. You'll be lucky to find space in the water.

"There's a benefit to being the only kid left in the world," he told Courtney. "She's got more toys than Michael Jackson. The crew never minds stopping at the toy store."

Shane thought to say something more about the crew, how the rest of the day hadn't gone as smoothly, but he held back. He wanted to spare Courtney the details. No reason she had to live the outside-world nightmare along with him.

His skin was still moist from his shower, Courtney observed. He wore shorts and no shirt, his stomach muscles ripped from months of cycling and hard labor. He had trimmed his beard to a narrow line that framed his face and he was wearing the nose ring.

Courtney chuckled. "You're trying to annoy them."

Before they'd arrived at the Settlement, Shane hadn't worn the ring very often. He'd told her it irritated him because of all the dust and grime.

Shane sat down on the bed. "I go out on the toughest job shifts to the stores, gas runs, and I bust my ass on the Gauntlet. The dirty looks I get are ridiculous. These folks aren't supposed to have resentments, but you could fool me. I'm starting to think if I don't use it, I'll lose it."

"The nose ring?"

"My individuality."

Courtney smiled. "You should make an Al-Anon meeting."

"You mean the ladies auxiliary? I'll pass."

"I like it. It helps me accept things, even though the women are ... I guess timid is the word for it. Angry, too, underneath. Who can blame them? I've been listening to the shortwave when I'm home alone with Beth. Hoping we'll find another settlement somehow.

"People keep looking at Beth, asking questions. They don't believe she's mine and they're so pushy, always wanting to take her for a while. I know we haven't heard the last from Mark and Dale about her education."

"It's like in *Poltergeist*," Shane said, putting on a spooky voice. "They're attracted to her light."

"I was so happy to find a safe place for her ... and us. But I'm not sure this is it."

Shane stroked Courtney's arm. "I'm glad you've been listening to the shortwave ... I can't imagine living here the rest of my life. The food is great and the hot showers are the shit, but it's their way or the highway here, maybe literally ... and we're definitely on the outs. That's the last thing you want when everyone carries guns and you're supposed to be fighting on the same side.

"I talked to the dude they call 'the Professor.' I heard he taught communications at Tennessee State. I thought I could talk to him ... brother-to-brother, you know? I asked him, honestly, why was he going along with all the brainwashing shit? You know what he said? 'Maybe our brains *need* washing.' Then he tells me like he's James Earle Jones: 'Boy, we have something that's working here. Why do you think we need *you* to change it?'

"The way he looked at me I could have been juggling crack on the street corner," Shane continued. "I knew that look. It's the one that says, Boy, you came from trash and you're gonna end up trash. But, shit, Courtney, that's not my story. This is a new world and I'm not bringing that old shit with me. I don't need to be brainwashed to know that."

"They're out of their minds if they can't see how amazing you are." Courtney kissed him and lay in the crook of his shoulder. "I did run into one of the woman on your crew, Amber, when I went running . . . She mentioned the toys for Beth."

"Amber definitely drinks the Kool-Aid here."

"She asked whether our relationship was approved."

"Really? They better not start that silliness."

"I can't even believe she asked." Courtney ran her fingers along his chest. "That train has left the station."

When the lights went out, Courtney, Shane and Beth went to the kitchen for dinner. They'd mostly kept up with their habit of eating together. Ana had made rice and beans with fried fish, and Shane happily dug in. Kai and Jared returned from Gauntlet duty and took a fast shower in the remnants of hot water then joined everyone for the tail end of dinner. Bill had eaten silently, pensively. "I hear you're moving into the rehab," he said to Jared.

"Yeah. I asked Keith to sponsor me. He wants me to move. I'll have a couple of sober brothers there, so that should be cool."

Everyone spoke words of encouragement. Patty had misgivings about Jared moving, but since the first day Keith had brought them bread, he'd been one of the more welcoming members of the Settlement, not as preachy as some of the others.

"I know you guys aren't that happy with the way things are here," Jared said. "Everyone knows."

"He's right," Bill said. "Mark gave me an earful. He reminded me of the need for unity. He cancelled your new meeting, Patty."

"What?"

"These people are crazy as a box of frogs," Shane said.

Kai pushed his plate away. "Worse every day."

"I've been patiently trying to offer different viewpoints in the meetings and one-on-one, but it's not working." Patty's face had turned red with anger. "Then they have a short list of what you can talk about. They still don't want people to talk about zombies. 'We're here to focus on alcoholism,' they say if you bring it up in a meeting. For God's sake! You can't talk about drugs or different interpretations of the Program or zombies! If you do, they assign you to harder, riskier jobs and I think the only reason they haven't put more pressure on Kai and me is because we have so much time sober. Jesus Christ, are they fucking crazy?"

"Whoa," Shane said, leaning back in his chair.

She breathed deeply. "Mark is out of his mind. Sponsors control every aspect of their sponsees' lives. Sponsors report everything to their sponsors who report up the ladder all the way to Mark. He has final say on job assignments, living arrangements and even who sleeps together."

Kai spoke matter-of-factly, "This is a cult. But what can we do about it?"

"That's an exaggeration," Jared said. "Mark is a really spiritual guy and people trust him. We don't have to do anything about it."

"I'm not staying," Ana asserted.

Bill worried. What if she actually took off? Mark was right about one thing. She was the most stubborn woman he'd ever met . . . although probably just a good mother. Mark didn't know about that. Bill hadn't told Mark about Ana wanting to find her kids. He liked Mark but his instincts told him that Mark wouldn't appreciate anyone being uncommitted to the community. And Bill was starting to sense that it could be a problem if Mark thought Ana was the wrong woman for him.

"Honestly, we've been thinking about leaving . . . but we have Beth and can't rush back into zombie country," Courtney said. "It wouldn't be fair to her. We were hoping to find another settlement to go to, not just head out with no destination."

"I agree," Bill said. "Like they say, 'if you don't know what to do, don't do anything.' We shouldn't rush out of here if we don't know where we're going. This place is a miracle even if it's not perfect."

Ana stood. "I'm not staying here!" Her eyes were wet and her voice raised, "You always knew I wasn't staying!"

She ran from the room, Bill following her. The others sat silently.

"I feel sorry for Ana," Patty said after a moment, "but her hometown is thousands of miles away, in the mountains. We could never make it there even if we tried."

They heard the sound of Ana sobbing and Bill trying to soothe her.

"I don't know about getting Ana home," Shane said. "No way we could do that, but leaving is definitely on my mind. Mark and his crew may even prefer we leave. It could get hairier if we stay and keep confronting them head on."

"Things weren't so bad on the road with just us," Kai added.

"It's a lot to give up," Shane said, "leaving here. Especially the hot showers . . ."

"And the safety for Beth," Courtney said. A picture of Beth in a house swarmed by zombies flashed across her mind.

Patty thought about her own safety. She'd been able to stay inside the Settlement—no trips outside—up to now. There were advantages to being treated like an old woman, even though it annoyed her to no end. Yet, she couldn't imagine how things could work out for her in this settlement. She hadn't felt so alone in a crowd since she'd gotten sober.

"Really, guys," Jared spoke what Patty was secretly thinking. "I'm learning a lot about myself here and I can honestly tell you—I can't handle the stress of living full time in zombie country."

"I think we should give it more time," Patty said. "Things will become clearer."

CHAPTER 23

Patty and Kai abandoned the idea of holding a meeting in the Club-house. But word got around that they had a small meeting running in their home. A few people started to attend. They showed up fur-tively, as if they were having an affair with the next-door neighbor. In each case, the person's sponsor learned of it and reeled them back. Each person's sponsor and "sober siblings" stopped speaking to Patty and Kai.

"It's your meeting," Fiona whispered to Patty after a morning of silent treatment from the psycho sisters. "The word is out, and no one's going to speak to you."

They saw Kerry looking at them as she tied her boat to the dock. Fiona abruptly turned away.

The phenomenon spread until virtually everyone had stopped speaking to any of the New Yorkers other than Bill, who continued to attend the big meetings. Now, Patty and Kai pulled back the chairs they'd arranged in a circle in the living room even though most of them had remained empty.

"It was a good meeting even with just the three of us," Kai said.

"You've got to be kidding," Patty said. "That guy was Mark's grand-sponsee. He was a spy. As far as I'm concerned, that was our last meeting."

Kai thought about it. "Every guy here is Mark's grand-sponsee or great-grand-sponsee. Cat told me Mark was a 'circuit speaker' before Z-Day, flown around like a celebrity to speak at AA conventions all over the country. People looked up to him then, but now he's like the messiah."

"Have you been spending much time with Cat?"

Kai frowned. "She's headed toward an arranged marriage with a more suitable person."

They both startled at the noise of the front door banging open.

Shane walked in. He was carrying a carton and looked grim. He saw that he'd scared them. "Sorry."

"What's that?" Kai asked

Beads of sweat glistened on Shane's brow. As usual, the house was cooler than the Tennessee sun. "It's a portable car battery charger. We were at a store a few towns over. I tried to take it without the others in my crew noticing . . . not sure if one of the guys saw." Shane shook off his concern. "I'll plug it in during Light Hour for a couple of days, so we'll have a full charge if we decide to go. Most car batteries are dead out there. We'll be prepared in case we don't have a car to use for a charge."

"That's great," Patty said, although the thought of living out there sent chills through her.

Shane put the box in a closet. "I'm telling you, the sooner we go, the better. I'm not worried about friendly fire *yet*, but I am worried about slow reactions. Today one of the guys ignored me when I told him to hold his fire. From where he was, he couldn't see what I saw. He ended up bringing a whole crew of zombies down on us with his loud-ass gun. How can I trust my back to people who don't think my opinions count?"

The doorbell rang.

"Mark wants you at the Clubhouse," the visitor said to Shane. "Now."

Shane returned to the living room. "Is Courtney here?"

"No," Patty said, frowning.

Dale and several others, the Settlement's founding group, sat on either side of Mark in the Clubhouse.

"Where's Beth?" Shane asked Courtney when he sat in a folding chair next to her, a few seats away from the others.

"With Ana."

"Okay, let's get started," Mark said. "We've asked you here because we've come to a decision. Your relationship . . . presents a problem. If you had sponsors it could have been prevented."

Shane stiffened beside Courtney. She put a hand on his arm.

"Our relationship is none of your business," Shane said.

"I can see why your personal philosophy would make you feel that way," Mark said. "But you're the first male Al-Anonic we've had. We know you each had at least one parent who had the gene that keeps zombies from swarming you. But we have no guarantee for your children."

"Children?" Courtney asked. "Who's thinking about children?"

"Once we were sure that Beth wasn't your child." Mark ignored her. "We ruled out the concept of third-generation immunity."

"I heard her talk," Dale added. "That kid hails from Kentucky, maybe Tennessee, but she sure ain't from New York. No way she's yours."

"A zombie can sense a non-immune human from miles away, through walls, up stairs. You both know that," Mark said. "If you two have a child or Courtney even carried a non-immune fetus inside her, it could bring thousands of zombies down on us. We can't take that chance. Some have argued to exile you, since we all know how hard it is to force a break-up of an existing relationship, but others have argued that we have to give you a choice. So, you have a choice: If you stay, one of you has to move out of your house and you can have no further contact. If you choose to stay together, you will have to leave."

"What don't you understand? I'm not having babies," Courtney shouted. She breathed deeply, lowered her voice. "I'm using birth control. I'm not going to get pregnant."

"I'm sorry," Mark said. "No birth control method is foolproof, and zombies might know you're pregnant before you do. Even a Plan B pill could be too late."

Shane put his arm around Courtney, felt her trembling. They wanted to get out of this place anyway and it was settled now, but the issue of Courtney getting pregnant was scary. They had a point about it. He wondered if the others in their group would leave with them now. They hadn't been able to agree on leaving even before. "You need to give us time to think," Shane said.

"Take a couple of days," Mark said, "but you're on notice: If we get swarmed by zombies, we will kill Courtney immediately. We won't have time to give her a pregnancy test. We're not happy about it, but the community comes first. Life is harder now than it used to be, in all ways."

Shane jumped out of his chair. "Motherfucker, you touch her, I'll kill you!"

Dale and the other men stepped between Shane and Mark. Shane backed off, shaking their hands off him. Mark stood and the others followed him out.

Courtney and Shane sat together, alone in the Clubhouse.

"What if somebody sees a zombie? They'll shoot me," Courtney said, weeping.

"I'm not letting you out of my sight until we're out of here."

"My body is a time bomb," Courtney said.

"We don't know that." Shane held her. "I wanted to get out of here anyway."

"Just us . . . and Beth? We'll die."

IT WAS ANA who began packing her belongings first. She did it angrily, throwing things in her knapsack. "That was all bullshit," she said to Courtney. "Next it will be me."

Kai and Patty signed on swiftly as well, agreeing that Mark's latest move was about control, not safety.

"No one really knows whose offspring will have immunity or anything about how that will work," Patty said. "This may be Mark's slick way of getting rid of dissidents without others realizing what he's doing."

Courtney packed, relieved that others were coming. She and Shane couldn't stay in the Settlement and live separate lives. They had to take their chances outside. She would get a diaphragm and take birth control pills, double insurance in case Mark was right. She hoped they'd get out with little fanfare. She chastised herself for being a drama queen but, despite Mark saying she and Shane could leave, she remembered the Jonestown story. Everything had been weird at Jonestown but the violence only started when a congressman tried to take people out of the commune with him.

When the time came, Shane and Kai packed the truck inside the garage attached to their townhouse, away from the eyes of their neighbors. Patty was off talking to Jared, just now telling him they were leaving. They knew he would consult with his sponsor about whether he should go with them and they wanted to get out quietly. Patty also planned to say goodbye to Fiona, the young girl from the fishing crew, if she could find a discreet way to do it.

Bill returned. He sat down on the bed near Ana, his eyes red. Ana's anger melted into sheer pain when she saw him, sure that he had decided not to come with them. She took him into her arms, his head leaning against her chest. She stroked his hair, tears running down her face. She had to find her children no matter what, and now was the time.

"I'm coming," Bill said. "I can't imagine a zombie apocalypse without you. Besides, I think these guys are Moonies. We could be next."

Ana laughed. *"Gracias a Dios."* She sat on his lap for a passionate kiss.

Jared came back to the house with Patty. She'd had no luck finding Fiona. Inside the dim garage, Ana and Bill were passing their backpacks up to Courtney. They all paused in their packing. Jared got down on one knee and gave Beth a doll he'd come across in one of his trips to the mall. Beth hugged him and actually said thank you.

"You can still come with us," Courtney said. "It's not too late."

"I'm finally staying sober. I know you guys don't agree with a lot of things here . . . I don't like what happened either, but I have a shot here."

"I understand," Courtney said.

"And, besides, there's a guy I really like . . . and he likes me." Jared looked at Bill to see his reaction. "I just have to get through the steps first."

Bill's jaw went slack.

"You have no idea how depressing it was to be the only gay guy in the group. I felt so hopeless."

"I didn't know you were gay," Bill said.

"There's that, too," Jared said, wryly.

Ana gave Jared a hug goodbye. Then, as an afterthought, she grabbed the shortwave radio they were about to load into the truck and handed it to him. "We'll get another one. We'll radio you if we find a safe place."

Patty was relieved that Jared would be able to reach them. "Someday it may be easier to travel if things don't work out here for you . . . if you wanted to find us."

"Okay," he said, his eyes glistening.

Kai pulled out a Geiger counter and handed it to Jared. "This is our spare. Keep an eye on this, just in case." Kai lowered his voice for only Jared to hear, "And keep an eye on Cat please. Tell her I said goodbye."

After they finished securing all the gear, the rest of their group hugged Jared. Patty and Jared both wiped away tears as they parted.

Bill told the others he had to say goodbye to Mark and Dale. "They treated me well."

The others weren't comfortable with it—they had no idea how Mark would react to the group leaving with Courtney and Shane, but they overrode their instincts or maybe just paranoia, and agreed. When they were inside the pickup, Jared opened the garage door. The light of the sun blinded them for a moment. Then they saw Dale's huge silhouette. Mark stood beside him. They were armed.

Courtney closed her fist tight on the butt of her revolver. She warned herself not to overreact. She saw that Shane had his hand on his gun as well.

Bill rolled down the window on the passenger side.

Mark spoke first, "You didn't say goodbye."

"We were coming."

Courtney thought: *Don't get out of the car, don't get out of the car.* But Bill did just that.

Mark and Dale hugged Bill. Patty opened the window on her side. Dale then Mark reached in to shake everyone's hand.

"I know we didn't see eye to eye," Mark said to Patty. "But you're always welcome to come back if you don't find a place that suits you better."

"Thank you."

Patty appeared relieved by Mark's attitude, but Courtney could see in Mark's expression that there was no love lost with any of their group other than Bill. She wouldn't feel comfortable until they were out of the gates.

Mark pretty much ignored Shane, Ana and her, but he smiled

sadly at Beth. "Goodbye, little one."

Beth looked down at her lap, not saying anything.

"You could leave the child here," Mark said. "It would be safer."

Courtney felt Shane's hand on her arm, or she might have shot Mark instantly. At least that was how she felt. She didn't respond.

Bill returned to the front seat and Mark hit the side of the truck as if it were the rump of a horse. They pulled out of the garage.

Kai drove to the guarded front gate. The guards weren't people any of them had been close with, so they just waved and proceeded through. They'd driven a hundred yards down the winding road away from the settlement when a shadow stepped out from the woods. It didn't walk like a zombie. Courtney's spine stiffened. The Jonestown ambush took place *after* a group left the cult.

It was a slight woman, her face in shadow. Then another figure came from the woods towards her. They all recognized the gait of a zombie.

Kai stopped the truck. Shane and he ran out to rescue whoever the zombie was stalking.

A cloud covered sun for a moment and they could see Fiona's face when she turned. Eyes opened wide, she shot the zombie. They had a glimpse of its face—the skin rotting off and the raging hunger imprinted on its features—before its head exploded.

Beth buried her face in Courtney's blouse the way she did whenever there was a loud noise. The others piled out to scan the woods for more zombies. It was quiet except for the sound of forest birds, which resumed chirping once the echo of the gunshot died down.

"Please let me come with you," Fiona said to Patty.

Patty knew everyone wondered whether Fiona would end up like Jared once she was outside the protected environment of the settlement. Fiona was newly sober. Outside, there would be booze in the houses where they stayed and all sorts of pills in the medicine cabinets. There would also be a lot more stress. But there was no way Fiona could return now. Others in the settlement would know she'd tried to leave, and she was already an outcast there anyway. Patty worried she'd commit suicide if they denied her. Patty looked around at the others. No one objected.

"Get in," Patty said.

Fiona piled in, yet another person on a lap.

"First thing we have to do," Bill said, "is get a second car."

"And another bike," Patty added.

They drove silently for a couple of miles, planning on stopping at a bike shop they'd seen during their forays into town. Kai suppressed his disappointment that it had been Fiona, not Cat who'd joined them.

Courtney patted Bill's shoulder. "Dude, you have no gay-dar. You didn't know Jared was gay?"

"No idea."

Shane laughed. "Me neither."

"You straight guys are always the last to know."

"I hope he'll be happy," Bill said, adjusting his weight where Ana sat on his lap. He thought about the camaraderie of the meetings and his work at the rehab house, and felt the gnawing loss of his old sponsor and all his friends from before Z-Day as if he were losing them all over.

Ana held his hand. He pulled her close, looking out at the road ahead. It was unbelievable how completely life had changed in just a few months, and how it kept changing. But he had a deep sense that he had made the right decision to stay with Ana and the New York group, wherever that led him. He watched the empty country slip by.

CHAPTER 24

They fought the dark edges of depression as much as the zombies. "It's hard to believe how bad our luck has been since we left," Shane said to Courtney.

Courtney's scalp sweated under a baseball cap that shaded her face from the relentless sun. The heat from the blacktop steamed her calves as she pedaled.

"Cars crash ahead," Shane said.

They approached cautiously, peering intently at the vehicles as they morphed from a multicolored blur into the outline of two cars, standing side-by-side like conjoined twins. This crash didn't look too bad, but they'd been dismayed time and again at the blocked and in-fested roads as they'd traveled through Arkansas. They'd been forced to devote hours to meandering travel, only to have to stop and find a place before nightfall. They could have been cycling in place judging by the crow-fly distance they'd ended up covering by each day's end—not that they'd found any new settlements to serve as a goal line.

They approached the cars, trying to scope out any hungry dead before they were spotted.

"There's room to pass to the right," Shane said.

"Two hostiles ahead," Courtney called out quietly to the other riders.

Where there were car crashes, zombies tended to congregate nearby, as if they were lost souls haunting the place of their last human breath. The group theorized it was due to the lack of prey in sparsely populated areas to draw them away on Z-Day, or maybe the undead had simply returned to haunt after they'd exterminated humanity.

The dead in the car crash launched toward them. In the heat of the midday sun, they were disgustingly decayed, bone glinting where muscle and skin had sloughed off.

Courtney and Shane stopped their bikes. With the ease of military sharpshooters, they put the zombies down with one bullet each. Then they remounted.

They passed human road kill a few yards beyond the crash, bones covered with brightly colored clothing. "At least the corpses are skeletons now," Patty said to Kai. "Much less gruesome."

"Good not to choke on the smell anymore," Kai agreed.

As Shane had foreseen, car batteries were dead in the vehicles they'd found since leaving the Settlement. They'd needed to use his battery charger a couple of times already, and mastered the art of pumping gas by hand, unscrewing gas pump covers and pulling the rubber belts until the gas came up. They had the blisters and calloused palms to show for their work. Yet, far too often, they were rudely interrupted by packs of "fans," as Jared had once called them. Already today, they'd needed to retreat by bike, leaving behind a pickup they'd spent hours working on. Add to that the problem of finding a five-year-old a place to pee in the midst of a zombie attack. Beth had wept inconsolably when she'd ended up wetting herself. It had been a bad day.

"Farmhouse ahead," Shane stated.

Dusk was closing in. The place appeared promising, and they were ready for food and sleep. Like everything else in their life, scavenging at farms was getting tougher. They'd barely seen a cloud in the sky since Ohio; the region was in deep drought. Vegetable gardens had wilted and dried out, farm animals lay dead and dust blew everywhere.

They stopped before the turnoff to the farm.

"Radiation is high," Kai said. "There are two plants to the North . . . I would have thought they were too far away."

"Dammit," Courtney said. Radiation was the worst for children. This was Beth's first time in a contaminated zone.

"We have to keep going," Kai said.

Bill noticed how worn out Patty looked. She would never complain, but he thought the harshness of the trip was taking its toll. "We're not getting out of this fast. Wouldn't we be better off inside? Maybe it will blow over."

Kai took in Patty's fatigue. "Okay. We will be hot. All the windows need to stay closed and we can't eat anything from the farm here. But the air might be clearer in the morning."

They rolled through the farm gates toward the house. An odd noise surprised them. They processed it, sorting through long-distant memories. A growl.

"A dog," Shane said, nearly in awe. They hadn't seen any sign of dogs since New York.

Shane crouched near a crawlspace under the graying clapboard home. "Hey boy."

"Te, te, te," Fiona joined him, making inviting noises.

A brick-red Labrador with protruding ribs wiggled from the space. The dog inched toward Shane, then sat and leaned on the inside of his muscular cycler's thigh. Shane scratched his neck. "Hey boy, hey boy."

"Doggy!" Beth squealed.

The dog nuzzled Fiona's hand, too, when she joined in petting him. Shane decided that this dog was going to be his. He wasn't going to leave him to fend for himself.

"He could be contaminated," Kai warned. "You'll need to get him cleaned off when you bring him in. Let's get inside."

Shane and the others approached the entrance to the farmhouse the way they always did, bats and guns ready. The dog followed Shane, but he reared back and growled when they neared the side door of the house. Shane understood. The dog had never gone off duty. He was guarding the house. If the live members of the family had ever returned, he would have been there to warn them. "It's okay, boy," Shane told him. "We're used to this."

They could see through the windows that the side door led to the kitchen. Shane walked in front with a baseball bat in his hands, his gun holstered. Kai came behind him, covering with his pistol.

Patty and Courtney tried in vain to hold onto the scruff of the dog's neck. They had to keep him from adding an extra uncontrolled element to the clearing of the house. But the dog turned, almost as if he were going to bite, and ran in through the open screen door. His shoulders bunched, he slunk low through the kitchen. He looked back only once to make sure the men followed. Sun seeped through Venetian blinds, striping the room and the dog with light and shadow. The house reeked.

The dog turned a corner and stopped outside a closed door. Shane stood against the wall and reached for the doorknob. He could hear footsteps mounting stairs from the basement. A lamp crashed toward the front of the house. Shane pulled his hand back from the knob, listening to make sure the others didn't need his help before he opened the door to whatever lurked below.

Bill and Ana smelled the undead the moment they passed through the front door. Bill took two running steps into the living room, his baseball bat held high. Ana held her gun out with arms straight, ready to implode the skull of the approaching dead if needed. Guanajuato. The Museum of the Mummies. That was the thought that popped into Ana's mind as she took in the naked zombie's leathery, bloodless skin stretched over her walking bones. The skull made a disgusting sound when the wood of Bill's bat swung through it. There were still brains in there, but they looked dried out like an overcooked pot of refried beans.

Ana approached the corpse, the woman reminding her even more of the mummies in the Guanajuato museum, a couple of hours drive from her home town. The climate in Guanajuato had something special about it that preserved corpses. When they were displayed in the museum, they had desiccated, hardened skin, and hair still covering their heads and private parts. Ana felt Bill's hand on her back, returning her instantly to the miserable sauna of a house they'd ended up in. The house was as dark, hot and airless as a tomb. It must have preserved the zombie body in a special way. She heard the thud of Shane's baseball bat down the hall.

The dog came to sniff the corpse at Ana's feet. He growled and stepped backward, clearly not recognizing his former master. Ana picked up an ankle of the woman and Bill picked up the other. They dragged her toward the front door to dump her outside.

"She's light," Bill said. "Like a shell."

"They all should turn to dust," Ana said.

"She was still fighting."

Ana hated this house. All of them hated staying in houses where zombies had been.

"We can't get out of here soon enough," Bill reflected. "Bad feng shui."

Ana didn't know what that meant, but she was sure he was right, and it was frustrating not to be able to find fresh food on the radiated farm. It struck her as a travesty to have food within reach and not be able to use it.

Kai and Shane checked every room, the dog leading the way. The house was clear except for the two zombies they'd killed. Kai helped Bill drag out the second body, a man who was as naked as the woman. They must have been having a midday tryst when Z-Day broke out.

"We have to go west, away from the plants," Kai said to Bill as they dropped the body on the dust-bowl lawn in front of the house. "Radiation is one hundred miles from the nearest plant. At that range, there are four plants to worry about. We're in a vice grip again, between the Texas plants to the south and the Arkansas plants north. We can go southwest, Ana's direction. It's as good a direction as any."

"Yeah, but I don't know how to get her to drop the idea of going to central Mexico. There are mountain ranges and deserts between here and there. And, shit, a lot of those cartel guys must have the alcoholic gene . . ."

"It could be dangerous even without zombies."

They walked around to the bike carts. Ana and Fiona were carrying plastic bags full of clothes into the house. Bill and Kai picked up their own backpacks.

"I'm taking it one day at a time," Bill said. "I'm just hoping things will work out, but Mexico is all Ana talks about now. She really thinks her kids are alive."

"It will be hard for her," Kai said as they returned to the house. His throat tightened as he thought of his own wife and daughter. "But at least she has you."

In a bathroom, Shane poured gallons of bottled water over the dog and himself. Then he scrubbed the dog with dish detergent and rinsed him again. The dog virtually inhaled the bowl of food Ana found for him. Kai held the Geiger counter next to the dog and gave

Shane the A-OK sign. "We can keep him in the house."

In the living room, Courtney nearly dove on top of Beth when the dog ran toward the girl. The dog was friendly.

"What's his name?" Beth asked, happily, after he'd licked her face.

Beth had begun to talk more but everyone noted the dog's positive effect on her. "What do you think?" Shane asked Beth.

"I don't know."

"I think I'll call him Ark, for Arkansas," Shane said. "Or I could call him Nuke."

"Ark," Courtney and Fiona said together.

"Ark it is."

Beth ended up falling asleep on the living room rug, Ark's side as a pillow. Courtney liked dogs but she didn't know how Beth could stand his fur in the heat of the house. Sweat beaded on the little girl's forehead.

After dinner, Bill, Kai, Patty and Fiona sat together in the kitchen. Despite hard days of dodging obstacles in the road, killing zombies, commandeering cars, hand-pumping gas, charging car batteries, and searching for a safe place to stay, they made sure to have meetings. They knew Fiona needed the structure and support. She was more emotionally fragile than the others and only seventeen years old as it turned out. The three older addicts were all grateful for her. They might have let their own meetings lapse if it hadn't been for her. Fiona had mood swings that made them dizzy, but she was the only one who didn't seem outright depressed.

So far, so good, Patty reflected, listening to Fiona chattering about how happy she was about having a dog. They all worked hard to make sure the meetings focused on gratitude rather than self-pity. Yet, this day had been especially hard, ending in a radiation zone again, without a vehicle.

Bill sighed, wondering how the dog would keep up with them when they cycled and how much radiation it had taken in.

"I'm going to think positive," Fiona said as if reading Bill's thoughts. "The radiation might have just started here. The readings aren't that high."

Patty wiped sweat from her face with a towel. The heat and fatigue were weighing her eyelids down as if invisible fingers were tugging them closed. She had to force herself to stay awake long enough to get through the meeting. She knew everyone felt stifled and exhausted, but she wondered whether her age was finally catching up to her. That frightened her. She refused to slow the others down or fail them in battle.

As soon as the meeting was over, Patty went upstairs to go to bed. It was still light outside—the sun had barely slipped below the horizon—but she didn't care.

Courtney knocked and entered. "Mind if I come in?"

"Sure." Patty waved her inside.

Courtney sat at the foot of the bed. "Are you okay? You've been looking really tired."

Patty's blond hair was turning gray. Her hair had grown long enough to tie back and she wore it in a ponytail. Courtney thought she looked more beautiful, softer now, but very tired.

"I'm fine," Patty said, noticing Courtney's glance at her hair. "You're just seeing the change in hair color. I'm overdue for my Botox, too. Look—" Patty arched her eyebrows. "I can frown again. I'm actually relieved. Do you know how bizarre it is not to be able to frown when you're being chased by a pack of zombies?"

The women laughed.

"Don't worry about me. Age is starting to win out over the Botox, especially with all the sun we're getting. I always thought that failing eyesight was God's gift to the aging woman, and now we have failing electricity, too. It's a blessing, totally stops me from seeing the wrinkles. Ha. Not that anyone could care less under the circumstances." Patty held Courtney's hand for a moment. "Truthfully, I've never felt more comfortable in my own skin. Botox and hair dye seem like ludicrous, old ideas . . . And look, I'm a grandmother now and can still cycle a hundred miles a day. How many people can say that?"

"How many grandmothers are there in all?"

"I like to think," Courtney said after a moment, "if my mother had lived long enough to recover from her addiction . . . she'd have been like you. But the more time that goes by, the less I believe that. You're more of a mother and friend to me than I could ever have asked for."

"And you're definitely the daughter the biological clock denied me. I'm blessed to have you and couldn't be prouder."

Courtney left, and Patty went to use the bathroom. Thankfully, they wouldn't be in this sauna of a house long enough to worry about lugging buckets of water in to flush the toilets. That was one good thing. Patty used the hand sanitizer they'd brought with them and looked at herself in the dimly illuminated bathroom mirror. Without thinking about it, she lifted up her arm and did a mini breast exam as a matter of habit, something she'd been doing for decades.

Her fingers felt a small but unmistakable lump. A shot of fear roared through her veins. A lump. There wasn't a doctor alive in the world and she had a lump.

CHAPTER 25

No one was sad to leave the next morning, although they worried about cycling in the oppressive heat dressed for winter. They were ready at dawn, wanting a head start on the sun's blaze.

"First priority is to get trucks, and keep them," Bill said. "We need to find clear roads to travel. The heat may be as dangerous as the radiation. We can't give up the shelter and air-conditioning of a car so easily."

Beth whimpered in long pants and a long-sleeved blouse but she didn't struggle when Shane put her in the hot trailer hitched to his bike. Already schooled in survival, she accepted the situation without the fuss of a normal child. In some ways Courtney thought that was worse. What if the heat made her sick and she didn't tell anyone?

Ark jumped in beside Beth in the cart. It would be even hotter with the two of them in there, but the trailer was made for two. Beth started chattering quietly with Ark, not just in sentences but in amazing paragraphs. Courtney handed Beth a bottle of water. "You can pour it on your head if you get hot, okay?"

Beth nodded.

"And you tell me if you feel sick."

Beth put her arms around the dog's neck. "Can I pour it on Ark, too?"

"Yes, but not too much."

It wasn't long before they made their first adrenaline sprint past a zombie-haunted car wreck. The road was blocked every couple of miles after that. They once had to walk their bikes onto a grass shoulder, down and up again through a drainage ditch, because of an eighteen-wheeler that blocked the road and the shoulder. The sun baked their backs. The road stayed clear for a while, and they began to look out for a vehicle to commandeer. A sign said: Welcome to Texas—Drive Friendly the Texas Way.

Ana remembered her last time in Texas. There had been nothing friendly about it. An older man who had once been a teacher in Oaxaca had buddied up with her for a stretch. They had traveled together in the back of a dark truck then walked through scrubland. It had been hot then, the way it was now. "Texas sits on the coals of the earth, at the very mouth of hell," he'd quoted.

Two years and four months later, a gritty wind whipped into her face as she cycled. It was hard to believe things had actually gotten worse than that time in her life. She tried to conjure up the cool shade of her hometown's streets. "My town is sixty-eight degrees all year round," she told Kai. "It's rainy season there now. In the late afternoon, it rains for a few minutes, maybe an hour. Once in a while a long rain, but not usually."

Thirsty just thinking about it, Kai grabbed his water bottle from the bike's holder and took a swallow.

"It is a beautiful village with mangos you can pick off the trees."

"There are mountains and deserts between us and there," Kai said, putting his bottle back. "And what if the drug cartels are there?"

"Maybe the zombies killed them," she said. "Accomplish one good thing."

"We wouldn't know until it was too late."

Ana looked at the parched fields and sparse trees they rode past. "This country is not so great anymore. And bad people were everywhere, even before."

Up ahead, Shane pointed to an overpass. "There could be a cool place—underneath," he called out. "Break time."

But when they pedaled closer, they saw there would be no break. They had come too close to a traffic hub. They could see the skyline of a city in the distance, its buildings glimmering as if a mirage. Some of its former citizens were on the overpass, and they'd spotted live prey. The undead were a rotten, nearly jellied mass of bones, sinew and shredded clothing.

"We have to outrun them," Patty said.

They tried to gain as much speed as possible, riding downhill. A zombie dive-bombed off the overpass trying to reach them.

Too late to reverse course, they sprinted toward the left side of the overpass where there were fewer undead. Courtney was reminded of jumping into Double Dutch ropes. She had never been able to time the entry to avoid the ropes catching on her legs. But she made it through now, hearing zombies strike pavement around her but not hitting her. She stopped in the cool darkness, fumbling for her flashlight and gun, and looking back for Shane, Beth and the others.

The zombies were busting like water balloons, one after the next. Shane stopped beside Courtney, safe. Fiona was covered with splattered zombie guck and crying when she reached them.

"Are you hurt?" Courtney asked as she shone the light on Fiona.

Fiona wiped the goop off her face with her sleeve. "I'm okay."

Courtney swept the pavement with the beam of her flashlight to make sure none of the zombies had survived their fall. Shane fired a couple of shots at those that were still crawling but most had dived headfirst onto the pavement.

"We're trapped," Shane said, pulling his assault rifle from the bike cart's side pocket. He looked down to make sure the grenade he kept in his backpack's netting was within reach.

A deafening roar of automatic gunfire sounded from the daylight they had just left. Bill and Ana had stopped their bikes short of the overpass. They'd removed their silencers and were spraying the zombies on the overpass.

Bill shouted, "Go to the left! Get out now!"

"Let's go." Patty mounted her bike in the darkness. "They're distracting them."

The group reached the far side of the overpass and dashed out before any of the undead could dive on top of them. They pulled to a stop twenty yards away. Shane yelled to the zombies on the bridge,

"Here boys, over here."

Ark jumped out of the cart and joined Shane in taunting them, pouncing as if he were itching for a fight.

"Silencers off," Shane called.

They lined up and began shooting when the zombies arrived on their side of the overpass.

"Hold your fire!" Shane yelled. "Ana, Bill, *now!*"

Bill and Ana sprinted into the dark of the overpass toward their friends' voices. They burst into the sunlight and kept going. All rode away at full speed. After several minutes, they stopped to collect themselves and calm Fiona down.

"None of us has ever gotten sick from being splattered," Patty told her.

"Let's go," Shane said. Adrenaline still pumped through his veins. "We're too close to a city."

They passed flatlands and scraggle-woods, mopping sweat from their brows and eyes, seeing only an occasional house. Fiona was doubly miserable with internal body parts adhered to her skin and clothes. At least her sweat had kept the stuff from drying, but it left a stinking film.

It felt as if they'd lived a whole lifetime before noon. As the sun became hotter, they knew they couldn't make it much further on their bikes. They scoured the driveways of the few homes they passed but saw no vehicles. Patty noticed that the houses looked as if they were falling apart, sinking into themselves. It was amazing how the lack of anyone to fix a loose shingle, leaking pipe or broken window was having a cumulative effect on the way the world looked. She thought the constructed world would return to earth a lot faster than she'd expected.

Patty ruminated on her new situation, too. Her life span, she knew, would be shorter by decades. In her old life, she had lived two blocks from Sloan Kettering, one of the best cancer centers in the world. She'd had information, medicine and doctors at her fingertips. Without surgery, chemotherapy, or even the most basic medical or dental care, they were all at risk now, even the younger ones. 55 was once again 55 and probably a lot older. A hundred years ago, 40 had been old age. In the Stone Age, 30.

Life was a thin thread, not guaranteed to any of them for even an hour. She had to accept that. So, what was a little lump in her breast at

55? Patty feared more for the others than herself, especially Courtney and Fiona, who seemed to need her most. She had no intention to add to their burdens by telling them her worries. She didn't even know the lump was cancer.

They came upon a ramshackle trailer home on a cinderblock foundation, surrounded by acres of unplanted fields. A dust-coated pickup was parked out front. The truck was a relatively new model but you wouldn't know it after two months of sitting unattended. It only had one row of seats. Three maybe four could sit inside.

Courtney saw that Beth was asleep, her face red and sweaty. The others appeared drained, too. Courtney felt as if she would herself pass out from heat exhaustion if they didn't find a way to cool off. "If we can get this thing started, three can ride inside," she told the others. "The rest of us can ride in the bed until we find a second car. At least we'll get out of the radiation faster." She opened the truck's door. "No key."

"Ark, here," Shane called.

The dog leapt out of the bike trailer and crept, growling, toward the side of the house. Shane and Bill followed. They opened the unlocked door to the kitchen. A zombie wearing a cowboy hat launched at them. He was a fast one. Bill shot him.

"I guess they really do wear cowboy hats in Texas," Shane said.

Bill chuckled. "Did."

Ark had relaxed and they figured they could, too, although they listened for any movement in the house. They scanned the kitchen's Formica counters to see if the car keys were there or hanging on a nail near the door. No luck.

Bill took a couple of dishtowels from a rack over the sink and threw one to Shane. "Here. We're gonna have to turn him."

They grabbed the corpse with the dishtowels and turned him on his back. Shane could see a bulge in the front pocket of his jeans. He gingerly reached into the jelly of the cowboy's pants and pulled out a ring of keys.

"Booya!" He held them up, grimacing. "Let's hope it starts. No saying whether the charger has any juice left."

Shane opened the truck's door, molten air bursting out at him. He turned the ignition. Dead.

Bill opened the hood and hooked up the portable charger. They'd already used this one three times. Shane turned the key. Silence. "Shit."

The others braced themselves to get back on their bikes.

Kai walked from a shed next to the trailer. He had a new charger in his arms. "Pay dirt!"

This time, the truck came to life.

"Fiona, Courtney, Ana and Beth ride inside," Patty commanded with unusual force. "Women of childbearing age and below. And don't any of you give me any shit about this."

"That's not an issue for me anymore," Courtney said, bitterly.

"You don't know that," Patty said. "In the car."

Kai and Patty wrapped themselves with tarps and squeezed between the bikes in back. Shane and Bill stood against the back windshield, balancing with a hand on the roof rack. The young women stripped down to t-shirts inside the cab. Courtney let Beth go topless, sitting on Ana's lap. The air conditioner barely fended off the heat or the zombie stench that emanated from Fiona, but the women started to feel guiltily comfortable.

After twenty minutes of driving, Ana called, "An SUV!"

In the middle of the road with its door open and no zombies in sight, a good break. It had keys in the ignition, and the owner had turned it off, leaving them a half tank of gas. After charging it with the pickup, Shane got in the back seat beside Courtney, Beth and Ark, feeling discomfort smoothing out now that he was back beside his family. The car swiftly stank of dog and sweaty, ill-washed humans as they waited for the air conditioner to kick in.

Kai set up the GPS on the dashboard and placed a walkie-talkie on the table that separated Patty's seat from his. He held up the Geiger counter. "Our lucky day, guys. The readings are going down. We just need to keep moving."

He took the lead in the SUV with Ana and Bill following in the pickup.

After another half hour, Kai checked the readings again and spoke into the walkie-talkie, "We're out of the radiation completely now. We just have to keep driving and the land will probably be fine."

Beth sat on Courtney's lap staring out the window. "Where did my mommy go?" she asked

The question took Courtney's breath away. She felt as if she could burst into tears at the pain and confusion Beth had been holding inside. "Do you remember?" she asked gently.

"To get help."

"Your mommy wanted to get help . . . but she died. Do you know what that is?"

Beth twisted her face into a psychotic-zombie expression.

Courtney hugged her. "No, she's probably dead-sleeping by now . . . When I was a young girl my mommy died, too."

"Oh."

"I think you're a gift to me so I can be *your* mommy now . . . because I understand so much about losing a mommy. Would that be okay?"

"Yes." Beth leaned her head against Courtney's chest.

Two hours later, everyone in the SUV but Kai, the driver, had dozed off. He saw the picture of a lake on the GPS screen. On impulse, he turned off at the rutted road that led to the body of water. "Going exploring," he announced on the walkie-talkie.

When his car-mates woke up, they found themselves parked in front of a large rustic house surrounded by towering pine trees. Half an acre behind the house was a lake with a small manmade beach and a dock beside it. The place was silent, devoid of any sign of life or death. There was no car in the driveway and Ark was calm. The lake behind the house called out to them.

All looked to Kai for the okay. He shrugged. "It should be safe."

They ran for it, squealing like kids on the last day of school. Shane and Courtney trotted along with Beth between them, holding her hands. Ark ran ahead, barking gleefully. He was the first one in. Everyone ripped off their sneakers and holsters then ran laughing into the water. Beth knew how to swim and paddled from person to person.

After sloughing off the layers of zombie goo that stuck to her, Fiona went back to the truck and retrieved soap from the pickup. She returned to the water, soaped up then passed the soap around to the others.

Each of them felt renewed, even hopeful. They tromped, damn near gleefully, to the house, which proved as empty as it had seemed. They threw open the windows and allowed the fresh scent of pine to permeate.

CHAPTER 26

Fiona and Patty found fishing rods and brought them to the dock, ready for some one-on-one sponsor/sponsee time while they fished for dinner. Kai took the plastic cover off a large grill on the deck. Its chrome shone as if it had never been used. He opened the cabinet below and found a metal propane tank. He tipped it and heard the liquid sloshing. The deck was shaded by tall pines and had a picnic table that would be perfect for eating outside.

Kai hadn't seen so many pine trees since Japan. A sprinkling of houses sat on the lake's perimeter. There was no sign of life. The place had been secluded even before. He stopped and enjoyed the surroundings, breathing in their good fortune.

After a while, he went inside to scout for seasonings in the kitchen and brought back a dozen potatoes he found there. At the picnic table, Shane, Bill and Courtney were teaching Ana how to play Spades. Patty and Fiona returned from the dock and cleaned the fish.

"Is the fish dead?" Beth asked.

"Yes, of course," Patty answered.

"It doesn't come back?"

"No," Fiona laughed. "Or else how would we eat it?"

Seeming satisfied and suddenly bored, Beth followed Kai back to the kitchen and returned with aluminum foil he gave her to carry. He showed her how to wrap the potatoes to put on the grill.

The breeze from the lake cooled them by the time the fish had been seasoned and grilled. They had an idyllic dinner.

"This can be our vacation house," Fiona said.

"We should stay here a few days," Shane agreed. "I could use a vacation."

Patty swallowed her food. "It's amazing here."

Courtney put down her fork. "Do you think we could stay here for good?"

Ana blurted out, "You have your family, and that's all that matters?"

Courtney's face reddened as if slapped. "But, Ana, do you know what you're asking? From all of us?"

"Too close still to the plants," Kai cut in. "We're safe here for now but not forever. And it will get cold in winter. Not as cold as New York, but cold enough to snow."

"How do you know that?" Bill asked, impressed again by Kai's knowledge.

"I'm not so smart this time," Kai said. "There's a family photo in the dining room, taken here. Very snowy."

Patty put her hand on Ana's arm with a peacemaking gesture. "We can all use a few days rest. We need to take opportunities to relax or we'll burn out."

Ana wiped away a tear. "It is beautiful here. I'm sorry to ruin it."

At nightfall, the alcoholics had their meeting, while Courtney and Shane went to their room to settle Beth down to go to sleep. Unnoticed, Ana walked through the screened-in front porch and out the front door. She turned on her flashlight, listening for the cracking of branches caused by undead intruders. She smelled the air, her senses finely tuned: Nothing but earth and woods.

The back of the pickup lay open, the way they always left it to cut down on packing time in case they had to make a speedy exit. She swept the flashlight around the metal bed until she came across the shortwave radio.

She set it up in the room she and Bill had chosen for themselves. No one had taken much note of how she kept herself busy during meeting time. But every night since they'd left the Settlement, she'd sat and listened to the static, hoping to hear a Mexican voice, any Mexican voice that would let her know that her people were still alive. But she only heard the broadcasts from the Tennessee settlement.

As they had driven southwest, no one mentioned that they were also traveling toward Ana's home. They were still over a thousand miles away, farther if one drove around and over the mountain ranges between here and there, but Ana felt drawn there more strongly the farther they traveled. It was as if her town had a gravitational pull. But she didn't need Courtney to remind her that they were impossibly far.

She was listening to static when Bill returned to the room after the meeting, ready for sleep. When his breath had fallen off to a quiet rhythm, Ana conjured up her children in her mind. They would be much older now, five and seven years old. She could smell the scent of their hair, feel their hugs. Their imagined voices called out to her, gradually becoming part of her dreams.

They all slept peacefully that night. Kai and Fiona took the first watch, and gratefully gave it over to Courtney and Shane. Just before dawn, Bill and Ana took the last watch of the night. They sat on the screened-in porch at the front of the house, Bill's arm around Ana's shoulder. Birds had started to chirp, and Bill thought that dawn was his favorite part of the day. He closed his eyes and meditated on the sound of the waking woods around them. He could keep watch confidently even with his eyes closed. With the rest of the world so silent, he could hear a zombie a city block away.

As the sun dawned, Ana saw a white-tailed deer and its two young ones walking out from the woods, unaware of the human presence. The deer had hit the jackpot. They chewed on lava-orange mushrooms that had popped up from the forest floor despite the dryness of the soil. Their ears twitched. They sensed something. They craned their necks, peering toward the back of the house and the lake. Something was coming. The deer ran through the underbrush into the woods.

Ana tapped Bill's thigh and drew her weapon, the peaceful moment already evaporated. Bill picked up his baseball bat and unsnapped his shoulder holster. Anxiety pumped their hearts, especially jolting because they had been so relaxed. Without needing to talk, they re-entered the house, heading toward the back door that led to the deck and lake.

The sun wasn't yet up above the trees. From the back door, they could make out the silhouetted landscape and shiny mist rising from the lake, but deep pockets of darkness still obscured the forest's underbelly. They peered into the blackness below the trees. Both registered the smell at the same time. Not zombies. Smoke.

Beyond the far right side of the lake, where a second ago there had been only pink sky, ebony clouds billowed behind the treetops. A line of fire closed in on the lake. Trees became torches. Jets of flame shot forty feet into the air. The wildfire advanced toward the far edge of the lake and started to head off to the south. But a second later, the desert-dry wind picked up and blew toward them.

Ana and Bill could feel the change in wind direction. The wall of smoke whipped fast around the bend of the lake. It would reach their house in moments. Falling trees crackled as the catastrophe sped their way.

"Everybody up!" Bill turned back toward the house, shouting.

"Fire! Fire!" Ana shouted.

The fire was coming at incredible speed. A cloud of ash covered the house in advance of the flames. Inside, Ark was barking and jetting up and down the stairs to alert everyone. The group tumbled out of their rooms, finding each other in the darkness. Bill and Ana ran upstairs and grabbed their backpacks and guns. They shrugged on their shoulder holsters then stuffed handfuls of clothes into their backpacks while they ran back to the hallway. Shane carried Beth down the stairs, and Courtney lugged their backpacks. There was no time to grab lanterns and larger supplies they'd brought with them.

"Everyone here?" Courtney shouted over the noise.

"Everyone's here," Patty said, her hand on Fiona's back.

Fiona hugged half a dozen rifles to her chest. They sprinted to the front door, into the smoke-blackened dawn. The crackle and boom of the burning pines sped closer. So much smoke and ash filled the air that they couldn't tell whether flames had reached the house. The roar of the fire hurtled toward them. A tree crashed into the house. They ran, coughing, over the hot ash that covered the driveway.

"Go, go, go," Shane shouted, running next to Patty.

Beth clutched a book Shane had given her. From the back seat of the SUV, Courtney grabbed Beth from him. By the time their vehicles started to roll, smoke billowed out of the windows of the house behind them. Rapid-fire explosions thundered inside the house.

"The ammunition!" Courtney shouted. "Let's go!"

Following Kai who drove the pickup, Shane accelerated as quickly as he could on the rutted dirt road. The house exploded with a flash of flames. Fire raced up the wooded side of the road, gaining on them. Beth's fingers clutched Courtney through her t-shirt. *Please don't let it catch us*, Courtney murmured, *Don't let a tree fall and block us. Please don't let us get a flat tire on this Goddamn, fucked-up road.*

With one bump, they made it back onto the two-lane blacktop.

Ahead, Kai had made a hard left and hit the accelerator, heading south. They were surrounded on both sides by dense pines. On Kai's side, the forest they'd just left had turned into a wall of smoke. He picked up speed.

Riding shotgun, Bill shouted to Kai and into the walkie-talkie, simultaneously, "A quarter mile ahead to the left! The fire's ahead of us, looping around!"

A line of flames spread instantly to the road and, incredibly, jumped to the forest on the other side. The road had turned into a wall of fire, thirty feet high.

"Stop! Turn it around!" Bill yelled.

Both vehicles about faced with the agility of NYC cab drivers. They floored their accelerators, heading back the way they'd come. The flames had almost reached the blacktop at the turnoff. If it jumped the road before they got through, they'd be trapped. They had no choice but to drive toward it, holding shirts to their faces to filter out the ash and smoke.

Courtney covered Beth's body with her own. She counted the seconds as they sped through the super-heated air. Hot as an oven. One . . . two . . . three. She could barely breathe, the heat was too much to bear. Then she felt the temperature dissipating.

She looked up. The air cooled and cleared. They'd made it.

Ten minutes later, they stopped at the top of a hill at a cliff-side scenic overlook. They stood outside and stared. In the distance below, thousands of acres of pine forest still burned. The fire was traveling south, away from them now, extinguishing itself in sections after it had charred the trees black.

Bill said what they all knew, "We're going to need new supplies,"

Dejected, they sat on boulders between the road and the drop. They didn't say anything, passing around bottles of water from a crate in the back of the pickup. They shared a box of Ritz crackers. Beth chewed multivitamins and ate crackers then drank from a milk box Courtney gave her. They all dutifully swallowed their iodine pills and stared blindly at the smoldering air over the forest. It was morning for better or worse.

"Do you mind?" Fiona said to them, taking a spray paint can from her backpack and signaling to the truck.

They all shrugged.

Fiona spray painted in a neat script with the sure hand of an experienced graffiti artist. For a few moments she was lost in the work, forgetting about everything while the others watched. Hot pink balloon letters emerged, wet and swirling along the side of the black pickup: "Occupy Zombieland."

Fiona stepped back and admired her masterpiece.

They all chuckled. She was an odd one but something about that hit them right.

THEY TOOK THE same road they'd been traveling before, driving southwest again past the turnoff to the house. The fire was burning itself out ahead of them. The road would be both fire and zombie-free for quite a while. They drove through a steaming moonscape, the breeze charbroiled, and the sun obliterated by smoky haze. In the first town they came upon, most of the houses had caught fire, too. The structures were either burning or had already reduced to embers. The place was a graveyard.

Yet, up on a hill, surrounded by the macadam firebreak of a large parking lot, the town's Wal-Mart stood untouched, a sentinel.

"When a Wal-Mart looks like heaven, you know you're fucked," Shane said.

Bill echoed the sentiment, "When a zombie-infested Wal-Mart looks like heaven, you're beyond fucked."

"We are in hell," Ana said.

"We lost some weapons and ammunition," Shane said. "We only have the smaller flashlights now. It's going to be tougher going in there but they must have sold guns and ammo."

"It *is* Texas," Patty said.

Patty, Courtney and Beth stayed behind again. Patty's inner feminist rebelled at waiting outside while the others took the greater risk. But she had to accept that she was slower and less agile than the others. No matter what her pride told her, she was more valuable as the getaway driver and backup for Courtney and Beth.

The three watched the rest of the group walk toward the Wal-Mart with weapons ready. Ark took point, walking in front of the group. He moved cautiously, his shoulders hunched. They all knew what that meant. The group rounded the corner of the building and disappeared.

The smell of the fire was sickening. Courtney made a concerted effort not to cry, she was so damn discouraged. "On top of everything, when they go shopping, I'm always terrified that someone won't make it out. I'm still waiting for the other shoe to drop. We haven't lost a single person in our group. Those odds seem too good to be true."

Patty didn't answer. She sat in the driver's seat with her gun on the dashboard, as discouraged as Courtney felt. Their eyes met for a moment but they quickly looked away, both knowing they were in danger of blinding tears.

"At least the fire thinned out the zombies in town," Patty said after a while, keeping her eyes peeled for any dead wanderers in the parking lot.

They heard the squeaky wheels of shopping carts. The dog and people came into sight. They returned with carts filled with camping supplies, ammunition and clothes.

Shane tried to be cheerful when Courtney came out of the car to greet him. "Just another day at the office," he said, kissing her on the lips. He smelled vaguely of zombie.

Ark nearly bowled them over, wanting to be petted now that his work was finished.

Fiona's cart included cans of spray paint. "The world will be my canvas now," she said. "It could be like ancient cave drawings, discovered by a future human race."

The grayness of the sky had lightened. Smoke still rose up in columns from the burning houses in town, but the sky had turned a white-blue laced with high stratus clouds. The sun was visible and hot. Beth was asleep, and Courtney was anxious to keep busy. She climbed onto the truck's bed. Bill and Kai passed cartons up to her. She packed them away and secured them with bungee cords. Everyone worked quietly, even the sound of birds absent now that the forest was dead.

Courtney thought she heard something different. She stood up and listened. A hum. A slight hum. Everyone looked up toward the sound, searching the sky. Not a hum. It was more a drone. High up.

"Oh my god," she gasped, "it's a plane!"

They all stood stock still, watching the plane fly away until it was just a speck in the sky. Then it was gone entirely.

CHAPTER 27

"It didn't see us?" Bill asked with disappointment.

"They were probably looking at the forest fire," Kai said. "Not a military plane."

"It was small," Patty added. "A puddle-jumper like the ones we used to take to the Caribbean islands."

While the others converged around the open door of the SUV, Courtney pulled up Points of Interest on the GPS. The closest airport it registered was in Dallas. "No way they're flying out of a big city airport. It would be packed with zombies."

Bill helped Kai spread a road map on the open tailgate of the truck. "There are probably a bunch of small airfields within flight range. Commercial airports, military bases."

"And drug runners, don't forget the drug runners," Shane said. "Not all of them are going to be on a map."

"We can at least look for the airfields that are on the map," Kai said. "But I don't think it will be nearby or he would have been flying lower.

"A needle in a haystack," Bill said.

"Maybe better that way," Ana replied. "We need to be careful."

Shane agreed. "Odds are that if the pilot has our special gene and a plane, he won't be the geek next door. We need to think about this."

"But we can look." Courtney was ready to start searching. "We're well armed. There's no reason to assume the worst."

Bill sighed, uncomfortable with the choices. "We have to look. How could we not?"

In the end, they drove south and west, the direction the plane had been heading and the way they'd been going anyway. They kept their eyes on the sky now in addition to looking out for zombies and obstructions. They had identified a few airfields on the map, which they would try to check out.

They left the burnt forest and gutted towns. The land shifted to open black-soil grassland. The sky was limitless. It lifted their spirits to have a goal again, any sort of goal. Despite their misgivings, the sight of a plane had made them think about civilization, as if they might be rescued like survivors on a desert island. They kept their hopes subdued, though, wary of the backlash of disappointment. None of them really thought that "rescue" was among the menu options for their future.

After one false lead requiring fifty miles of driving that got them to a deserted dirt airfield, they weren't any closer to finding the pilot before the afternoon sun had waned.

"We should pack it in for the day," Shane said. "We've got a ways to go before the next airfield. I'm not huge on checking out a place like that at dusk."

"I second that," Bill said over the walkie-talkie.

They found a clapboard house that looked empty. At least ten miles from the nearest house, it was surrounded by empty land with no trees nearby. A quick perusal of the house confirmed that the place was theirs for the night. They felt relatively safe so far, and Shane brought Beth out to play fetch with Ark, both the dog and child needing a run.

Fiona sprayed a fast mural on the white siding of the house. Patty sat upwind from the fumes in the shade of the porch. Finally trusting her, Fiona talked about her ill-begotten high school life with its humiliating drunk sex and her defiance of parents and teachers. It was as if the pain had been time-stamped on her. Patty knew she needed to get it out or she could never leave it behind. As Fiona spoke, a portrait of the eight of them (including Ark) emerged on the wall in silhouette. When Patty came to look, she easily picked out who each person was. Fiona had scrawled the words "New York" along the bottom, even though she had never been there.

The next morning back on the road, they heard rumbling.

"Is that thunder?" Fiona asked, excitedly.

There were clouds in the sky for the first time in weeks. They all heard the noise, getting louder. It wasn't from above. Dust rose on the horizon. They drove toward it with trepidation, everyone silent. They stopped in the middle of the road, the SUV and pickup side by side. Out of the dust, a herd of cattle appeared, hundreds of long-horned steer.

"Wow," Courtney exclaimed. "Look at that, Beth. Cows."

Courtney took off Beth's seatbelt so she could stand and see better. In the driver's seat, Patty recognized the noise of the cattle as if it were an old friend. She had heard those sounds—the intense clattering and mooing—in Western movies. But this was so much louder, and the pounding of hooves shook the car. They sat for five minutes watching until the last steer passed.

A short while later, they reached a gas station and diner located in the proverbial "middle of nowhere," as if anywhere was somewhere nowadays. The place had giant horns sticking out over the entryway, probably for the benefit of long-dead tourists. There were cars and a couple of old pickups in the lot to choose from, but they decided to keep the vehicles they had. Although they were low on gas, both the SUV and the "Occupy" pickup had handled perfectly. Now that they were in open plains, they'd been able to skirt even the worst obstructions by driving off the paved road and back on again.

They parked the trucks next to the gas pumps and got out to stretch their legs, guns and bats ready. They could already hear stirring within the diner—they were not alone. Kai and Bill unscrewed the cover to a gas pump. The men and Courtney took turns pulling the rubber belt inside it to bring the gas up.

The other women faced outward, watching the diner. Any zombies that had been outside when the outbreak struck had apparently wandered off, but some were definitely stuck inside. Shrieks and groans filtered out from the wooden building. Then a rhythmic banging began, the sound of an inhuman battering ram. The team at the gas pumps worked as fast as they could. The zombies might have been pounding at a wall or door for weeks, weakening it structurally. With fresh meat within earshot, they might finally break through.

When the two vehicles returned to the highway, everyone breathed out the tension. Patty sat in the back seat of the SUV with Courtney and Beth, reading Beth *Don't Let the Pigeon Drive the Bus*, a picture book about a pigeon obsessed with driving buses.

"How about I give you five bucks?" Patty read. "What's the big deal? It's just a bus."

"No!" Beth said, shaking her head, vehemently.

"Pigeons can't drive buses," Patty agreed.

Shane was glad to see Patty so animated. She had become so pensive over the last couple of days. They'd taken for granted that they could turn to her for optimism whenever things were bad, but now she seemed emotionally exhausted. Patty had kept her concerns to herself, but he was worried. Something was bothering her beyond the day-to-day stress of being outnumbered ten million to one by zombies.

"In half a mile, turn right at Airport Road," the female GPS voice said.

They had found the airfield on their map and entered the coordinates in the GPS. They hadn't seen the plane again, so they didn't have high hopes for this place, yet, they all relished the sense of possibility.

Airport Road was in poor repair but paved. They could make out a couple of buildings in the distance. When they came closer they saw two wooden hangars, originally painted white but now a sad gray. A wind sock on top of one was blowing west to east. Weeds reached skyward from cracks in the runway pavement.

They parked several yards from the first hangar. The airfield was empty and silent.

"The runway still looks usable," Patty said, as they exited the air conditioned vehicles into withering heat.

Dark clouds were blowing in. A flagpole clanged, and the wind sock blew full. Courtney walked, holding Beth's hand in her left and a gun in her right. All of them wished for rain.

"We should check for an office to see if there's any sign of someone," Bill said.

They walked quietly, guns ready, ears open for the sounds of zombies.

They walked around the first building. It looked as if the hangar had been abandoned long before Z-Day. Kai shone a flashlight through a dirty window. No sign of movement. The office door was boarded up from outside. "No one's been using this one. We should check the next building."

Rain began to bang like an amplified drum roll on the aluminum roof of the hangar at the far side of the runway. The noise was deafening by the time the rain was visibly racing toward them across the runway pavement. A rumble of thunder followed.

The first drops felt like heaven. Fiona raised her hands and let the water sluice down her arms. Beth was enjoying it, too. She laughed and hugged Courtney around the hips. A bolt of lightning lit up the sky, then thunder crashed, startling the little girl. Courtney turned to take her back to the car. Ark walked next to them, jumping excitedly in the rain.

Fiona spun around, laughing. They heard another closer crash. The boarded-up office door exploded outward, slicing Fiona with shards of glass and stake-sharp pieces of wood. Fiona screamed. A huge zombie landed on top of her.

Shane placed his gun on the zombie's rotted scalp and blew its brains out. Rain streamed off Fiona, bright red.

Patty ran to her, holding the hysterical girl who wailed in Patty's arms. They couldn't hear anything now except the screams, barks, thunder and the sound of rain. Fiona's shoulder had been ripped apart by the zombie's bite. None of them had ever been bitten before or even seen anyone bitten since the first days. But they knew that many people with the "immunity" gene had probably died on Z-Day.

Kai tried to pull Patty away from Fiona. Patty grabbed onto the girl, not letting go.

Kai yanked on Patty harder. "Patty!"

Fiona became silent. The sudden absence of screaming seemed to pause all the noise: the rain, the barks, even the sound of their breath. Fiona fainted into Kai and Patty's arms. Then Kai yelled as her teeth clamped down on his biceps.

Another sudden crash of thunder. Fiona's head blew apart. Then Kai's. Brains splattered everywhere, covering Patty.

Bill's gun smoked before the rain cooled it. His hair was plastered wet against his head. He let out a sob.

Patty screamed at Bill, "He hadn't turned! He might not have turned! What have you done?"

It was so fast. A split second. Bill pushed away a momentary doubt but continued to sob.

Ana shouted back at Patty over the noise of the storm. "He was dead! There was no time!"

Realization sunk in for Patty. It was her fault. She had killed Kai by resisting him. "Oh no! Oh my God!"

For the first time since Z-Day, Bill threw up. Ana held his bent-over back without taking her eyes or the sight of her gun away from the maw of the hangar door. Tears and rain streamed down her face.

Shane helped Patty up, gun pointed at the door. "Let's get out of here."

They inched backward toward the vehicles. Patty leaned on Shane, her legs trembling.

They drove away, silently. The rain pounded against the SUV's roof. Gusts of wind pushed it from the side. Courtney began to cry. She couldn't help herself. Shane swiped the tears off his face, staring through the driving rain at the road ahead.

Beth had fallen asleep, her upper body sprawled on Courtney's lap. Courtney leaned her head back, knowing now how Beth dealt with the worst sort of trauma. Unfortunately, the grown-ups were wide awake. Courtney stared straight ahead, steeling herself: *There was no room for much emotion in their world. They were survivors, not tourists.*

"Where's the walkie-talkie?" Patty asked, barely whispering.

"Glove compartment," Shane said from the driver's seat.

Patty pulled out the walkie-talkie and pressed the talk button. "Are you there? Over."

"Yes, over," Ana said from the other vehicle.

"Bill . . . I'm sorry," Patty cleared her throat, choking off a sob. "You did right. Thank you."

Bill's hoarse voice came through, speaking from the background. "I know . . . it's okay."

THEY AIMLESSLY PACED the small house where they spent the night. Patty couldn't eat or sleep. She could barely breathe with the guilt she felt for taking Fiona from the safety of the Tennessee settlement and for being such an idiot when Kai tried to pull her away.

Courtney told Patty that she had to move past what had happened or die. "We've gotta do the next right thing," she said, surprising even herself when the AA saying came out of her mouth.

"I killed him." Patty said. "I don't know that I can ever live with that."

"It was a matter of a second. We don't know what would have ended up happening."

"No, Courtney, I think we know." Patty exhaled raggedly. "I just need a little time . . . to pull myself together."

"Okay, but we need you now . . . or at least soon."

They returned to the road in the morning without discussion. Bill asked Patty to ride shotgun with him. As they drove, the land turned to desert punctuated by short grass and brush. Jagged ridges rose on the horizon.

"On Z-Day, Kai argued with his wife," Bill said.

"He told you that?"

"He hated talking about it but he knew he needed to get it out. He told me he stormed off to the store that morning even though he was scheduled to work from home that day. He said he was stupid to think that whatever they were arguing about was really important. He thought that if he hadn't stormed off, his wife would still have become infected but he would have been able to save his daughter. He thought his daughter had the gene."

A sea of red-purple paddle cactus blossoms suddenly spread for acres on both sides of the road.

"In the end, he had to kill both of them," Bill concluded. "He told me he had to accept that regret and find a way to be of service. He didn't believe the AA Promise that he wouldn't regret the past. But he still saved all of us from radiation poisoning. He brought farm animals to the Settlement. That was only a small part of what he accomplished in the months he stayed alive. Despite what he believed, if he'd been home on Z-Day, his wife would probably have killed him and their daughter, and we'd all be dead or dying of radiation poisoning now.

"A wise woman—I think it was you—said that it's hard to know what the domino effect is of any event. I think your point was that you can use the experience for a divine purpose, even if you wish you could press the replay button on it."

Patty looked hard at Bill, watching his profile as he drove. She breathed deeply, taking it in. "Thank you, Bill."

The walkie-talkie crackled from the dashboard. Courtney's excited voice came through, "To the East. A plane!"

The plane came toward them this time, lowering its altitude. It was four-seater, a different plane.

It circled around them. Then it dipped its wings and flew ahead as if guiding them down the road.

In the SUV, Ana dug her nails into her armrest, hopeful but deathly afraid of who the people in the planes might be.

Shane took his gun from its holster, remembering the adage an old dope fiend from the neighborhood once told him when he was a kid: "You may think it's the light at the end of the tunnel," he'd said, "but it's really an oncoming train."

The plane landed a few miles to their west. They took an obvious turnoff to get to it. The road cut through a narrow space between stunted trees and bushes. The bushes scraped the sides of their vehicles, sounding like chalk on blackboard. Finally, they came upon an airfield surrounded by low barbed-wire. There was one long runway down the center, a wooden hangar, and a gas tank on stilts. Three planes were parked outside the hangar: The small plane; the larger sixteen-seater they'd seen before; and a cargo plane with a purple and orange FEDEX insignia on the side.

Bill drove toward a motor home with a corrugated roof. Chickens wandered out front, scattering away calmly when the trucks approached. A pot-bellied pig lapped at a trough of water alongside the home. A spit of a river ran through a gully behind it, surrounded by scrubby trees. Solar panels lined the roof, as if they were a personal shout-out from Kai, who would have said that solar panels were a sign of civilization. Patty gave Kai a mental nod, feeling as if he were right there with her.

In the dusty shade under the roof awning, a scraggly-looking man sat on a wooden chair, apparently alone. He watched the vehicles approach, a TEC-9 machine pistol in his lap. He finger-combed his shoulder-length salt and pepper hair from his grizzled face and smiled warily at them as they pulled to a stop.

He was not alone in his wariness. Ana eyed him suspiciously. She knew a drug runner when she saw one, or at best, *un coyote*.

CHAPTER 28

B ill and Shane stepped out of the vehicles, holding their weapons unthreateningly at the side of their legs.

"I guess y'all come in peace," the man said.

Bill spoke, "Yes. We're traveling through . . . glad to see anyone alive." Bill looked around. "We'd hoped there'd be more to it when we saw the plane."

"This is it, sorry." The man took a long look at them. "Why doesn't everyone come out of the trucks? I'd feel more comfortable if I knew who was here."

Bill motioned for the others to emerge. Ana stood by Bill's side.

The man spoke to Ana in fluent Spanish, "*Los güeros, que tal de ellos?*"

Her expression conveyed a hint of defiance. "*Son buenos. De Nueva York.*"

"You gotta be shitting me." He eyeballed the rest of the group. "All the way from New York?"

Ark approached, wagging his tail.

"Oof." The man grimaced. "Take your dog. I hate dogs."

Shane snapped his fingers. "Ark."

The dog sat next to Shane's leg, looking longingly at the water trough.

"Go 'head, boy." Shane nudged him toward the water. Ark drank next to the pig, which was more than twice his size.

The man seemed at ease with what he saw of the group. "Let's put all the firearms away, yes? Ain't nothing worth fighting for between humans nowadays. Guns are for zombies, and they hardly get out to this Godforsaken place. This is just about the safest place in the country from what I can tell."

"Are you alone here?" Shane asked, looking around before he put his gun away.

"Yup, like it that way. I was living out here long before the undead took over. The apocalypse has treated me well. A lot less people hassling me now. A lot less assholes—even out here."

"You've seen others?" Patty asked.

"Oh yeah, there's folks trickling through. I help 'em out if I can. Ain't seen no kids though." He peered at Beth. "So, what did you do on your summer vacation, *niña?*" She clung tightly to Courtney's legs. "I bet you'd like a nice cold soda pop."

Beth nodded, but the others felt as much yearning for a cold drink.

"Where did the people go—the ones that passed through here?" Bill asked. "Is there any government?"

"Plenty of time for that. Come on under and take a load off." He put his gun on an upside down milk carton next to his chair.

They stepped under the makeshift porch roof while he reached beside him to a half refrigerator that was plugged into an outlet on the side of the trailer. He offered soda and beer. Everyone took the Pepsi and he popped open a sweating Dos Equis for himself.

They sat on wooden benches and lawn chairs, although Shane stood, leaning against the porch poles where he could keep a better eye on their surroundings.

"My name is Jesus." He pronounced it the Spanish way, the "J" sounding like an "H."

Patty raised an eyebrow.

He chuckled. "Not *that* Jesus. Nowadays, it's easy to get it confused . . . any port in a storm. Things are so fucked up for folks." He turned to Courtney. "Excuse my language but don't seem no other way to describe this shit storm. Not used to having kids around."

Courtney was cautious about any attention from the man but didn't sense threat. She figured cursing was the least of Beth's problems. Shane assessed him, too, and reserved judgment. He wasn't hitting on the women. But he was drinking, and alcohol changed people. Plus, the guy must have been a smuggler. Why else would he have been out here with an airstrip so close to the Mexican border?

"Have you seen much of the country?" Patty asked, bringing him back to the question on all their minds. "Are there any settlements?"

"The U.S. is pretty much dead from what I can tell. I haven't seen any sign of people grouping together. There's fires, animals and zombies running in packs, like you've probably seen. No government, far as I can tell. I've only flown a few hours in any direction. I don't fly near the big cities to the East anymore." He lit a cigarette with a disposable lighter. "All I needed was to see Comanche Peak on fire. That's one of the nuke plants near Fort Worth. I'm no expert, but it was enough for me. I stay the fuck away from the cities. They got plants near Houston, too. If there's people hiding there, it's on borrowed time."

"We passed through some hot spots," Bill said. "New York is contaminated."

"New York must've been something."

"What about Mexico?" Ana asked.

"It's better down there. I don't think they had many nuclear plants. Believe there's only one down by Veracruz, on the Gulf. But Mexico got hit by the zombie epidemic or whatever you wanna call it. Passed over the country in a single wave just like here."

"The cartels," Bill asked. "Do they control Mexico now?"

Why was Bill talking about Mexico?, Courtney wondered. If Ana wanted to make that trek, they would have to split up. Bill was losing his mind. She looked at Shane with exasperation. He didn't share it, telling her silently that she didn't need to worry.

Jesus took a drag on his cigarette. "Funny thing . . . some survived, the ones who used to close down the *cantinas* at dawn and sniffed their own product. I guess y'all noticed . . ."

Everyone knew he was trying to assess whether they were all drunks and addicts. They looked pretty grungy by now, Patty thought.

Mother Theresa would have looked like a dope fiend.

"In the beginning, I wandered around in the planes more, trying to get a picture of what was going on. The cartel guys were a lot better armed than the average person when shit-time came. So, yeah, there are still a few hard-asses out there but anyone else who managed to stay alive is pretty well armed by now, too." He laughed. "Plus, the dudes holding drugs and money are up shit's creek. There's no one left to buy the drugs and nowhere to spend the money. You want pills, you go to the drugstore and take them. You want coke and don't mind clearing out zombies, you go to a dead dealer's house and take it. A person wants drugs, there's no end to it . . . and it's free."

Jesus gazed at the horizon, ruminating. "Sort of takes the fun out of it, if you ask me . . ." He looked at them. "Not that I'd know personally."

They observed him skeptically.

"Shit, the people who took that path are dead of overdoses or sloppiness by now . . . You can't get high and fight zombies at the same time. Bottom line, it took the zombies to end the drug wars." He stretched. "Can't say I miss the DEA, Immigration, the sheriff, the I.R.S.—I could go on and on about all them ball busters."

Jesus flicked away his cigarette and stood. "Let me show you my pride and joy."

Beth had taken a liking to the huge pig and was squatting next to him. Courtney called her and they all followed Jesus, walking on the dusty ground toward his airplanes. Ark ran ahead, his tail wagging, not seeming at all suspicious.

Jesus took them to the FedEx plane. "This one's my baby. A Cessna Caravan Super Cargomaster. I don't fly it much. Uses too much gas. But when I do, damn." He grinned in admiration. "865 horsepower engine . . . a beautiful aircraft."

Everyone followed him around the plane.

"When I realized how bad shit had hit the fan, I took her from San Anton' airport. Traded in an old bucket I had. I shit you not, that was one hair-raising mission. There must have been five hundred dead motherfuckers chasing me down the runway. I just barely got off the ground."

He showed them the nose of the plane. "See that metal plate under her nose? That's an old trick come in handy. It protects her from gravel and loose rocks when I have to land on dirt. She's got high wings and I put on extra-large tires. This baby can land anyplace there's a couple of thousand feet of earth."

"So, the planes all work?" Bill asked.

"Yeah, they work. I'm just hoping the damn zombies die out before I need to re-up on parts. Once I can get into the airports more easily, I'll take enough parts to keep them going forever."

"You think they're dying out?" Shane asked. "Have you seen any of them actually dead?"

"Not yet. Ya gotta hope though."

They paused in the shade of the plane.

Bill brought up his question. "You said people have passed through here,"

"Not often I see gringos." Jesus turned to Ana. "I guess you're P'urhepecha?"

Ana stepped back, shocked. "What?"

"P'urhep—?" Patty started to ask.

"P'urhepecha," Ana said. "Those are my people. But why—"

Jesus was enjoying himself. "Well now, girl, you've got the map of Michoacán on your face . . . but I'm no Einstein. P'urhepecha's mostly all that comes through here. Not many but a trickle. Some have whatever that special something is that we have. You know, they've got a shot at hiding from zombies."

"What?" Ana took a step toward him, her hands flying to her chest as if trying to keep her heart inside.

"Yup." He turned to Patty as if he hadn't noticed Ana's reaction. "The P'urhepecha are Indians of Central Mexico. Everyone learned in school about the Mayan and Aztec, but there were still something like a hundred thousand P'urhepecha before the zombies. They speak Spanish but they always kept their own language. Before Shit-Day, they stayed pretty much to themselves unless they had to migrate to work. Nowadays, they pass through here, going back home. A reverse migration I guess you'd call it. Self-deportation." He smirked. "Heard it called that on Fox News. The Aztecs couldn't conquer the P'urhepecha and the zombies couldn't either . . . not entirely least-ways."

"We call it immunity, the way we're able to evade the zombies," Bill told him.

"We think it's a genetic anomaly we all share," Patty added, "like plants that are genetically modified so insects won't want to eat them."

"Not to say all the P'urhepecha have the immunity thing going on," Jesus said. "Most of them definitely kicked the bucket on Shit-Day, but if I see a Mexican coming through here, hands down he's P'urhepecha."

Jesus walked back to the trailer. Ana stood stock still, stunned, her mind trying to work through what he'd said. She had known it all along, deep in her heart. She was sure her kids were alive now. She collapsed into Bill's arms.

Back at the trailer, Jesus gestured toward Ana. "I think I got a little of their blood. I prefer to think that. I'm Chicano—American mom, Mexican father."

He grabbed another beer from the fridge and took a swig as if to emphasize his explanation. He scoped their expressions.

"I never had any trouble sobering up for a flight." He held up the beer. "I don't have a problem with this shit—just like the taste on a hot day."

Ana stood before Jesus and wiped away tears. "The P'urhepecha. Where do they go?"

"The ones who come through here?"

"*Si, si.*"

"*Dime*, are you from Anchengari?"

"Yes." She frowned. "That's my town. How did you know?"

"Every last one is from there. It's just one little town where folks are immune, enough of them to put down the zombies and set up defenses before the epidemic could destroy them. It's one of God's mysteries I guess." He turned to the others. "Most of the people from that town, or their grandparents at least, survived the volcano at Paricutin in the 1940s. Everyone got out in time but they had to set up a couple of other towns for the refugees. Anchengari was already there but tripled in size when the Paricutin folks moved in."

"An isolated gene pool," Courtney said.

"Maybe." Jesus shrugged. "Then there was a piece of luck, even though it didn't seem lucky at the time . . . A couple of years ago, the town was overrun by La Familia, the drug cartel that controlled Michoacán. La Familia had joined forces with illegal loggers. With La Familia's protection, they were stripping down the town's forests."

Ana gripped her hands together. "That's true. We needed the forest for timber to sell and for our medicines. They were destroying whole forests."

Jesus took a swig of beer. "La Familia kidnapped or killed anyone who tried to stop them. Anchengari wasn't the only place where that happened. La Familia had forty-five thousand people working for them in Michoacán. But the folks at Anchengari did something different. They got together and took back their town. One day, they drove out the cops who were helping La Familia and confiscated their weapons. Then they ran out *Los Federales*, the corrupt bureaucrats from Mexico City. They set up their own government, schools and clinics, and settled in for a long siege because La Familia didn't take shit like that lightly.

"So, before the first zombies attacked, the town had already cleared out the outsiders likely to be infected. They had armed checkpoints on the roads and through the forest to keep the loggers out. There was no place in the world more ready for Z-Day, at least not a place where people had what you call immunity."

Ana began speaking to herself in Spanish mixed with the P'urhepecha language that nobody understood. She had no doubt she was going home now. Her head was spinning, joy with fear.

"I fly there quite a bit," Jesus went on. "I guess I've had what you'd call a change of heart since the zombie thing started. I feel a tad more of a kinship with human beings . . . as long as they keep a respectful distance. You might say I keep a vacation home there. The townspeople don't need me, but it's nice to get a hero's welcome when I come in, bringing home their relatives."

"You would bring us?!" Ana asked.

"That's a possibility. I've got a girl there, too, although I'm still waiting for her father's approval." He smiled. "The P'urhepecha have what you'd call traditional values."

"But why haven't we heard from them on the shortwave?" Bill asked.

"Why would you? The town doesn't want to be found. They figure they'll leave well enough alone. No cartels, no feds."

Jesus lit another cigarette. "My only business nowadays is a sort of taxi and freight service. It's about two hours flight time." He looked the group over. "The cost is very reasonable—reasonable to the P'urhepecha who come through anyway. I don't know about the rest of you folks. You all thinking about going with her?"

Ana looked around at her friends, expectantly.

"Yes," Bill answered.

There was a long moment. Patty cut in. "I think we need time to consider."

CHAPTER 29

As the afternoon sun arched toward the mountains, Jesus suggested they spend the night in a ranch about ten miles down the highway. "I already looted anything of value in it, but it has four walls. Either that or you all can sleep out under the stars here. It's a little cold at night but safe enough."

Courtney gave him a look. "You're joking, right?"

None of them could imagine sleeping out in the open.

Jesus shrugged. "Suit yourselves. Take a right at the highway and hang another right on the first dirt road. You can't miss it."

They drove the rutted road back to the highway. Each mulled over the new developments. During their summer together, Ana had regaled them with stories about her town's beauty and climate. She hadn't said much about the danger there before Z-Day, but she wasn't one to talk about her own hardships. They understood that about her. Still, who would have thought they'd spend the rest of their lives in a little mountain village in Mexico?

"It would be a new language to learn—not even Spanish," Patty reflected as she bounced in her seat in the SUV, riding with Courtney, Shane and Beth. "What if we don't like living there any more than the Tennessee settlement? We'd be so far away."

"Far away from where?" Shane asked. "If we end up on our own again, one dead country's as good as another."

"We can't drink the water in Mexico," Courtney countered. But her thoughts went back to her father, how he'd said, "You can't go home again," when he told of the happy parts of his childhood. Now there was truly no home. "It's scary to travel even further into the unknown . . . but if we can believe Jesus, there are thousands of people in that town now, and they're managing to make things work. That's encouraging. Can you imagine him in the Tennessee settlement?"

They all laughed.

"It's the way my people are," Ana insisted a short time later when they sat on the weathered deck of a deteriorating ranch house. "We were pushed too far by the *traficantes* but we are an accepting people."

The deck at sunset was cooler than the insides of the house and provided a glorious mountain view. The sky behind the ridges and mountain tops had turned pink, orange and purple.

"My people weren't the conquerors or the murderers. It was the Aztecs, then the Spanish." Ana counted on her fingers. "Then the Americans came, the corrupt *Federales* and the cartels who made a mess of things . . . It is a good place. You know I am going no matter what. But you are my friends, my family, and I want you to come, too."

"And, guys, I'm begging you," Bill said. "I suck at foreign languages. I need you."

When the sun vanished behind the mountains, the desert cooled. They moved inside the house, which was comfortably furnished with soft couches and armchairs, fairly well equipped despite Jesus' disclaimer. They lit a fire and talked until well after dark. Did they trust Jesus? Within limits, yes. Was it true that he actually sobered up before flights? Time would tell. They tended to believe him. The aircraft appeared to be in great shape, and he seemed to have a pretty sane life set up for himself, considering his personality quirks. Other than Ana, they were all nervous about the idea of going to live in Mexico. Courtney paced as they debated (Beth's eyes following her as if watching a tennis match), but Ana's joy and enthusiasm were contagious.

"Also, Courtney," Ana delivered the coup de grace, "there will be other children for Beth."

When morning arrived, they returned to the airfield, the decision made. It would take two days to get enough supplies to make it worth the gas for the cargo plane. Their help with Jesus' shopping mission was his price for the flight. They all agreed it was reasonable.

Before they left on the shopping trip, Patty pulled Jesus aside and showed him a piece of paper she'd taken from Kai's backpack. It was a receipt with the address of the supplier where he'd bought his solar panels.

"Not far," Jesus said. "Never knew they were there. I bought mine on the internet from the Chinese. We can drive in ninety minutes."

By mid-morning, they were ready to head out in three vehicles to go shopping for supplies. When Bill suggested Patty stay behind with Courtney and Beth, she waved him off. "Not on your life," Patty said. "I've got unfinished business. I'll ride with Jesus."

"Don't forget water-purifying tablets," Courtney reminded them.

They followed the same routine that day and the next, everyone returning safely to the airfield and packing supplies in the plane. Jesus didn't pop open a single beer until his day's driving was done. He performed flawlessly on their missions and won over everyone.

ON A BRILLIANTLY sunny morning, everyone piled into the FedEx plane, arranging themselves amidst the strapped-down cargo, which included a dozen solar panels. Jesus chose Bill as his co-pilot. He lit a cigarette and held it between his teeth. Bill waved away the cigarette smoke that was already filling the cabin.

"Your main job is to watch the clouds," Jesus said. "Not much you can do about it, but if you see any big black ones, just shout out. That's the big difference between flying before and now. No weather reports."

"I hadn't thought about that."

Jesus looked straight ahead. "I didn't want to worry the others but it will take every drop of gas in this baby's tank to make the trip to Anchengari. If we hit bad weather and can't land, there won't be enough gas to get back or even circle very long."

"Jeez."

"The good thing is, if we make it, the P'urhepecha have a whole field of gas trucks to fill me up. And y'all still have your bikes in case of an unexpected landing."

Bill remembered what Shane had said about the light at the end of the tunnel. He felt nauseous. "That's encouraging."

"Don't worry. Ana told the truth about the weather there. It almost never rains until late afternoon. The climate is damn-near perfect. I expect a smooth landing in paradise."

The desert floor fell away below them. The Rio Grande became a glittering snake slithering through leathered earth. Bill said a silent goodbye to a country he would probably never see again.

After they'd flown for about an hour, Patty replaced Bill in the comfortable co-pilot's seat. Patty waved her hand in a vain attempt to dispel the cigarette smoke. Jesus launched into his monologue again, "Well since you're here, your job is to look out for the big black clouds and the lightning . . ."

Patty caught a glint of humor in his eyes. The sky was clear, she marveled at the verdant red-soil mountain ranges below. The plane flew with barely a bump of turbulence throughout the trip.

"See that lake there?" Jesus said. "That's where we're headed."

She took in the sight of undulating wheat and corn as they flew lower. "Are those farms?"

"Yup."

Jesus descended toward a sliver of highway below. Patty felt a rush of blood to her face as they neared the blacktop. A screech and Jesus touched down, light as a feather. She breathed.

Jesus patted the steering wheel. "Let's go."

They reunited with the others in the back. Jesus unlatched the cargo door. They all stood, appreciating the fresh, temperate air. Patty didn't see any sign of undead in the fields or on the road. But three Jeeps approached from the distance. Although the sun was in her eyes, she could make out the shape of men with machine guns. She froze. What if Jesus had lied? What if he was a member of a drug cartel? What if this place was really a drug cartel's den? She imagined Jesus shipping in slave labor—them. Why didn't she think of that earlier?

"Come on out," Jesus said. "Meet your new neighbors."

He climbed down the ladder. Patty held back, reluctant.

Enthusiastic voices of the men greeted Jesus from below. "*¡Hijole!* Bro'der!"

Ana walked to the door, tentatively, excited but scared of bad news now that she was finally home. She took in the sight of the men. "*¡Primo!*" She looked back at Bill, her face ruddy with excitement. "It's my cousin!"

The others headed to the door.

There was a great commotion outside as the men below recognized Ana. "My children?" She asked in P'urhepecha. The man, who looked so much like Ana he could have been her twin, spoke in a tongue the Americans couldn't fathom.

Ana turned back, cheering and sobbing. "They are fine. They are with my mother . . . as always." She kneeled in front of Beth. "Wait Beth, wait until you see. My children are your cousins!"

Riding in the Jeeps, they passed an armed checkpoint, then thousands of head of grazing cattle in pastures beside the road. "We rescued cattle from ranches all over the countryside," a driver told Patty in Spanish.

Tropical forest crowded and canopied their way. Women with assault rifles waved them past an unlit fire pit beside the road.

"We have many checkpoints," the driver told Patty. "This checkpoint was here even before the zombies. It is our most famous one. The women who were here when the dead attacked saved everyone. They killed the first of the zombies, *Federales* who were supposed to protect us from La Familia. Then the women radioed the town that it must defend itself from an even greater enemy than before."

The Jeeps emerged from a copse of trees to a burst of sun. They passed white adobe homes with maroon tile roofs. The blue lake glinted like Morse code from a valley below. At the center of town, people were already gathering in the plaza. Palm trees swayed in the center square. An ancient Spanish church at one end towered over wide sidewalks around the plaza. There were café tables at the restaurants under the shaded arches of the buildings, although no one sat at them.

Patty wondered how this amazing town's life would improve with the cache of solar panels she and Jesus had found. There had been hundreds of them, and Jesus would bring them, little by little. Kai's legacy. She hoped she had done him proud.

The Americans were overwhelmed by the number of people filling the plaza. A Mariachi band played, and the scent of corn tortillas and flower blossoms permeated the air. Many of the women wore traditional clothing, long flowing skirts and blossomy cotton blouses, but others wore jeans and t-shirts. The group walked from the Jeeps into the plaza, numbed by the energy of the crowd. They had been accustomed to the silence of a dead country.

"It's Sunday," Jesus explained. "People were already out enjoying the day when they heard the plane. More coming—the word spreads fast when I bring somebody home."

Townspeople hugged Ana and shook the hands of the Americans. A weeping middle-aged woman and two children broke through the throng. The entire town seemed to part. They heard the excited call of children: "*¡Mami! ¡Mami!*"

"*¡Mis niños!*" Ana sobbed.

She grabbed her dark-haired boy and girl in her arms, breathing in the smell and feel of them. Ana's mother wrapped her arms around them all, kissing Ana. Ana took turns embracing her mother and each of the children. "*Tan grande. Vivo y tan grande.*"

She proudly introduced Bill; Ana's mother hugged and kissed him. Ana translated her mother's thank you for bringing her daughter home alive. She was the only one to make it home from as far as New York, the mother said. Ana's brothers and sisters, seven of them, took turns thanking Bill and the other Americans. Standing a head taller than the crowd, Bill found himself yearning to call his sponsor, his friends, his parents to talk about this new world, so elating and disorienting, different from anywhere he'd ever been. He still missed them all. But he was relieved by the warmth of Ana's family. He knelt to shake hands then hug Ana's children.

Patty turned to the driver she had ridden with. "*Hay un medico aquí?*" Is there a doctor here?

"*Claro que si.*" Of course, he said, with an open smile. He switched to halting English, "Would you like me to take you there. We have a hospital."

"*Mañana.* There will be enough time for that."

They all watched as Ana's children began speaking to Beth in P'urhepecha.

Courtney held Shane's hand and beamed with happiness, seeing Beth light up in the presence of children.

"I never thought I'd see that again," Shane said. "Happy kids."

He patted Ark, feeling the enormity of everything they'd all lost and gained. Sitting in a precinct cell just a few months ago, he'd never dreamed of a fresh start like this. He wondered where they'd live and what they'd do here, but mostly he was amazed they'd survived. He squeezed Courtney's hand.

An elderly woman was talking to Courtney. She didn't understand a word the woman said. The woman gave up, patting her on the shoulder, saying in accented English, "It's okay. It's okay."

One day at a time, Patty had told Courtney, and she tried to focus on that. Today was what mattered: they were both safe and had a lot to learn. She and Shane would raise Beth, and maybe one day, they'd no longer have to fear having a child together if that ever made sense. She wished her father could see her now. She remembered him telling her before middle school that she had to be like a tree, bending with the wind, not breaking when faced with change. In a world stripped of everything they'd ever known, she was proud of herself for doing that.

Beth came to her and she opened her arms.

Bill glanced over at Courtney hugging Beth. The memory flooded back to him of the morning when she walked into the Lotto office with her coworkers, the moment before their world turned upside down. Now, Courtney's face was flushed from excitement and the strong Mexican sun. Her hair was pulled back in a ponytail, unruly wisps framing her face. She looked up and met Bill's eyes. For a split second in time, they shared the joy that rose above all their loss and trepidation. They were safe, with the people they loved, with hope for a new life. They had finally hit the Lotto, and collected.

ACKNOWLEDGEMENTS

Thank you to David Wellington, author of Monster Island, and Scott Kenemore, author of Zombie, Ohio: A Tale of the Undead, which Jared and I thoroughly enjoyed. A special thanks to Max Brooks, author of World War Z and The Zombie Survival Guide, for his advice on how to survive a zombie apocalypse.

Special thanks go out to my editor, Richard Marek, as well as Ellen Roberts, Ellen Weinstat, Karen Mason, Isabel Pinedo and Ashley Prentice Norton for their support and comments on the manuscript. Thanks also to Jackie Danicki, my social media guru; Kerry Brooks, my cover artist; Dorri Olds, my web designer; and Jaye Manus, my ebook producer. And an extra special thanks to my family, Jerome, Kai and Shane Miller.

My apologies and thanks to every NYC subway rider who I accidentally bumped or otherwise annoyed as I edited pages, hanging onto a pole, during rush hour commutes.

Last but not least, thank you to the Rooms, without which nothing.

MICHELE W. MILLER

A former urban desperado, Michele W. Miller has settled into a "happy, joyous and free" life over the last twenty years. Married to a New York City high school chemistry teacher, mom to ten-year old twins, and black belt in the Jaribu System of Karate, she practices law and lives in Manhattan. *The Thirteenth Step: Zombie Recovery* was a quarter-finalist selection in the 2013 Amazon Breakthrough Novel Award competition. It is her third novel.

You can connect with Michele W. Miller
Twitter: @zombierecovery1
Facebook: facebook.com/zombierecovery
Webpage: www.michelewmiller.com
Email: zombierecovery1@gmail.com